The *Magic* of *Robola*

EFFIE KAMMENOU

Publication date - November 2025

Printed in the United States of America

First Edition:

10 9 8 7 6 5 4 3 2 1

ISBN 13: 979-8-9932207-0-3

Library of Congress Cataloging-in-Publication Data
TXu 2-383-113

Kammenou, Effie. The Magic of Robola

Cover Design by Deborah Bradseth of DB Cover Design
www.dbcoverdesign.com

Author photo by Elizabeth Dugan Photography

In memory of my parents,

Eleni and Nicholas,

reunited for eternity.

A NOTE TO READERS

For those who have read my other books, you will have noticed that I always incorporate an element of historical fiction into each one. It's never the plot's primary focus, but usually a backstory for supporting characters who play an essential role in the main character's life.

In this case, I didn't delve into a period that impacted the country or the world. This glimpse into the past was about the history of two families and how they strengthened their bond while establishing a small vineyard and forming a business alliance.

Like in all my books, there are common themes:

- True friendship.
- Solid family relationships.
- Appreciation for heritage.
- The importance of lessons learned from the past.

And let's not forget the romance.

The Magic of Robola is set on the Greek island of Kefalonia. It's a beautiful island, very different from those on the Aegean advertised in travel magazines.

Kefalonia is located in the Ionian Sea, on the west coast of Greece, across from southern Italy. The topography is mountainous, with sky-high pines lining its peaks and cliffs overlooking the most indescribable blue water on the other side of the island. Wildflowers grow everywhere, and caves that could be described in mythology await exploration. Another unique aspect of the island is robola, a wine grape indigenous to Kefalonia alone. The vines are grown in gravelly limestone soil on mountainous terrain with rich, clay earth. Robola is considered one of Greece's finest wines.

If all of this sounds familiar to my loyal readers, it is. *Chasing Petalouthes* was also partly set in a vineyard on this island. However, the stories are quite different and do not intersect in any way.

I suppose I'm a bit partial to this island as it's my grandfather's origin. He was one of thirteen children who had to make their own way once their father passed early in their lives. I don't know what became of most of my grandfather's siblings. One became a priest and stayed on the island, and another moved to NYC. My mother lived with that uncle when she studied at NYU. It was the only way she could convince her father to allow her to attend a university so far from home. There would be no dorm living for her. As for my grandfather, he had made his way to Athens and eventually became a prominent businessman.

My mother fondly recalled her summers on Kefalonia, especially the feast day celebrations on the island for the Panagia—the Holy Mother —and Saint Gerasimos, the island's patron saint.

I've featured many locations in my stories throughout the seven books I've written, yet I've never written about where my father's side of the family was from. Unfortunately, I've never been to the island of Lesvos, but I've heard it's a beautiful place. I hope to finally visit and write a story set there one day.

The main characters of this story are Nikko and Eleni. These names were intentional, as they belonged to my parents. My mother died thirteen years ago, and I still miss her terribly. After her passing, I spent more one-on-one time with my father. I had always dedicated one day a week to spending time with my mother. She loved going to the east end of Long Island during the summer, and we would take day trips exploring towns, wineries, and restaurants. Once she passed, my dad wanted to do those things with me, even though when we had invited him to go with us back then, he'd consistently declined, wishing us a nice day. It was a gift to have that time with him, and when he passed in November 2022 at the age of one hundred, it was a terrible loss for our whole family.

Unlike my other books, which are comprised of two series, *The Magic of Robola* is a stand-alone. I have yet to complete the final book in *The Meraki Series*. Theo's story is waiting to unfold. Thank you for reading. I genuinely appreciate your support all these years.

Xoxo
Effie

ACKNOWLEDGEMENTS

To my husband, Raymond, and my daughters, Eleni and Alexa, for your never-ending love, support, and encouragement.

To my grandchildren, Michael and Mia for bringing so much joy into my life.

To my sisters, Kathy and Jeanine, who inspire me with their compassion and kindness. We have sadly lost both our dear parents, yet we've kept their spirits alive through tradition and treasured memories.

To my grandfather, Andreas, who grew up on the island of Kefalonia. He passed away when I was young but my mother's stories of her summers on this beautiful island inspired me.

To my editor, Katie-bree Reeves of Fair Crack of the Whip Proofreading and Editing, for years of a valuable working relationship. I couldn't do this without you.

To Bryn Donovan, for your advice to expand this book from a novella to a full-length novel, and to add a little spice into it. Your second-round edits helped me to dig deeper.

To Deborah Bradseth of DB Cover Design, for all the incredible covers created for me over the years.

To all my friends and family, too many to name, who support and inspire me every day—you know who you are. You may have even found traces of yourselves within the pages of my books.

To my parents for all their love, support, faith, and a foundation of morality and human kindness.

Turn to the back of the book to reference the glossary
if Greek words and expressions.

The

Magic of

Robola

PROLOGUE

Eleni

Kefalonia, Greece
Thirteen years ago

I am depleted—of tears, of will, of joy. I sense all eyes on me, searing me with sympathy as I lumber unsteadily from one casket to the next to the next. Woeful whimpers echo off the church's stone walls—for me, for my deceased family, and for their own grief.

A guttural, bellowing wail rips from the depths of my soul as I cry out their names, disbelieving and enraged at the injustice and finality of the moment.

I wrap my arms around my mother's coffin, resting my head on the hard wooden surface, but my legs give way, and I slowly crumble to the ground.

He's by my side in an instant. My Nikko. Two days ago, I was floating on a cloud. I had everything—a mother, father, brother, and the promise of a future with my love.

But now I can't bear to look him in the eyes. I don't want to feel his compassionate arms supporting me. I don't deserve him. And he doesn't deserve to be pulled into the dark abyss that is now my life. I flinch and shrug from his embrace. He must intuit—my sudden antipathy and reluctance to be near him—understand I am no longer the same girl he loved. I am dead inside. My heart is numb. My spirit shattered. I have nothing to offer and vow never to return to this island again. For as many happy memories this land has given me they have now been obliterated by immeasurable sorrow.

"There is nothing permanent except change." Heraclitus

CHAPTER 1

Eleni

Present Day

Eleni kicked off her four-inch pumps and collapsed onto an asymmetrical pink velvet sofa, exhaling in relief. She could confidently say that the event was just one more success for Eleni's Affairs to Remember.

A few short hours ago, Glasshouse Chelsea, a venue with floor-to-ceiling windows overlooking the Hudson River, had been transformed from an empty space into a social media groupie's haven. Brand-sponsored kiosks designed for Instagrammable opportunities had been painstakingly assembled to Eleni's specific directions and arranged in neat rows, creating an easy-to-follow pathway for viewers.

As guests entered, they stepped onto a pink carpet; a wall of fresh flowers in graduating pink hues from bright to pale had been erected above it. Photographers were on sight, snapping pictures to make each ticket holder feel like a star. But that wasn't all. Each corner of the room was set up for maximum selfie potential—a plush sofa, a boudoir vanity, a garden swing, and a backdrop picnic scene in a Holland field of colorful tulips.

Eleni had worked tirelessly for months organizing the event, and she was more than pleased at how well-received it was by the enthusiastic stream of ticket holders moving from one display to another. She and her assistant, Angela, tactfully kept the flow of people moving steadily without rushing fans as they posed for photos with their favorite influencers. The abundant variety of complimentary gifts offered by Eleni's assistants kept them from growing restless as they waited in a line stretching out onto the street below.

Now that the last group had weaved their way through each section, eventually disappearing into the night after their last filtered photo snap, Eleni took a much-needed break. Leaning back into the sofa, which had been utilized as a prop that evening, she kicked off her designer stilettos, wiggling her toes in relief as she watched the men from the rental company dismantle her handiwork, stripping it back to the bare space it once was.

"Great job today, Angela," Eleni said as her friend sat beside her. "I couldn't have done this without you, as always." Closing her eyes, she sighed, her dark, wavy hair fanning out over the sofa's backrest.

"I'm not so sure about that," Angela scoffed. "You handled those out-of-control social media fangirls like a pro."

"And you would have too. Just like you did with the bridal party scuffle last week."

Angela slapped a hand over her mouth, laughing. "That wasn't a scuffle. That was a knockdown drag-out brawl. I settled it, but almost at the cost of my hair extensions."

Eleni rested her head on her friend's shoulder. "I love what we do," she said in a sleepy voice, "but every once in a while …"

"Yeah," Angela agreed.

Realizing she was about to drift off, Eleni sat up straight, shaking the weariness out of her bones. "Why don't you go? I have it from here."

"No, I'll leave when you do," Angela said through a yawn.

"Go home. Get some rest. I insist," Eleni said, nudging Angela and urging her off the sofa.

"Are you sure?" Angela asked as Eleni glanced at her friend to see her topaz eyes soften with concern. "You're exhausted, too."

"It's a content type of exhaustion." Eleni smiled reassuringly. Angela was not only her assistant; she was her closest friend. And though Eleni appreciated her concern, Angela had already done far more than was expected of her role. "I'm fine. I'll make myself a cup of coffee to wake myself up with. The rental company has only a few more things to load into the truck, and then I'll leave, too."

Okay, but only under one condition. You sleep in tomorrow," Angela bargained. "I don't want to see you in the office until noon."

Eleni massaged the fatigue from her face and chuckled humorlessly. "I can promise you won't see me before noon, but unfortunately, I won't be sleeping in. I'm having breakfast with my grandfather and I'd never disappoint him. Then I have a client meeting, followed by lunch with Gregory."

Angela scowled at the mention of the man Eleni had been dating for eight months. "Cancel him and go home. You'll probably be so tired you'll fall asleep on him anyway while he waxes on endlessly about his boring-as-shit career."

"Tell me how you really feel. By all means, don't hold back." An offense could be taken by her friend's apparent dislike of her boyfriend, the less-than-flattering comments she spews about him, or the faces she makes behind his back. But coming from Angela, who has always had Eleni's back, she could never be insulted.

*　*　*

The following morning, Eleni dragged herself from the comfort of her bed, wishing she could have slept in as Angela had suggested. But she had a client meeting to discuss an upcoming event right after her standing weekly breakfast date with her grandfather or, as he called it, an appointment. The event was a fundraising gala for a well-known cancer research center where her grandfather donated large sums of money. Eleni's grandmother, who, along with her grandfather, had raised her after the death of her parents, had died from colon cancer. Eleni felt honored to have the opportunity to organize the event and had offered to significantly reduce her fee as a gesture of goodwill.

Usually, Eleni reserved a conference room at a cooperative office building for such occasions, but this particular client preferred to meet at their office. Afterward, she had a lunch date with Gregory. It had been a few days since they last talked in person as they were both busy people with opposite schedules, so their time together was limited.

If she were being truthful, and not because Angela put ideas in her head, she was beginning to question their relationship. Gregory worked in finance, something Eleni knew little about. In turn, he had no understanding of how demanding her career was. And that would be fine if he didn't sometimes make her feel like her work was less important than his. She hoped, with time, after witnessing how she managed an event and how demanding it was, he'd come to appreciate what it took to run her business. But it was more than that. It was about what her heart revealed. It never raced in anticipation of seeing him. Gregory was a handsome man. There was no denying it—above average height, a toned body that looked irresistible in his designer suits, and a smile that could charm anyone with a pulse. Women flirted with him shamelessly, often right in front of her. Those damn chocolate eyes rimmed with thick, dark lashes made women melt when he looked in their direction. But though he was hot to look at, and she enjoyed his company in and out of bed, Eleni didn't get a flutter in her stomach when she thought of him. Maybe it was his practical nature and formal manner she found off-putting. Or perhaps she was just no longer capable of such feelings for anyone. In all honesty, it seemed she hadn't been for a very long time.

July was the height of tourist season in NYC, not counting Christmastime when every store window was elaborately dressed for the occasion. During that time, lights were strung from one side of the street to the other, and the aroma of roasting chestnuts neutralized the usual unpleasant city odors. The city felt more serene and magical, even with the crowded streets.

Summertime brought out Times Square crowds with their annoying selfie sticks, street vendors cluttering the sidewalks, and intrusive furry characters from various much-loved cartoons peddling themselves for photo ops. They had to die of heat under those heavy costumes, and Eleni wondered how they could stand it. Bypassing the commotion, she headed down an alternate avenue, taking a parallel street and swinging around to Gregory's office. When she arrived, he was standing in the lobby tapping out a message on his cell phone.

"Sorry I'm late," Eleni apologized, patting him on the shoulder to get his attention. "The meeting ran longer than I expected."

Looking put out, he stated, "Well, I only have about forty minutes now."

Eleni's brow creased at his curt response but she shrugged it off. "We can just grab something quick then."

They chose the sushi bar around the corner. It was a small restaurant, but the food was good, and they frequented it regularly, ordering now without even looking at the menu.

"So how was your little event yesterday?" Gregory absentmindedly asked as he scrolled through the messages on his phone.

"Major event," Eleni emphasized with a touch of annoyance.

"Hmm?"

"How about we unplug during lunch?" she suggested, snatching the phone from his hands. "Or at least let the calls go to voicemail."

"It's business." He extended his palm, impatiently gesturing for her to return the phone.

Eleni was about two seconds away from getting up and leaving the restaurant. His preoccupation with everything but her was beginning to become a pattern.

"And you asked me about mine, which was not a *little* event. It was a pretty big deal."

Gregory lifted his hands in surrender. "Okay, I get it. It was a big deal for *you*." He sighed. "Although you walked away from a position that was a much bigger deal."

"One that wouldn't have made me happy," Eleni pointed out for the hundredth time.

"I thought we were thinking of a future together." Gregory softened his approach. "A house, kids … That all takes money." He reached across the table, taking her hand in his. "We need to be realistic. Not count on pipe dreams."

Eleni withdrew her hand away from his and placed it on her lap. "Maybe *you* were thinking of a future. But you never asked me what I wanted or how I imagined my future would look. You only ever spoke in hypotheticals." Nervously fiddling with the blue zircon ring her grandfather had given her on her eighteenth birthday, she sighed. She didn't know how else to make him understand. "And it's not a pipe dream," Eleni defended herself, anger beginning to thrum through her veins at his audacity. "My business is growing."

"Giving your services away to charities isn't the way to grow," he insisted, his gaze chilling her.

His brown eyes, which had once reminded her of the chocolate fondue dripping off the strawberries they'd once shared during a romantic date, had now taken on the unpleasant image of murky sludge at the bottom of a pond.

She didn't like it when he did this. Gregory had a way of making her question her choices, making her feel like she never quite gained his approval or measured up to his standards. But Eleni was coming to realize she didn't need to. "Stop, Gregory. Just leave me to my business, and I won't tell you how to run yours."

Eleni wanted to be supported, and so far, he had done nothing but discourage her at every turn. For months, she had tried to brush off her growing apprehension as Gregory took a different approach to business than she did. A more conservative, less risky one. In all fairness to him, she had, too, once. But it had left her unsatisfied and bored. And if there's one thing she had learned in life, it was that it could be snatched away without notice. So why shouldn't she reach for the stars while still on this Earth?

The server approached with their orders just as Gregory was about to respond. Instead, he closed his mouth, picking up a spicy tuna roll with wooden chopsticks and dipping it in a small bowl of wasabi. Eleni had only ordered a salad drizzled with ginger dressing and a spring roll. She was just about to take her first bite when her phone rang. She glanced at her phone screen, facing up in her open handbag. Curious about why a hospital called, she almost let it go to voicemail, but instinct told her to answer. If they were calling for business, they would have dialed her office.

Gregory raised an eyebrow, shooting her an accusatory glare for doing the very thing she had just complained about.

"Sorry," she mouthed, raising a finger to let him know she'd only be a minute.

"Yes, this is Eleni Pangalos," she answered. Eleni's heart sank as the woman relayed her message. Paralyzed by fear, Eleni shook her head in denial. Tears welled before spilling down her cheeks.

"Ms. Pangalos? Are you there?" the caller asked after her stunned silence.

"Yes, forgive me. I'll be right there," Eleni gasped, trying to gain some semblance of control. "What is his condition?" she asked, grabbing her bag and rising from her seat.

"I'm sorry. I can't give out any further information over the phone."

"I'm on my way," Eleni said before ending the call.

"I have to go!" she said in a panic, resting a hand on Gregory's shoulder to get his attention away from the text he'd been writing.

"What's going on?" Gregory asked in confusion.

What's going on? Didn't he hear the distress in her voice? Her end of the phone conversation? But this wasn't the right time for her to address his lack of self-awareness. Her focus at the moment was singular. Her grandfather was her world, and nothing was more important than ensuring he got the best care.

Eleni barely choked out the words. "My grandfather had a heart attack. He's at New York-Presbyterian."

Standing, Gregory reached into his pocket, pulling out a money clip. He threw several bills on the table. "Let's go," he ordered, escorting Eleni out in a rush.

CHAPTER 2

Eleni

Present Day

Eleni sprinted past the automatic glass doors leading to the emergency waiting room. The receptionist behind the Plexiglass barely looked up as she approached.

"Excuse me. I'm here for my grandfather, Andreas Pangalos," she offered, trying to remain composed despite the shake in her hands.

The middle-aged woman—who, judging by her bored expression, might've been at her desk for hours—tapped at the keys of her computer.

Suddenly, the woman's hooded green eyes changed from expressing apathy to something unreadable. She glanced back up at Eleni.

"Wait here," she said with more kindness in her tone than Eleni expected. "Someone will be out to speak to you in a few minutes."

Eleni turned to Gregory. Her stomach churned as she waited nervously for answers. "I don't have a good feeling about this."

"I'm sure everything is fine," Gregory assured her, cupping her shoulders. "They probably want to update you on his condition before sending you in to see him."

Several minutes passed before an attractive female doctor of Asian descent approached them. "Ms. Pangalos?"

"Yes. I'm Eleni Pangalos," she confirmed anxiously.

"I'm Doctor Aimee Chen. I was on your grandfather's case." She sighed, looking at Eleni with compassion. "I'm sorry to inform you that your grandfather suffered a massive heart attack." She paused a beat, then continued. "We did everything we could, but by the time he was brought in, it was too late. I'm afraid he didn't make it."

A gut-wrenching sob escaped from within Eleni as her mind struggled to absorb the doctor's words. "No! That's not possible. I was with him a few hours ago," she cried. Gregory put his arms around her, but nothing could console her. If anything, his proximity suffocated her and kept her from seeing her *pappou* for herself.

"I'm truly sorry, Ms. Pangalos," Dr. Chen said, guiding her to a chair.

She didn't understand. He'd seemed fine that morning. He complained of lethargy, attributing it to his age and refusal to slow down. But she should have known something was off. She should have insisted he saw the doctor. Not that he would have listened. The man had been as stubborn as they came.

Her grandfather, her dear *pappou*, was the last of her immediate relatives. Rationally, Eleni understood that she would lose him someday, too, but she had hoped to have him for several more years. At twenty-nine years old, she was now alone in the world and had seen more loss than anyone should bear in a lifetime. How many more stabs to the heart would it take to drain it dry? Eleni didn't know, but she was sure it was awfully close now. There wasn't much more she could possibly take. Or many more loved ones she could lose.

Gregory handed her a Kleenex from a side table. Wiping her tears, Eleni composed herself as best she could. Numbly, she asked Dr. Chen, "What do I do now?"

"You can see him if you like, and then we will transfer him to the funeral home of your choice," she replied, sitting beside Eleni.

"Oh." Eleni thought about this for a moment. "I need to call his lawyer first. When my grandmother died, he had her body flown to Greece to be buried in their village. He made it clear that's what he wanted as well."

Dr. Chen nodded. "I understand. Still, you must arrange with a funeral home here to coordinate with a funeral home there."

"I see. I didn't realize." Eleni felt weak and distant—oddly removed from her body, as if she were on the outside looking in and someone else was moving and speaking through her. And now she had to get ahold of herself and do …what? What else didn't she know?

"I was nineteen when my grandmother died," Eleni explained. "The details of how the arrangements were made weren't shared with me." Now it was all up to her and she was at a loss. Overwhelmed and grief-stricken, none of it seemed real or possible. She determined she would go down the corridor, find her grandfather, and then they would head home together. He was alive. He had to be alive. This was nothing but a bad dream she'd soon awaken from. But it wasn't, and the doctor's voice roused her back to reality.

"I'm very sorry for your loss." Dr. Chen pulled out a business card from her lab coat. "Here is my number if you have any questions."

* * *

Once Eleni and Gregory left the hospital, they hailed a cab. Eleni remained silent, her mind racing with images and memories of her grandfather. At first, as he'd laid there on the hospital bed, she might have fooled herself back into the delusion that he was merely sleeping, but the coldness of his hands and cheeks as she kissed him goodbye immediately dispelled that conviction. What signs had she missed over these past few weeks? Guilt took hold as she dwelled on what she could have paid closer attention to.

Gregory didn't offer conversation on the way home. Instead, he kept his eyes trained on his iPhone. That in itself wasn't unusual, and she wondered if this time it was out of consideration for her need for solitude or if he was once again prioritizing business over her. It was impossible to tell, but Eleni didn't have the constitution to worry about it.

When they arrived at her building, Gregory escorted Eleni to her apartment, inviting himself inside. Once they settled in, he uncorked a bottle of wine from the vineyard her grandfather had half owner-ship of, made from the Robola grapes that grew there.

"I thought you could use this," he said, handing Eleni the glass.

Gregory sat across from her, swirling the wine in his own glass but never taking so much as a sip. Even in her grief-stricken state, the snub to her family's wine didn't escape her. He'd made his distaste for it apparent on more than one occasion. A contemplative expression creased his brow. Finally, he spoke.

"Eleni, I know your heart is in the right place, but it might not be practical for you to bury your grandfather in Greece."

She set her glass down on the coffee table, looking at him in confu-sion. "Why would you say such a thing? Those were his wishes."

"Aside from the expense, think of the time you would have to spend away from your work. You have events scheduled, and contrac-tually, you must uphold them."

"How dare you? I just lost my grandfather. A man who raised me and who I loved dearly." She rose from the sofa, pacing angrily.

Gregory remained seated, his expression impassive, seemingly unaffected by her reaction. This annoyed Eleni all the more.

"Earlier, you dismissed my business as unimportant, frivolous even, and now, suddenly, it's imperative to keep it running?" Eleni raised an accusatory brow, her tone rising. "As for the expense, my grandfather provided for that long ago."

"I'm only trying to help. If you're set on this, I suppose you can temporarily recommend your clients to another event planner."

Eleni narrowed her eyes, assessing this man she was now begin-ning to see in a new light. Or rather, what had been bothering her in his attitude since the news of her grandfather that she couldn't quite put her finger on. Shaking her head in disbelief, she didn't know whether to laugh at him or tell him what he could do with his unsolicited advice.

"Oh, sure, I'll just hand my clients over to the competition." She shook her head in incredulity. "If you want to kill my business, and it sounds like you do," she insinuated, pointing an accusatory finger at him, "that's how to do it."

He began to reply, but she shot her hand out to stop him. If only he knew the meaning behind the gesture the way she meant it—full open palm, fingers spread out—*the moutza*—a big fat Greek fuck you!

It wasn't like her to be vulgar, but at this moment, she didn't care. Right at that moment, she made a decision. Eleni placed a hand firmly on his forearm and urged him off the sofa.

"Gregory, I appreciate you coming to the hospital with me, but I think I'd like you to go now."

Gregory stared at Eleni as if she had just told him that little green women from Mars were coming to visit her. "There's still so much to decide, though."

"You're right. I have so many decisions to make, and I want to be alone to think." She walked over to her front door and opened it. "I'll make sure to say goodbye before I leave for Europe," she added in a clipped tone.

Gregory was speechless. He set down his glass of wine and rose. "So you don't expect me to come with you?"

"Were you planning to?"

"It would have been a stretch, I admit. I've got client meetings all week. But I would have tried to make it work."

"Right. I'm sure you would have *tried*." Eleni took a deep breath, steeling herself for what she instinctively knew she should have done months ago.

"Gregory, you're a good man, but I've been giving this some thought lately and realized our lives don't fit together. I think it's best we part on a friendly note and go our separate ways now." She tried to say it nicely, to spare his feelings, but all she felt for him was indifference. Perhaps the day's events had left her empty and she had nothing left to give. Or maybe all the little things about him that annoyed her, niggling uncomfortably in the recesses of her mind, had finally come to the surface.

"Eleni." He reached out to cup her cheek, but she stepped back, pinning him with a warning stare. But he plowed on. "You're grieving. This isn't the time to make rash changes in your life. We make a good team. Surely, you can see that."

He infuriated her. It was so like him to place the blame where it wasn't. She *was* grieving. She couldn't deny that. But it was his callous interference that had finally pushed her over the edge.

"It isn't rash. I'm sorry, Gregory, but this relationship hasn't worked for me for some time. I'm not even sure why you're interested in me. You disapprove of my career choice. You make no effort to know my friends. You can't even stomach a sip of wine from my family's vineyard," she pointed out, folding her arms across her chest.

Still holding the door open, Eleni gestured for him to walk through it. "And I don't want to be *half of a team*. I want to love and be loved." It wasn't like Eleni to be harsh, so she softened her tone. After all, it wasn't Gregory's fault—they were just very different people. "I know you'll find someone who will meet all your expectations. But I'm sorry. That person just isn't me."

He began to speak, but she cut him off. "Please." She closed her eyes, sucking in a deep breath. "I can't handle any more than I've had to deal with today. Just go."

With a frown, Gregory nodded in defeat. "I'll give you the space to think things through more clearly. We'll revisit this when you get back." Then, respectfully, he turned, walking away without further argument.

CHAPTER 3

Eleni

Present Day

Rain bled through gray stratocumulus clouds, threatening to continue for hours. Eleni watched luggage loading onto the plane from the floor-to-ceiling gate window, wondering if her grandfather's casket would also travel on the same plane she was about to board. The blackening sky mirrored her gloomy mood and the reason for this disheartening voyage to her family's homeland.

Everything about this trip gave her anxiety. She had ended her yearly visits to Kefalonia after her parents and brother had been killed in a car accident thirteen years prior. When her grandmother passed away three years later, she accompanied her grandfather to the funeral but flew home as soon as soon as he'd allowed. Eleni's reluctance to return now was as strong as it had been then. The island that had once brought her so much joy now only blanketed her in grief and traumatic memories. Soon, all her loved ones—her entire family—would be reunited. But that gave her no comfort, for she could only visit them in a graveyard.

* * *

Ten hours later, Eleni landed in Kefalonia. Much of that time she'd spent on her laptop corresponding with Angela, reassuring her friend that she could run the scheduled events on her own during Eleni's absence. Eleni emailed her elaborately detailed instructions to ease Angela's mind, though it wasn't necessary. Her friend was more than capable. Eleni considered her more of a partner than an assistant.

Satisfied she had sent Angela the pertinent information, she attempted to sleep during the flight, but her mind raced with trepidation—not only for the solemn days of mourning ahead, but also over who she had left behind all those years ago and would likely have to face again now. It was for the best, she had rationalized at the time, if one could justify anything in a state of abject grief.

As time had passed, she'd convinced herself it would have been an impossible situation to deal with, and that they were both better off. At nineteen, Eleni hadn't yet discovered how she fit into a world where she could only rely on herself and her beloved, heartbroken grandfather. And now, all these years later, he was gone, too. There was nothing about this trip that didn't fill her with dread.

When she finally disembarked and retrieved her luggage from the baggage claim area, she was achy from sitting for so many hours in one spot and longed for a relaxing soak in a hot tub. But though that might pull the tension from her muscles, Eleni wasn't sure anything could truly soothe her soul.

So many times, she was tempted to ask her grandfather about *him*—the one she could never forget—the one who haunted her dreams. Her one love that fate had mercilessly stolen from her. As she was about to head to his family's home after all these years, her stomach twisted into knots. But hopefully, he was long gone from the island. He'd once shared his dreams and aspirations with her, which never included a life on the vineyard. Maybe she wouldn't have to face him after all.

CHAPTER 4

Eleni

Thirteen years ago

Anticipation overtook Eleni as their plane landed in Kefalonia. Soon after they had retrieved their luggage, her father pulled onto the road in their rented car. Rolling the backseat window down, Eleni breathed in the fresh air as the wind hit her face. Faint notes of wildflowers, thyme, and honey mingled with pine tickled her nostrils. The sun was brighter, the sea bluer, and life in general was just better here.

Eleni looked forward to her summers on the island each year. The ability to meander through the towns, lounge on the beautiful beaches, and stay at the vineyard offered a sense of freedom she didn't have in New York. Not that she didn't enjoy the city too, but this place was her sanctuary. Maybe because she waited all year for the novelty of this different way of life, or maybe it was spending the summer with the Varvos family she found appealing. Or perhaps it was just one particular Varvos—Nikko—her oldest and dearest friend. But he wasn't just a friend anymore, was he? And the thought of seeing him again gave her all kinds of nervous, jumbled feelings in her stomach.

Eleni rolled the window up and leaned against the headrest, closing her eyes. Daydreaming for the thousandth time of their kiss and what had led to it made her heart leap. She just wished it hadn't happened at the end of the summer so that more, and more, and more of them had followed.

Eleni, Nikko, and both of their younger brothers were for the most part inseparable. This had always been by choice. However, Eleni and Nikko had hoped to forge some time alone over the last few years. Somehow, the brothers showed up no matter how hard they tried to lose them. Trying to ditch the youngsters had become a game of sorts, and it was all in good fun, as there had been nothing but friendship between Eleni and Nikko.

But something had shifted between them. While the boys looked for shells and sea glass, Eleni and Nikko walked along the beach, quiet with their thoughts.

Stopping, Nikko took Eleni by the hand, guiding her to sit with him at the shoreline. Lacing his fingers with hers, Nikko inched closer until his legs wrapped around hers. An unexpected jolt of electricity ran through her as she looked into his eyes. Suddenly shy, Eleni turned away.

"I don't want you to return home to Brooklyn tomorrow," Nikko admitted.

Eleni laughed, shaking her head. "Astoria," she corrected.

Nikko brushed a strand of hair from her face, the simple act unexpectedly making Eleni shiver.

"But I can't call you Astoria. That doesn't suit you."

"And Brooklyn does?"

He nodded. "It's the only place I know of in New York unless I called you The Big Apple."

"You *can* just call me Eleni."

"But that wouldn't be as much fun."

"Then I need a name to tease you with, too. So what can I call you then?" Eleni smirked.

An unreadable expression came over Nikko's face. Was it uncertainty or maybe a bit of nervousness she saw reflected in his eyes?

"Your boyfriend? Only call me your boyfriend and no one else."

She stared into his eyes, believing their honesty, knowing she wanted nothing more. He leaned in, Eleni's heart hammering violently in her chest. Nikko was about to kiss her. But before his lips made the contact she suddenly craved, they were interrupted by shouts of excitement and kicked-up sand pelting them in the face— their brothers. Eleni expelled the breath she didn't realize she was holding.

"Look what we found!" Eleni's brother, Peter, bragged, waving a large piece of sea glass at her.

It was pretty impressive. It was rare to find anything larger than five or six centimeters. And as if their timing wasn't bad enough, Yanni, Nikko's brother, dumped an entire sand bucket of shells, sea glass, and sand onto their laps.

"Thanks for the mess, *Malaka!*" Nikko berated his brother.

"Nikko!" Eleni shoved him. "That wasn't necessary."

"It's meant with love." Nikko laughed, brushing himself clean.

She wasn't sure that embarrassing your brother by calling him an idiot or, more literally translated, an idiot who masturbates too much was a loving notion.

"Come on, let's clean this up and go," Nikko said.

After they placed the shells and sea glass back into the pail, the boys ran ahead while Eleni and Nikko kept their pace for a leisurely stroll. An awkward silence fell between them. "What's wrong?" Eleni asked, breaking the tension.

"Them!" he raged, pointing to the boys. "Us," he softened. "The older they get, the less time I have you to myself. And ... you didn't answer my question."

Smiling, Eleni threaded her fingers through his. The moment had passed for their first real kiss, and she wanted it to be perfect, special, something that would stay in her mind forever. Instead, she lifted herself to her tippy-toes, planting a kiss on his cheek. "Yes, I want to be your girlfriend. We'll text, email, and write letters. I'll mark my calendar for when I come back next year."

"It's going to be a long year, Brooklyn," he admitted as they returned home.

* * *

Dinners were usually enjoyed outside on the back patio. A scarred wooden table seating more than a dozen people was set under a pergola of magenta bougainvillea. Eleni's and Nikko's grandparents sat together at one end, their parents in the middle, and the four children were positioned at the far end.

With their heads huddled together, Eleni and Nikko devised a plan to steal some time alone before she returned to the States the next day.

"Everyone should be in their rooms by eleven o'clock," Nikko whispered. "We'll sneak down to the wine cellar. Just be careful of those two," he said, pointing to the boys.

Eleni giggled. "They'll probably be in their room playing video games. I think we'll be in the clear."

"Meet me in the back of the wine-tasting building at eleven-fifteen, and we'll walk down to the *káva* together."

At the other end of the table, Andreas and Kostas, the family patriarchs, looked suspiciously at the pair. Their odd behavior worried Eleni; she wondered if they suspected what she and Nikko had planned.

"Why are they looking at us that way?" she asked Nikko.

"Who?"

"Our grandfathers. They keep looking our way, then shoot knowing glances at each other."

Giving her the side-eye, Nikko discounted where her mind was taking her. "Relax. Unless you want to forget the whole thing?"

"No," she assured him, resting her hand on his lap. Eleni was fifteen years old and determined her first kiss was going to be with

Nikko. It was now or never.

As Eleni observed everyone, she knew Nikko was right. No one was paying attention to them. Nikko's grandmother—his *yiayiá*—scolded the boys for shooting cinnamon peas at each other before returning to the discussion with her grandmother. Their parents were nearly in hysterics over a story her father was relaying, wine splashing on the table when he set his glass down too forcefully.

And then it hit her. She was leaving all of this tomorrow—the laughter and ease, the dinner under the stars and the frolicking through the vineyard, the sunsets on the beach. And Nikko. This time, more than at any other, it would be impossible to say goodbye.

* * *

"Nikko."

"I'm here," he announced, coming into view from behind the building. "Here." Offering Eleni a sweater, he said, "I had a feeling you'd forget how chilly it is down there."

"Thanks. I wasn't thinking about it." Eleni slipped the cardigan on, stepping beside him as they walked to the wine cellar hand in hand.

When Eleni descended the stairs, she was struck by what she saw—solar lanterns were set about, illuminating the dimly lit space. Nikko must have arranged them and covered the cold floor with a blanket just before she arrived. Turning, she smiled at him as he guided her to sit on the quilt.

Taking her hand in his, Nikko stared into Eleni's eyes. "I've wasted the summer afraid to say how I feel," he started, the tremble in his voice punctuating his apprehension. "I worried you wouldn't feel the same and it would ruin our friendship."

Eleni cupped his cheek. "Never," she assured him breathlessly.

"And now you're leaving. Just when I found the courage."

"Don't you know you can tell me anything? That whatever you're feeling, I'd mirror?" she asked. "Surely you must sense that. I've never known life without you, and yes, it's hard when we part, but I know you'll be here when I return. Knowing that gives me something to look forward to."

"But it will be a whole year before I see you again. That was okay in the past, but it's not enough now."

"Did you bring me down here to complain or put what time we have left to better use?" she asked shyly.

"Much better use," Nikko whispered, pulling her close. "With no buckets of sand or brothers to interrupt," he added, stroking her cheek.

Eleni felt a blush rise as Nikko leaned in, softly grazing her lips. Too quickly, he pulled away, looking at her in question. For what? If he was waiting for permission, the answer was yes! She wanted more of his kisses, eager to be engulfed in his arms.

Eleni was the one to lean in this time, and the moment their lips touched, a shockwave ran through her body. Her skin tingled, and her heart pounded. Her stomach performed Olympic-worthy gymnastics that shot straight to her core. And it was all because of this boy.

In an urgent collision of lips, teeth, and tongues, they fell onto the blanket tangled in each other's embrace. Eleni ran her fingers through Nikko's dark hair, drawing in his head to deepen their kiss. She wanted to savor the moment and etch it into her heart and mind for the rest of her life. This was not only her first kiss with Nikko but her very first kiss ever. And sharing it with him was all she could ever have asked for.

Finally, when their hold broke, Nikko rolled onto his back, panting. "Pandora's box," he breathed.

"Huh?"

"Pandora's box," he repeated. "We pried open the lid and now it can't be shut."

Eleni rested her head on Nikko's chest. "I suppose not," she said with a sigh. "And I don't want to, but we need to shelf it for about ten months."

Nikko groaned, dragging Eleni on top of him. "That's too long."

"I know, but look at it this way, in a few years, we'll be old enough to decide our own fates."

"And what are your hopes for the future?" Nikko inquired.

"I'm not sure yet,' she answered honestly. "Maybe I'll become a vintner and live here."

"I hope not. I'm leaving this island for more exciting adventures."

"Like what?" Eleni asked.

"Maybe marine biology. But not here. Australia, perhaps. Or California so we can live on the same continent."

"I thought you loved it here."

"I do when you're here. But I don't necessarily want to get locked into what my father and grandfather do. I have my own interests."

Hearing this, an ache settled in Eleni's chest. "It's getting late. We better get back."

Nikko gathered the blanket in his arms and headed back up the old stone stairs.

"I can't imagine the vineyard without you," Eleni murmured sadly. Silently, they walked back to the house, a foreboding feeling settling in the pit of Eleni's stomach. Nothing was forever, and she wondered how many more summers she'd have with Nikko before everything changed.

Eleni was roused from her reverie when Peter announced they'd arrived. Opening her eyes, she looked out the window as the long, gravelly driveway leading to the house came into view. She and Nikko had kept their promises, texting, writing, and occasionally calling each other. At least for now, she was sure his feelings hadn't changed, and this summer would be one to remember.

Eleni's father honked the horn as he always did when they arrived. Within seconds, the Varvos family ran out to greet them. Eleni exited the car, watching Nikko approach her with a brilliant smile. How could he possibly be even better-looking than last year? At seventeen, he was now even taller than last year and, from what she could tell, more muscular. Mesmerized, she was taken aback when he picked her up off her feet, engulfing her in a huge hug. Burying her face in the crook of his neck, Eleni inhaled sea salt, earth, and a scent unique to Nikko alone.

"I missed you so much," Eleni cried as tears of joy dripped onto his shoulder.

"I didn't sleep a wink waiting for you to arrive," Nikko admitted. "This is going to be the best summer of our lives."

CHAPTER 5

Eleni

Present Day

Rolling her suitcase along behind her, Eleni stepped out to the airport curb, searching for the blue Toyota pickup truck that would be her lift to the vineyard. A blast of dry Kefalonian heat took her breath away, and a whiff of nostalgia had her momentarily remembering her carefree summers on this island. But that was before grief eclipsed the good memories from the forefront of her mind.

Returning was bittersweet. Tragedy overshadowed the joyful innocence of childhood, back when her only worry was whether to frolic amongst the rows of grapevines or spend an afternoon at the beach.

A car horn's harsh, metallic sound roused Eleni from her thoughts. A truck marked with the Pangalos Varvos Vineyard logo pulled up at the curb, and she waved the vehicle down. But when she opened the passenger door, Eleni froze. She'd been expecting Nikko's father, Stavros. But Nikko, the one person she hoped to avoid, was behind the wheel instead.

"Eleni." Nikko's monotone acknowledgment lacked emotion, as did his blank expression.

Eleni had been anxious about the possibility of facing him after all these years and the emotions it might stir. Still, despite her preparation, Nikko's stony reception rattled her. It was clear he harbored nothing but hostility for her.

He didn't so much as glance in her direction while she stood staring at him in utter shock. "Nikko." She mimicked his tone, her heart traitorously hammering in her chest. Even with the scowl on his face, he looked better than he had ten years ago. Not that she dared spare him more than a moment's glance. But Eleni couldn't mistake the brilliant hue of his blue eyes, even if a chilling frost had replaced the warmth he'd long ago offered her with affection.

Exiting the truck, Nikko approached her, purposely avoiding eye contact. Lifting her suitcase, he hoisted it into the open bed like a bale of hay.

Eleni glowered over his haphazard handling of her expensive designer luggage. With a complaint on the tip of her tongue, she thought better of it, instead flashing him an indignant glare to get her point across.

By the look on Nikko's face, he seemed as pleased over having to pick her up as she was to be subjected to his belligerent attitude. They quietly settled into their seats, and Nikko pulled back out into traffic.

After several minutes of awkward silence, Nikko spoke. "I'm sorry about your *pappou*. He meant a lot to all of us."

"Thank you." Eleni sniffled, struck by a sudden wave of sorrow. "He was everything to me," she croaked out. "And all I had left in the world," she muttered nearly inaudibly.

Nikko kept his eyes trained on the road. "You have family here," he said, his tone flat.

Eleni didn't respond. In a sense, what Nikko said was true. Her grandfather and Nikko's grandfather had been the best of friends. Long ago, they were young men sharing a single dream. With hard work and an unbreakable bond, they formed Pangalos Varvos Vineyard, combining their names to create an emerging and ever-blooming business.

Three generations of Pangalos and Varvos family members had contributed to their success and legacy in one way or another. Even as a young girl, she had learned the ways of the vines. But once her parents and brother died, she abandoned everything she knew and loved on this land, including Nikko, her first love.

Eleni solemnly looked out the window as Nikko drove. She'd almost forgotten the allure of this island. A forest of dark green pine trees, so tall they pierced the clouds and reached into the heavens, blanketed the majestic mountainside. On the other side, cliffs overlooked crowded beaches, miles of crystal-blue water, and a shoreline dotted with gently rocking boats moored to the docks.

Soon the truck turned, passing through open wrought-iron gates, the tires crunching as they drove down a long gravel driveway that was lined with symmetrical rows of grapevines. As they pulled up to the front entrance of the estate, Eleni couldn't help but smile through her mix of jumbled emotions when Nikko's mother and grandmother pushed their way through the front door, immediately embracing her before she barely had a chance to exit the car. It was heartwarming to see these women again, and she had to fight back tears as they greeted her affectionately. She only hoped Nikko appreciated how blessed he was to still have his parents and grandparents with him.

"*Éla pethí mou*," Maria, Nikko's mother, said, guiding her into the house. "You must be so tired and hungry. I have a plate of food waiting for you."

This, Eleni had not forgotten. Her own family had been the exact same way. You always offered—no, insisted—your guests ate until they couldn't lift themselves from their chairs. It was true, though. She was exhausted. But her grumbling stomach won the battle over her heavy-lidded eyes. Especially when the aroma of lamb, garlic, and oregano permeating the kitchen threw her salivary glands into overdrive, making her hungrier than she had been only moments before.

"*Kátse*," Maria urged, pulling a chair out for her at the kitchen table. She placed a plate of salad in front of Eleni. Without hesitation,

Eleni broke a corner off a slab of creamy feta cheese that was sitting on a bed of juicy red tomatoes and fresh cucumbers and popped it into her mouth.

The women sat beside her, offering their condolences and expressing their grief at losing their dear friend and business partner. It wasn't lost on Eleni that Nikko had disappeared. She supposed he had fulfilled his obligation and left at the first chance he had.

"Where is Stavros?" Eleni asked of Nikko's father.

"Out in the field with his father," Maria replied.

"Kostas still works on the vineyard in the heat of the day at his age?" Eleni asked incredulously.

"Just for long enough to feel useful. Then Stavros sends him into the vat room where it's cooler."

"That's smart. He mustn't be made to feel redundant." Eleni sighed, thinking of her own grandfather, who always worked more hours than he should have. A wave of sadness washed over her. "Have you heard from the funeral home yet?"

Nikko's grandmother, Thalia, placed her hand over Eleni's. "Everything is in order. The funeral is arranged for the day after tomorrow. Rest easy, *koukla.*"

The term of endearment stung. The last one to call her his little doll was her *pappou.* Yet, it oddly comforted her, too. "Thank you, Thalia."

"Please call me *Yiayiá.* You always did as a child."

Tears blurred Eleni's vision. She hadn't referred to anyone as *Yiayiá* since her grandmother died ten years ago. She was grateful to have this family to embrace and support her now. She swallowed the lump of emotion clogging her throat, wiping away her tears and nodding silently.

However, before Eleni attempted to reply, Maria slid a plate of roast lamb stuffed with garlic, lemon potatoes, and fresh string beans in front of her. Eleni couldn't help but laugh at the amount piled up before her. But this was Greek hospitality at its best, and she'd forgotten how comforting it could be.

After Eleni finished her meal, she respectfully retreated to the guest room. Though they had allowed many others to have occupied the space over the years, she found it very much how she had left it so many summers ago. A framed photo of herself with her brother and parents still rested on the dresser. Seashells she had collected over the years filled a glass vase, and a candid snapshot of her and Nikko was still taped to the vanity mirror.

Eleni closed her eyes, imagining she was a teenager again; the future had yet to unfold. She wanted to hang onto this fantasy for a moment longer. But, more than that, she wanted to change its course. Opening her suitcase, Eleni tried to force back the myriad of emotions plaguing her. Crying would do her no good, nor would wishing for things she had no control over. Instead, she methodically unpacked her garments. When that task was done, she ran a hot bath, pouring the contents of aromatic bath oil into the water. As the steam rose, the scent of lavender, known to relax the mind and body, floated in the mist, a balm on her senses. Slowly, she relaxed, letting her worries float away with the steam as she soaked in the free-standing tub for as long as the water remained warm.

LEG OF LAMB

Preheat oven to 350° F

Ingredients
Leg of lamb
2 heads of garlic, peeled and chopped
1 teaspoon salt
½ teaspoon pepper
1 stick of unsalted butter (8 tablespoons)
1 tablespoon oregano
3 lemons
1 cup water
Salt, pepper & oregano to taste
5 pounds of medium-sized potatoes

Method
Place the leg of lamb in a large roasting pan. With a knife, cut several deep inch-long slits into the lamb. In a small bowl, mix together the chopped garlic, salt, and pepper. Stuff the slits with the garlic.

Break approximately 6 tablespoons of the butter into pieces and stuff into the top of the garlic-filled slits. Squeeze the juice from 1½ lemons over the lamb and sprinkle with oregano. Pour the cup of water into the pan and add the remaining butter.

Roast for 1 hour. In the meantime, cut the potatoes into quarters. After the hour, add the potatoes to the pan, arranging around the lamb. Use the remaining 1½ lemons to squeeze over the potatoes. Add salt, pepper, and oregano to taste. Turn the heat up to 400° F. Place a small piece of aluminum foil over the top of the lamb. Just enough to keep the top from over-browning. Do not cover the sides. Roast for another 2 hours. Every once in a while, check the potatoes, turning them so they brown evenly.

When the roast is done, remove it from the pan and place it onto a cutting board. Remove the potatoes immediately, or they will soak up all the natural gravy.

Slice the lamb and place it onto a serving platter.

"Times and conditions change so rapidly that we must keep our aim constantly focused on the future." Walt Disney

CHAPTER 6

Eleni

Present Day

The following day, Eleni, dressed in a casual floral print sundress and flat sandals, emerged from her bedroom only to find the house empty. She called out to Maria and *Yiayiá* Thalia, but no one answered.

"Hello?" she called again, wandering around the empty rooms sprawled throughout the big family home.

"Out here," Maria said, greeting her by the French doors leading onto a back patio. "*Kalimera*, Eleni," she said, stepping into the kitchen and offering her a double-cheek kiss. "*Éla!*" She ushered Eleni over to a counter laden with an assortment of breakfast foods.

Rustic Greek bread torn into chunks filled a basket. *Melitzanosalata*, an eggplant dip, and *taramosalata*, a fish roe spread, sat beside it in twin ceramic bowls. Kalamata olives, *dolmathes*—stuffed grape leaves—and an assortment of cheeses were neatly arranged on a ceramic platter.

"You don't have to ask me twice!" Eleni said, her eyes widening with delight as she helped herself to her favorite morning starters. She took a bite of a *dolma* and moaned. "I forgot how much better everything tastes here."

"These don't come from a can," Maria declared proudly. "Homemade. Even the leaves are from our own vines. I'll teach you."

"I'd like that," Eleni said. "Though my talents in the kitchen are pretty non-existent."

"*Kafé?*" Maria asked.

"I can get it. Thank you."

After pouring herself a strong cup of coffee, Eleni juggled her plate and mug in one hand as she opened the door and stepped onto the patio. She sat at the table beside *Yiayiá* Thalia, greeting her with a kiss on each cheek.

It was a little past eight o'clock in the morning, but Eleni could tell it would be another scorching hot day. The sun was already blaring, blocked only by the bougainvillea-covered pergola that shaded the table.

Eleni glanced around. "I'm assuming Stavros and Nikko are in the vineyards, but where is *Pappou* Kostas? Don't tell me he's already working in the field?"

Both Kostas and her grandfather had been the same age. She couldn't imagine him working in this heat at seventy-seven years old, especially in the uneven terrain where the Robola grapes grew.

Thalia laughed. "Yes. He checks on the vines but doesn't do much manual labor anymore. He mainly works with Nikko, teaching him the secrets of our label. Nikko has become quite the winemaker himself."

"Nikko?" Eleni asked skeptically.

"Why does that surprise you?" Maria asked.

She shrugged. "No reason, I guess. I just remember he had other dreams."

"Dreams change. Children grow up." Thalia cocked her head knowingly. "You should consider getting reacquainted."

Maria caught her mother's eye, nudging her elbow ever so imperceptibly. As subtle as it was, it didn't escape Eleni's notice.

Changing the subject, Maria cheerfully asked, "What would you like to do today, Eleni? You can borrow my car if you'd like to explore the island."

"Maybe later. Thank you, Maria. Would it be okay if I roamed around the vineyard for now?"

"Of course! But I suggest a different pair of shoes," she advised, eyeing her open-toe sandals.

* * *

Eleni began her exploration where she had first entered the day before, down the gravel path toward the entrance to the vineyard. The vines here were planted in neat rows, much like the ones she had seen in Napa or on the east end of Long Island when she ventured out of the city. Dark purple Mavrodaphne grapes were easily spotted on one side of the property among the lush green leaves. On the other side, clusters of golden Muscat grapes could be found camouflaged amongst the foliage.

With a sad smile, she remembered running up and down the rows, playing tag and hide-and-seek when she and Nikko were too small to venture too far from the main house.

After a while, Eleni meandered past the entrance gates, deciding whether to turn right or left. Stretching her memory, she turned left, confident she was heading in the right direction. Once she and Nikko grew older, they climbed the rocky hills where grapevines seemed haphazardly planted with no pattern or order. It was also on these hillsides that Stavros had taught her how to tend the vines. So much of that knowledge was lost to her now, like everything else she held dear on this island.

Maria had been right to loan her a pair of work boots. Even her Converse high-tops would have shredded in this terrain. She labored up the mountainside, pushing through a maze of vines and stepping over jagged limestone rocks. Finally, she found Nikko's father squatting, his expression intent, inspecting the leaves on a vine.

"Good morning, Stavros."

"Eleni! *Kalimera*," Stavros greeted her warmly. "I thought you'd rest today. Not venture up here."

"I decided to explore," Eleni explained. She looked around, taking in the view. In the distance, tree-covered mountain peaks stood silhouetted against the sky above, while below, beyond the vines, wound a narrow dirt road. "I forgot how uniquely these vines are planted. New York, California, and France ... Those vineyards share one thing in common. Their vines are planted in perfectly placed rows, each tree measured out at an equal distance from one another, all in rich soil." Eleni bent down, scooping up a pile of rocks. "But here, it's as though the vines found roots wherever the wind dropped their seeds. And somehow thrived." She held the stones a moment before letting them drop to the ground. "It seems impossible."

Stavros chuckled. "Nothing is impossible if you want it badly enough. Andreas and my *babá* cultivated this from nothing." He gestured at the land before them. "With a little luck, a lot of prayers, years of hard work, and these stubborn vines, two young men with a dream created magic."

A sad smile crossed Eleni's face. "My *pappou* used to say that Robola was magic in a bottle."

"Yes, yes he did," Stavros mused. "Did you know that Robola is only grown on Kefalonia? Nowhere else in the world," he informed Eleni, his chest puffing out with pride.

"Of course, I knew. *Pappou* may have mentioned once or twice ... or a few dozen times." She reached for a cluster of grapes. "It's the magic of Robola," she whispered, her eyes glossing over with tears.

Stavros opened his arms, and Eleni welcomed his embrace. "I miss him, too."

"I didn't mean to disturb you. What were you doing before I interrupted?" she asked, stepping out of his hold.

"I'll show you." Stavros motioned her over to inspect a vine closely. I'm cutting back the leaves blocking the grapes from the sun and checking for insects and viruses."

"You go through every one of these vines?" Eleni asked in awe. "There have to be hundreds."

"A good portion of them, yes," Stavros replied. "I employ a grape farmer permanently. But soon, I'll call upon temporary field workers, and we'll have a full staff for the harvest."

"Already? I didn't think that happened until sometime in September."

"Not here. The Robola and Mavrodaphne grapes are subject to early ripening, so they harvest sooner than other varieties. And by the time we finish picking those grapes, it's time to harvest the rest."

"Do you have an extra pair of clippers handy? I could help you."

Stavros took her face in his hands affectionately. "Go enjoy your day, Eleni *mou*."

"Are you sure? I want to do my part while I'm here."

"There's plenty of time for that. But not today. Settle in first."

"I'll see you later then," Eleni said with a smile, kissing him on the cheek.

Carefully, Eleni descended the steep hillside and returned the way she had come. But she didn't enter the house when she approached the estate. Instead, she strolled over to the public area where guests visited to enjoy an afternoon of wine and appetizers. No one was sitting on the patio or strolling the property now, though, as the winery was closed today. A cottage, purposed as a tasting room and retail store displaying and selling the wines the estate produced, sat just beyond the seating area. Eleni popped her head inside the shop. She remembered helping out at the cash register once in a while when she was old enough. It was quaint in a rustic sort of way. On one side, a weathered bar stretching the length of the building was set up for tastings. On the other side, tall shelves stocked wines, stored horizontally for proper keeping. But the middle of the room was, in Eleni's opinion, a complete waste of space. Her event-planning mind was already churning with ideas on better utilizing the cottage's unused sections, maximizing its full potential. There was so much she could do here! But it wasn't her place to interfere. With a sigh, she exited.

Eleni scanned the grounds, shielding her eyes with her hand. A building she didn't recognize stood about fifty yards away, looking out of sync with the property's aesthetic. It had no character and was seemingly more suited for a factory setting than this beautiful landscape. She vaguely remembered an old barn once standing on that spot. Had they replaced it with this sterile industrial structure instead? Why? But what she saw when she entered answered her question. They had modernized with state-of-the-art equipment. Stainless fermentation tanks dominated the main room. In another room, she found an updated destemmer and a wine press. After inspecting each piece of equipment, she opened the door to another room to discover the labeler and corking machines. These contraptions fascinated her most of all.

The last room, however, looked like a scientific research laboratory. But as Eleni stepped into it, her stomach dropped when she spotted Nikko engrossed in whatever he was doing with his beakers and droppers. Pivoting silently, she went to leave without his notice.

"Come on in, Eleni," Nikko said without turning to face her. She could almost hear the smirk in his voice.

Silently, she groaned. Did this man have eyes in the back of his head? It was too late to back away now, but she chose to hover by the door rather than step into what was quite clearly his domain. Though she had to admit, she was intrigued by what Nikko was doing. "I didn't mean to break your concentration," she began.

"Getting reacquainted with the place?" Nikko asked, turning around toward her.

His tone wasn't particularly welcoming, nor was his stance. With his arms crossed over his chest, Nikko exuded an air of suspicion or perhaps accusation.

"I've been wandering about," Eleni answered defensively. "I'll let you get back to work." Curiosity won out, however, and instead of backing away, she took one step forward, pointing toward his work-space. "It all looks very scientific," she said with interest. "But not the scientific path I'd have expected you to take." The moment she said it, Eleni wished she could take it back. That was too personal a comment when they hadn't even exchanged more than a few sentences since their teenage years, though there was once a time when they'd shared their hopes and dreams for the future.

"Sometimes paths lead you back to where you're rooted," Nikko replied, staring at her coldly.

Unsettled, Eleni tamped down a shiver. She could practically see the air between them frosting over.

"As long as it makes you happy, that's all that counts," she said softly.

"Are *you*?" he asked suddenly, throwing the question out there and taking her by surprise. He kept his eyes trained on hers; the pull of his sapphire pools made it impossible for her to look away.

"Am I what?"

"Happy. Are you happy, Eleni?" he asked, his tone clipped.

"Yes, of course," she answered quickly, tripping over her words. "Aside from being terribly sad over my *pappou's* death, of course."

"Naturally." His expression softened. "Excuse me. I didn't mean to imply that you should be happy during this time of mourning." After an awkward pause, he asked, "Have you been down to the *káva* yet?"

"The cellar?" Eleni questioned, the word catching nervously in her throat. She didn't want to read into it, but with the level of animos-ity emanating from him since she'd arrived, why would he mention that place at all? She and Nikko had experienced their first kiss down there. "No, I haven't been to the *káva*."

A faint blush spread across her cheeks. She couldn't bring herself to meet his gaze as the memories swam to the surface. Instead, she looked down at her worn-out, borrowed work boots. "They comple-ment my outfit, don't you think?" she nervously joked, changing the subject.

Ignoring her self-deprecation, he smiled. "I can take you down there if you like."

"Sure, if I'm not interrupting your work. I think it's the only place I haven't nosed around this morning."

"I have time for a quick break."

They walked in silence as he led the way, her heart beating at double rhythm. She wondered if the memories flooded his mind, too. Or had he blocked her from his mind completely? Still, her inquisitive spirit couldn't resist exploring below.

It was just as Eleni remembered, with roughly carved limestone walls, a ceiling of cedar planks, and a terracotta floor. French oak barrels ran down the center length of the space, and wooden floor-to-ceiling racks stored hundreds of bottles of the vineyard's yield.

She shivered, running her hands up and down her arms to warm herself. "I don't remember feeling such a chill in here."

He pinned her with an unreadable stare before regaining his focus. "It's always steady at fourteen degrees Celsius," Nikko informed her. "You've been away too long. Your tolerance has changed."

She took that as a dig. It was time to go. "Thank you for bringing me down here. I'm going to let you get back to work now." Eleni walked briskly toward the cellar stairs.

"Hold on." Nikko jogged after her. "You seem angry."

"*Me*? You've made yourself abundantly clear." Eleni whirled around, her eyes blazing. "But you're right. I don't belong here. I haven't for a long time."

"Wait a minute," Nikko said firmly. "I never said—"

"You didn't have to."

"You were the one who left," he reminded her, raising his voice. "You didn't call or write. You had a choice, and you chose never to come back."

Tears flooded her eyes. She didn't want to do this. Not here and not like this. She had promised herself she would keep her distance from Nikko. "Would you come back to a place that only reminded you time and time again of all the people you've lost? Why can't you understand I was grieving? I couldn't bear to return!"

"I know, I know," he said softly. Nikko reached out to embrace her but dropped his arms when she stepped back. "But what about after? I wanted to be there for you."

"What was the point? You live here, and I live an ocean away. How would a pair of teenagers make that work?"

"My feelings hadn't changed when you returned three years later, but you barely acknowledged me then, either."

Eleni laughed through her tears. "Again, I came to lay my *yiayiá* to rest. I wasn't in the right frame of mind to renew a friendship, Nikko." She wiped the tears from her cheeks. "Happy times," she whimpered sarcastically. "And now, I'm here for the third time to bury my last remaining relative."

She couldn't take it anymore. Turning, she climbed the stairs, mumbling a thank you to Nikko for taking time out for her. She could tell by how she left him standing there, watching her go, that he wanted to say more, but all she wanted to do was flee as quickly as possible. Nikko might think her heartless, but he had no way of knowing the rivers of tears she had cried over him.

CHAPTER 7

Eleni

Ten years ago

Hollow. That was the only way to describe how Eleni felt inside. She was numb, broken, empty, and had barely uttered a word during the nine-hour plane ride home. Instead, she clutched the sodden tissue she had used to wipe her face each time a new stream of tears fell unbidden.

She should have been offering comfort to her *pappou*, who had just buried the love of his life. But he was the one patting her hand affectionately in a show of strength. They were both forlorn, having done this one too many times. And she imagined the lump in his throat restricted conversation as much for him as for her.

When they finally arrived at their apartment back in the States, Eleni abandoned her suitcase in the corner of her bedroom and flopped onto her bed. Maybe she wouldn't have to face her grim reality if she stayed holed up forever. She had dealt with enough of that for a lifetime.

Later, when the door creaked open, she pretended to slumber. In her current state, there was nothing she could do or say to help her grandfather. She would only make matters worse. As darkness fell, he checked on her again, this time stepping into her room.

"Eleni *mou*, you need to eat something," he pleaded.

A sliver of moonlight sneaked its way through the window blinds. Eleni could barely make out the silhouette of the man. Fitting, she thought glumly. They were both merely shadows of who they once were.

She roused herself, guilt slicing through her for not being more helpful to him. "I'm not hungry, *Pappou*. But if you are, I can prepare something for you."

His sigh was laced with worry as he sat down beside her. "No. Let me order what you like. A pizza? Shake Shack? Chopped salad?" he listed, throwing out suggestions.

But she scrunched up her face in disgust at each one.

"*Manoula mou*, losing my Katerina was unbearable. But I was blessed to have her for over forty years. My life won't be the same without her," he croaked.

Eleni sat up in alarm when his voice cracked, and she embraced her *pappou* affectionately. Pallid skin, outlined more prominently from weight loss attributed to grief, made him look ten years older than he had seemed just weeks before.

"You and I, we've weathered many storms. We'll get through this one, too," he promised. "But this isn't just about your *yiayiá*, is it?"

Eleni didn't want to answer that question. It was her turn to be selfless. Ever since she was placed in their care, her grandparents had wholly dedicated their lives to her. Now, she was all her *pappou* had left in the world, and she would stand by him forever.

"I've lost everyone I love." Eleni wiped away her tears. "You understand that better than anyone. You've lost them too." She reached over and kissed him on the cheek. "We'll get through this together."

Andreas was an observant and astute man. Eleni knew this, and she loved her grandfather all the more for not pressing her on what else distressed her. She thought she'd come to terms with her feelings for Nikko three years ago. A choice had to be made—one that was best for everyone, even Nikko. The thought of stepping foot on the island again was just too painful. So she had left it all behind. She would never see Nikko again. And that reality ripped her heart to shreds in a different way than the finality of death.

But in an ugly twist of fate, Eleni had been thrown back into the fire the second she glimpsed Nikko again. Pandora tormented her by reopening the lid, which, she knew in her soul would never be completely sealed shut. But Eleni had no choice but to try to lock it all away as fast as it opened, knowing she and Nikko could never be. Her duty was by her grandfather's side in New York, now more so than ever.

CHAPTER 8

Nikko

Present Day

When Nikko had been told Eleni was returning to the island, he'd decided to avoid her at all costs. It had taken him a long while to get over her. Brokenhearted, he eventually accepted a life without her once he faced the painful truth that their love was not reciprocal. How could it have been when she'd dismissed him and everything they shared without a second thought?

But so much for the distance he needed. Nikko's father threw him the keys to the truck, ordering him to pick Eleni up from the airport. There was no arguing, even when he offered to take up the slack at the vineyard while Stavros went for her. 'Get over it,' Stavros had said. 'Act like an adult. What's past is past,' he had gone on with a wave of his hand.

If Nikko hadn't known better, he would have thought his father was deliberately trying to throw them together. This was a total waste of time and energy since, even if they somehow managed to get along, Eleni would be on the next plane home before the ground over her grandfather's grave even had a chance to settle.

Still, at the sight of her flagging down the truck, Nikko's heart plummeted to his knees. Steeling himself to resist the hold she evidently still had on him, he remained stony-faced. Until Nikko expressed his grief over Andreas, and Eleni began to shed tears of sorrow, slowly melting his frozen heart. One look in her direction, one sob escaping from her lips, was all it took to crack through his veneer.

The next day, well before dawn, Nikko went out to the fields to work. Sleep had eluded him, and he eventually gave up, creeping out of the house early, hoping to execute his original plan. Avoid Eleni at all costs.

But even after all these years, their connection hadn't been broken. Nikko immediately sensed Eleni at the doorway of his workspace. She was an irresistible force field drawing him in against his will. Should he have ignored her in the hopes she'd slither away? Yes. Did he? No. The pull was beyond his control. Instead, without turning to face her, Nikko let her know he was aware of her presence.

That was a mistake. Mentioning the wine cellar was a mistake. Taking Eleni down there was an even bigger mistake. The last thing he needed was to resurrect the past. What was he thinking? Upsetting her was another mistake. But seeing her had stirred up feelings he'd tried to suppress over the years, and it pissed him off. She wasn't in the right frame of mind to renew a friendship? That's what their relationship had been reduced to? Granted, a summer that started out with promise ended tragically. But that didn't erase what had been undeniable between them. And it sure as fuck wasn't just a friendship. He would have stood by her and helped her through all of it. But she wanted no part of him then, nor had she let him into her heart three years later. And now, it was Nikko's turn to keep her at bay.

Contradictory wants, needs, and emotions collided as they ran confusing circles in his mind: hate-love, remember-ignore, hurt-heal. But most important was what he had promised himself—protect and survive.

CHAPTER 9

Nikko

Ten years ago

Nikko had just finished his shift at the National Oceanography Centre Southampton when his mother called to let him know Katerina Pangalos had passed away and that Andreas and Eleni would be arriving on the island to bury her. He had just completed his second year at the University of Southampton, England, and his advisor had recommended him for a highly competitive summer internship.

Needless to say, his close-knit family was disappointed Nikko didn't return home between semesters, but they were proud to learn he'd been offered the opportunity. He knew, without his father outright saying it, that he and his grandfather hoped Nikko would take over running the vineyard one day, but they never tried to persuade him away from his ambitions.

After two years of biology, math, and physics, Nikko wasn't entirely sure this was his path, either. Although he loved working hands-on with the sea life, next year's classes promised to become more intense, and the idea of spending most of his days locked away in a dorm or a library didn't make him happy.

Without a second thought, Nikko booked a flight home and

informed the department he had to leave due to a death in the family. He hadn't been home for almost eleven months if he didn't include the few days he managed at Christmastime.

Nikko sincerely wanted to pay his respects to the woman who was like another grandmother to him in every way. But, if he was completely honest with himself, it was Eleni drawing him home. It had been three years of thinking about her and wondering if she missed him as much as he missed her. It took a while before he entertained dating, but eventually, he did. So far, no one had come close to penetrating his heart like Eleni did, and his longing for her lingered no matter how hard he tried to put her out of his mind.

Had Eleni written him off as ancient history, a youthful first love never meant to last, or would seeing him reignite the flame between them she'd deliberately snuffed out? Nikko would find out soon enough.

It was after midnight when Nikko's flight landed. By the time he arrived home, everyone was asleep. Facing Eleni at her grandmother's funeral for the first time was not ideal, but there was nothing he could do about it now.

Lying in bed, Nikko stared at the ceiling. He was restless. And anxious. And hungry.

The house was silent except for the hardwood creaking below his feet as he crept downstairs. With his head buried in the fridge, seeking a snack, Nikko was startled when he heard a gasp.

"Eleni!" Nikko exclaimed, turning in surprise.

She stared at him as if he were a food bandit raiding the house for all the feta and leftover *moussaka*. "Nikko. I ...um ...sorry." Slowly, she backed away. "I'll leave you to it."

"No, stay," Nikko implored. "You must have come down for the same reason. Hungry?"

"Not really. I just can't sleep." Eleni crossed her arms over her chest, rubbing them as if chilled. "No one told me you'd be here."

"You sound disappointed."

"No. No. I just wasn't expecting you."

Nikko shut the refrigerator door and moved a few steps closer to her. "I'm so sorry about *Yiayiá* Katerina."

She nodded, her eyes reflecting the same sorrow he'd last seen in them so long ago. "I'm going to head up."

Nikko was a sight—his hair mussed, two days of stubble on his face, and flakes of phyllo stuck to his lips from the *tiropita* he'd sampled. But he was also bare from the waist up, his pajama bottoms hanging low on his hips, and Eleni hadn't reacted to his near nakedness. Before, at the very least, she would have needled him about his two a.m. snacking habits. More than that, her obvious discomfort injured him.

The following day dredged up painful memories for Nikko. He was reliving his worst nightmare. If he felt this way, it had to be ten times more painful for Eleni. He recalled remaining by her side throughout that awful day, though, with her state of mind, she barely acknowledged his presence. But now Eleni wasn't his to comfort anymore, so he hung back and let the rest of his family console her at her grandmother's funeral.

Nikko kept his distance at the church, the gravesite, and, for the most part, during the afternoon at home, where mourners offered her their condolences. But when Eleni left the crowd to sit alone on the front porch, Nikko stole the opportunity to speak with her.

"Can I sit with you?" Nikko asked.

"I'm not in a talking mood," Eleni mumbled.

"Okay, then I'll talk, and you can listen."

"Nikko ..."

"Just hear me out," he pleaded. "You owe me at least that."

He took Eleni's silence as a sign to continue.

"I still love you," Nikko said, hoping that would elicit some response. "We're old enough to decide our own futures now, and I still want what we dreamed of."

"Age has nothing to do with it. Responsibility does," Eleni said, her eyes trained on her lap.

"Look at me, and at least tell me you still love me," he whispered.

"I can't," she said nearly inaudibly.

"Then face me and tell me you don't love me," Nikko challenged.

She rose from her seat. "I can't do that either," she said, walking to the door. Halting, Eleni met his gaze. "Go back to England and finish your program. I begged my grandfather to take me home right away. I never want to see this place again."

If Eleni thought she had placed finality on the matter, she was wrong. *Tell me you don't love me. I can't do that either.* That would fuel his hope through every letter, text, and email he wrote from then on. He would win Eleni back eventually.

CHAPTER 10

Eleni

Present Day

Eleni's *pappou* couldn't have wished for a more perfect day to be laid to rest on the island of his birth had he planned it himself. The sky was as blue as the sea below, not a single cloud marring its splendor.

Solemnly, Eleni steeled herself as she approached the seventeenth-century stone chapel. Then, wishing this was only a moment of déjà vu because God knows she'd been here before, she exhaled, praying for the courage to step inside the church.

Sensing her anxiety, Thalia and Maria, trailed by an army of relatives, flanked her on each side, supporting her by the elbows. They looked like a cluster of nuns, the whole lot dressed head to toe in black, delicate gold filigree Byzantine crosses dangling from their necks.

Unlike other Christian funeral customs, the casket remained open during the service. But Eleni didn't want to look at her grandfather in that state. Instead, she stared at the mosaic icons set into the walls of the church, each one depicting various pivotal points in Christ's journey, the various saints, and the archangels. She looked up at the ceiling where the Venetian influence on the island was evident. A breathtaking Renaissance fresco of the Virgin with the Christ Child dominated the space. She tried to focus on the intricate details of the art, distracting herself from her current situation.

But Eleni could no longer ignore what was happening or contain herself when the elderly priest, dressed in a black cassock and gold stole, censed her grandfather's body while chanting the memorial hymn. *'May his memory be eternal. May his memory be eternal. May his memory be eternal.'* The chiming of the dozen small bells on the thurible made her shiver. That sound and the pleasantly identifiable aroma of the incense that had once filled her with a sense of peace had long since been replaced with a correlation to death.

A deep sob bellowed from Eleni, the echo off the stone walls punctuating her grief. Turning when a gentle hand landed on her shoulder, she found Nikko's sympathetic gaze looking down at her. Yesterday, his sapphire gems could have cut glass. Today, though, there was a softness in them she had only recalled in her dreams. She thanked him with a small smile, though the sadness bleeding through her anguished expression was unmistakable.

After the service, the procession leading to the gravesite seemed to drag on when, in fact, it was only minutes away. Eleni's and Nikko's families had established a private graveyard at a far corner of their property when they had developed the vineyard in the late 1950s.

This was the moment Eleni dreaded most. It was brutally final. All too real. Though some people found comfort in visiting their loved ones at their 'final resting place,' that wasn't true for her. She wanted to believe they were always with her in spirit—that on some level she didn't yet understand, they watched her progression in life. Time for them was eternal, a blip compared to what they all experienced on Earth. They were in the ether around her, in the heavens above, in paradise, just as the church promised. Not several feet under this mountain of dirt and rocks. The thought of being entombed here made her feel like she'd suffocate. Tears streamed down her cheeks and clogged her throat as her eyes darted from headstone to headstone, marking the names of everyone she loved. She was truly alone in the world now.

Suddenly lightheaded, Eleni's vision blurred, and she began to sway. But before her knees buckled and she fell to the ground, someone rushed to her side, supporting her waist with one arm and lacing his fingers with hers with his other hand.

"I've got you, Brooklyn," he whispered.

"Nikko," she breathed. That was all it took for Eleni to not feel so entirely alone. He'd always come to her rescue, even when she pushed him away or broke his heart. Nikko's old endearment was the warmth and comfort she needed at that moment. He had insisted on the nickname no matter how often she told him she wasn't from that borough of New York. It became a joke between them, but the name stuck, and that was that.

After the burial, the Varvos family invited the mourners back to their home. Friends from all over the island had come to pay their respects, and even families from rival vineyards had shown up to offer their condolences. After hours of being pulled into several conversations, many relaying stories Eleni had never heard, and practically being force-fed plates of food she couldn't bear to eat, she was ready to escape from the house for a few hours of solitude. She stepped out onto the front porch for some air.

Suddenly, Nikko snuck up behind her, whispering in her ear, "Are you ready to get out of here?"

"How did you guess?"

"Ah, Brooklyn, I can still read you like a book. Though I must admit, once you turned into a mystery novel, you confused the hell out of me."

Eleni tilted her head to one side, squinting. The jest in his tone did little to disguise the innuendo. "There's no mystery," she retorted with enough honey in her voice to sweeten a liter of tea. "I'm an open book. You just had to bother to read the pages." She smirked.

"You did always have an answer for everything."

"And right now, my answer is yes! Get me out of here. I can't take any more sympathetic pats on the cheek."

CHAPTER 11

Eleni

Present Day

Nikko suggested driving to one of the many beaches on the island. Eleni picked up the dress she had discarded on the floor after she had changed into a swimsuit and a pair of shorts. She would have loved to make a bonfire and add it to the flame. She would never wear the dreaded garment again, hoping it would be her last black dress for a long while. If ever.

Eleni attempted to sneak out without seeming rude to those still lingering behind, paying their respects. But as she tried to leave inconspicuously, she came face to face with *Yiayiá* Thalia. Speechless, Eleni couldn't find an excuse for her outfit change and worried about what the older woman thought as they stared at each other.

But then Thalia surprised Eleni by smiling mischievously, her eyes twinkling with approval. Placing a finger to her lips, she hustled Eleni through a side door. "Nikko is waiting for you in the car," she whispered, pushing her along. "Come this way so no one holds you up."

"Thank you, *Yiayiá*," Eleni said, kissing her cheek. "I hope you don't think I'm being disrespectful."

"Not at all! Now go. Andreas only wanted your happiness, never your tears."

Eleni walked around the front of the house, expecting to see Nikko in the blue pickup truck. Instead, he was waiting for her in a black BMW convertible.

"Hop in." Nikko opened the passenger door. "I packed a basket of food," he said, referring to what looked more like a cooler than a picnic basket.

"So where are we headed?" she asked, slipping into the car.

"Kanali Beach," Nikko replied, driving off. "I thought someplace quiet would be best."

Suddenly, Eleni felt self-conscious. She remembered that beach only too well. It was unlike the other over-crowded ones, lined with rows of occupied lounge chairs and loud, bustling tavernas, all within earshot. Kanali was where she and Nikko had spent their time, spilling their secrets, walking hand in hand along the shoreline and kissing under the clear skies while wading in the gently rippling water. Eleni's heart raced, remembering how they had almost made love there, but the risk was too great at being discovered.

There were so many memories of her summers on this island that Eleni had blocked from her mind, but not that. Not him. Not even on that other dreadful, fateful day when they finally learned what it truly meant to love each other, body and soul.

"I remember Kanali," Eleni whispered more to herself than Nikko.

"I brought enough food to hold us over until sunset if you like."

"Thanks for being so nice," Eleni said regretfully. "I know I'm not exactly your favorite person."

Nikko took his eyes off the road for a split second to glance at Eleni but refrained from comment. "We're here," he said moments later.

Eleni reached for the beach blanket and towels in the backseat of the car, and Nikko grabbed the heavier items. The pair then headed down the path to a secluded area.

The sun felt like an elixir on Eleni's skin, and she pondered why, even on the warmest days in New York, it didn't have the same effect on her. Yet the same sun shone down on her here as it did there.

"Wine?" Nikko asked, offering her a stemless glass generously filled with white wine as they sat on the beach blanket overlooking the azure waters.

"One of yours?" she inquired.

"One of ours," he corrected. "Yes."

"Ours?" she asked with a puzzled frown.

"I can only assume that, as his only heir, you own your grandfather's half of the vineyard now."

"I just buried my *pappou*," Eleni snapped. "Inheritance is the last thing on my mind."

"Eleni—"

"Don't." She held up her hand. "Is that why you brought me here? To see where I stand with his half of the business?"

"No, no. I'm sorry," Nikko said quickly. "Is that really how little you think of me? I didn't mean to insinuate anything. I apologize for not being more sensitive."

She saw the sincerity in his face and pulled back her accusations. Perhaps she had overreacted. "No, I'm sorry. Being here has my emotions all over the place."

"Here in Kefalonia or at this beach?" Nikko asked, forcing her to hold his gaze.

She laughed humorlessly. "Both, I suppose." Eleni hugged her knees. "We had so much fun here—me, you, and our brothers. I was the lone girl, but I kept up with your antics," she said, not addressing the elephant on the beach.

"Kept up!" Nikko laughed. "You were more of a daredevil than the three of us combined."

"How *is* Yanni?" She smiled, thinking of Nikko's younger brother.

"He's great. He's finishing culinary school in Italy." Nikko dug into the basket, ripping off a piece of bread. He spread a generous portion of *melitzanosalata* onto it and offered it to Eleni.

"Impressive, but not surprising," Eleni said fondly. She took a bite of the bread, mumbling her thanks around a mouthful of exploding flavor. "I recall he'd spend much of his time in the kitchen instead of helping us on the vineyard."

A wave of sadness washed over her. Nikko couldn't ask about her brother in return. Any pleasant memories she had on this island always ended up overshadowed by ones that cost her unbearable pain.

Had her brother, Peter, lived to choose a career, what would he be doing today? Would he have made this his home? He'd always loved shadowing Nikko's father in the field, firing off questions about the winemaking process while they worked. But he also liked to tinker with engines and often assisted in the repair of broken equipment.

As if Nikko could read her thoughts, he placed his hand over hers. "I miss him too," he said softly.

Silence fell between them. Eleni pulled her sunglasses from her bag, slipped them on, and lay face up on the blanket. Then, without turning to face Nikko, she asked, "You wanted to be a marine biologist. What happened?"

"After two years at the university, I changed my mind," Nikko explained. "I missed the vineyard more than I'd expected, and I decided I'd rather scuba dive for pleasure than take the required classes I hated and study the intricate biological aspects of marine life."

"That's fair," Eleni said, propping herself up on her elbows.

"What about you?" Nikko inquired. "How did you end up in event planning?"

"By accident, really," she said, lifting her shoulders in a shrug. "Friends would ask me to help plan their parties. I came up with fun themes and creative ways to execute them. A guest approached me at one of those parties and asked if I could plan her child's fifth birthday party. Little did I know, the woman was socially connected, and before I knew it, I was getting requests for sweet sixteen parties, bachelorette bashes, and bar mitzvahs. It just seemed to snowball from there."

"How old were you?"

Eleni laughed, still in awe of how it all came about. "I was in my first year of college. I quickly changed universities along with my major, shifting to Event Management." She lifted her hand, palm up. "Who knew there was such a thing! By the time I graduated, I had gained a respected reputation, and suddenly, I was organizing trade conventions and fundraising galas."

"So you're happy?" Nikko asked.

Eleni looked at him thoughtfully, not sure how to answer the question. She sighed. "Happy enough, I suppose. Work takes up much of my time, and I enjoy what I do."

"And your personal life?" he asked hesitantly.

"I have great friends." She knew that wasn't what he was really asking.

"No one more important than a ... friend?"

"I was seeing someone, but we just split up."

"And by 'just,' you mean in the last month or so?"

"No." She blew out a long breath. "A few days ago." She scrunched up her nose, waiting for his reaction.

"What?" Nikko shot up from his relaxed position. "You mean to tell me he broke up with you just when your *pappou* died?"

"Something like that. Well, actually, I broke up with him. It was a long time coming. I brushed off certain signs that we weren't right for each other until I just couldn't anymore."

Nikko stared at her, his eyebrows nearly touching his hairline as he waited for more details.

She sighed in defeat. "Gregory, my ex," she clarified, "didn't think I should leave my business obligations to bury my grandfather in Greece. He said it wasn't fiscally practical or something like that." Eleni made a face. "He didn't get it, even when I tried to explain it to him. But then again, he didn't get me. Our priorities weren't the same. And not just over the importance of carrying out my grandfather's wishes. Over everything … work, life … I'd just had enough."

"Asshole."

"Maybe. Or maybe we were just too different." Eleni shook her head. "The suggestions coming from his mouth after we left the hospital had me reeling. Gregory made it seem like he had my best interests in mind. It was an eye-opener. And that was right after he insulted a huge event I had just successfully organized, referring to it as 'my little event,'" she added, air quoting.

"He wasn't for you," Nikko stated. "Plain and simple. People say love is complicated and messy. Complicated, maybe sometimes. But messy? No. If the so-called relationship is too much work, your lives don't fit together, and you feel like it's a constant struggle, then that's not love."

"It sounds like you're speaking from experience," Eleni said curiously. It was her turn to raise her eyebrows, waiting for his truth.

"Let's just say some people won't let go even when it's plain as day the relationship is toxic."

"That doesn't sound like fun."

"No," Nikko confirmed. "Especially when she conveniently pops up just about everywhere I go. But enough about Antonía," he said, waving away the topic.

"Wait? What?" Eleni's eyes grew wide. "Did you say Antonía?"

Nikko pulled a face. "I suppose you remember her then?"

"She was unforgettable, to say the least. You hated her, but one of your best friends *liked* her," Eleni emphasized, her hands outstretched to make her point.

"It's not what you think."

"You said *relationship*," Eleni said, elongating each syllable.

"No relationship. Except maybe in her mind." Nikko ran his hands through his hair. "I wish I never mentioned her name."

"And now that you did, I want details."

Nikko groaned.

"I told you about Gregory. It's only fair."

"All right," Nikko relented, scrubbing his hands over his face. "Right before leaving for university, I went to a bar and had too much to drink."

"Let me guess, Antonía showed up," Eleni interjected.

"One drink led to another, and we …"

Eleni raised a hand. "I get it. I don't need those details."

"After that night, Antonía seemed to think we were in a relationship. After I left for school, she constantly messaged me on Facebook and Instagram. When I came home for the summer, I tried to drum it in her that we weren't together."

"But that was over ten years ago. And now?"

"She finally gave up when I didn't come home the following summer except for …your grandmother's funeral."

"Oh, wow," Eleni murmured. She tried not to let this bother her, but she remembered Nikko admitting he still loved her, yet he'd already slept with that girl—Antonía of all people. Eleni had no right to be upset. She practically pushed him into the arms of another by her rejection, but a heaviness settled in the pit of her stomach over learning this.

"When she found out I was home and had no intention of seeing her, she finally got the message. Eventually, Antonía found someone else to annoy."

"Yay, for you," Eleni cheered lacklusterly.

"Right," he chuckled. "Except is anything that simple? The poor *malaka* married her. It lasted a few years, and now that she's divorced, she thinks we can pick up where we left off—which was nowhere, I keep reminding her." He pulled a bottle of Robola from the cooler, refreshing their drinks. "You got rid of your asshole, and I'll figure out a way to keep mine far away from me once and for all. They clinked glasses. "To moving forward," Nikko toasted.

Eleni smiled. "To moving forward," she repeated, unsure of what that meant for her.

After finishing the first bottle of wine, Nikko suggested walking along the shoreline. Slowly, Eleni began to let her guard down. They caught up on their lives, strolling side by side in ankle-deep water yet conscious of not making any physical contact. There was no reason why they shouldn't regain the friendship aspect of their former relationship after all. Anything romantic was long over, and besides, it had been between two completely different individuals who no longer existed—naive young teens who were foolish enough to believe they could survive a long-distance relationship. Surely now, as adults, they could simply enjoy each other's company for as long as she remained on the island.

Still, as they strode back to the blanket, a jolt of electricity passed through Eleni when Nikko reached out to guide her, his hand resting on the small of her back. She closed her eyes, mentally convincing herself that her reaction was just a residual response to the memory of his touch—nothing more.

They took their places on the blanket, side by side, to view the spectacle of metamorphosing colors above. As the sun dipped lower and lower, it appeared as if the massive marigold orb was about to be swallowed by the Ionian Sea.

Eleni sighed with appreciation. When had she last stopped long enough to watch a sunset? Did turning around as she walked down a NYC street last May just in time to catch the phenomenon known as Manhattanhenge, as the sun aligned itself between skyscrapers as it dipped below the horizon, count? It was worth viewing but in no way compared to this natural seascape. Life had always been different here. Serene. Peaceful. Until the worst had happened, of course. Meanwhile, her existence in New York was like running on a perpetual treadmill. But that was her fault. Keeping busy kept her from dwelling on what was missing in her life.

"Ready to head back?" Nikko asked after a while.

"No," Eleni laughed. She never wanted to leave this breathtaking view, and the thought of returning to everyone at the main house filled her with dread. Still, it was getting late, so she sobered. "But I guess we should."

They collected their belongings and made their way up the path, illuminated only by the pale light of the moon and the twinkling stars above.

MELITZANOSALATA

Ingredients
3 large eggplants
1 head of garlic
¼ cup seasoned breadcrumbs
½ cup extra virgin olive oil
1 teaspoon balsamic vinegar
Juice from ½ of a large lemon
3 tablespoons freshly snipped dill
1 teaspoon sugar
1 tablespoon paprika
Dash of cayenne pepper (optional)
Salt & pepper to taste

Method
Pre-heat oven to 400°F

Place the eggplant on the rack of the baking dish. Puncture each eggplant in several places so that any excess water will drain as it roasts.

Place a head of garlic on aluminum foil. Slice off the top and drizzle with olive oil. Wrap the foil around the garlic and place it in the same baking pan as the eggplant.

Roast for 1 hour. Remove from the oven and cool for approximately 45 minutes.

Peel away the skin of the eggplant and remove as many seeds as possible. Squeeze the roasted garlic from the skin.

In a food processor, pulse the eggplant, garlic, breadcrumbs, olive oil, balsamic vinegar, lemon, dill, sugar, paprika, cayenne (if used), salt, and pepper until thoroughly blended.

*Remember that each eggplant is different in size and water content. You may need to adjust the amount of oil or breadcrumbs to achieve the desired consistency.

Serve on crostini, crackers, pita, or crusty bread.

CHAPTER 12

Eleni

Present Day

The ride back to the house was silent. Not because of any lingering tension between Eleni and Nikko; they were simply content and relaxed. Eleni's sigh as she reclined back in her seat punctuated her mood. It was the first time in more months that she could recall feeling so at ease.

Though she loved her career, it was demanding; she was always running on deadlines and catering to sometimes challenging clients. As a result, she rarely took a day to simply be, with nothing on her mind but beautiful surroundings. And the last several days had wrung her out. Her grandfather's death, arranging to have him flown overseas, the breakup with Gregory, and scrambling to fill Angela in on the workload so she could take the reins was just too much all at once.

Even though Eleni had buried her beloved *pappou* earlier that day, this few-hour respite helped to shed many burdens, if only temporarily.

When they pulled up the driveway, Eleni was relieved that the house seemed still.

Nikko exited the car and came around her side to open the door for her. Offering his hand, he helped her out. Moonlight bathed his face, Eleni's heart beating rapidly as their eyes locked. Time hadn't faded her memory of Nikko's attractiveness—not one bit. What time had done was transform a cute boy into an exceptionally handsome man. How could his eyes be even more hypnotic blue than before? Hypnotic, alluring, irresistible. 'He's just an old friend,' she drummed into her head, forcing herself to break her stare.

"Thank you, Nikko, for tonight." Not sure what to do or how to properly show her gratitude, Eleni awkwardly leaned in to hug him. Her heart lurched as he embraced her in return. She sighed, forgetting her mantra from seconds before as a comforting sense of familiarity overcame her. At that moment, Nikko seemed very much the boy she had once loved, though it felt different to be in his arms now. He was broader. More muscular. Toned. She stayed in his hold a bit too long for her own good. On his part, he seemed reluctant to release her. With a final hug, she patted his back, breaking their embrace.

Before Eleni stepped away, Nikko grabbed her wrist, pulling her back to him. He breathed her name as a question, their eyes meeting. It would be so easy to reach up and kiss him—how she longed to— but it wouldn't be fair—not to her, and especially not to him. Yet that undeniable pull of desire was testing her restraint.

"Goodnight, Nikko," Eleni whispered. "Thank you for today."

After such an emotional day, Eleni should have fallen asleep as soon as her head hit the pillow. Instead, her mind was reeling from the day's events and the dichotomy of it all. The intense sorrow of her grandfather's burial brought the years of grief she held for her family to the surface. But later, with Nikko, the sorrow had floated away with the sea's ebb and flow. And because of him, she didn't feel entirely alone. Soon, her eyelids grew heavy, and she finally began drifting off. The last image in her consciousness was the look of affection reflected in Nikko's eyes and his disappointment as she walked away.

* * *

Nikko lay wide awake in his bed. He'd vowed to keep his distance from Eleni while she was on the island. Of course, that was nearly impossible while living in the same house. Already, he'd broken too many promises he had made himself to remain detached. It only took one whimper from her during the funeral service, and his resistance had cracked.

He remembered how broken she was all those years ago when she learned her family had been killed in an automobile accident. Eleni's parents had left the house that morning to visit friends from New York who were staying with relatives on the other side of the island. They had a son the same age as Peter, so he was happy to go along with his parents.

Nikko and Eleni were excited to finally have an entire day alone. The day began with hope as they shared their dreams and brainstormed how to build a future together. They were only teenagers, but soon, they would make decisions about college, and neither wished to spend more years apart. Everything about that day had exceeded his expectations. Eleni was his, and nothing would ever keep them apart—or so he thought.

They arrived home in the most joyful spirits that evening, but that mood was broken when they were met with tragedy. It was Stavros who broke the news. Her family's car was struck at an angle by a speeding car coming around the bend of a mountain, which caused their vehicle to roll down a ravine. There were no survivors.

Eleni collapsed into tears. Stavros and Nikko each grabbed her by the elbows, helping her to the sofa. The next few days were a blur. Not only for himself but most definitely for Eleni. She was in shock. She didn't speak or eat. Nikko's mother had to help dress her for the funeral. And Nikko couldn't even reach through to her. Everything they had talked about and shared was forgotten.

68

It had been a devastating time for everyone. Though they were two separate families—Varvos and Pangalos—in their hearts, they were one. The loss was immeasurable.

Observing Eleni again, having to endure all that goes with saying goodbye to a family member, brought back the memories of that horrible day. Though as much as she adored her grandfather, nothing could compare to that horrific day. But as he'd watched Eleni's weary face while she politely spoke to each mourner, Nikko knew something had to be done. So he'd pulled his *yiayiá* aside, and the two of them conspired an escape while she filled a basket of food.

Now, the memories of their youth flooded his mind. No one had ever occupied his heart the way Eleni had. He tried to tell himself it had only been young first love. Idealistic love. Something everyone goes through and eventually gets over. He had kept those thoughts on repeat since she arrived back on the island—until he held her under the moonlight, the stars twinkling their approval from above. Having Eleni in his arms felt right, and he didn't want to let go. But once they parted for the night, he reminded himself Eleni was only here for a brief time. She wasn't his. Maybe she never really had been.

CHAPTER 13

Eleni

Present Day

The following day, Eleni poured herself a cup of coffee and headed to the back porch, where she knew she'd find Maria and *Yiayiá* Thalia.

"*Kalimera*, Eleni," the women greeted in unison, each wearing the same conspiratorial smile.

Eleni sat down beside the women, conscious of their stares.

"Did you and Nikko have a nice time yesterday?" Maria asked.

"I—I hope you didn't mind that I left," Eleni started, flustered. "I just, well … and Nikko offered—"

"No need to explain, *koukla*," Thalia said affectionately. "It was a long, difficult day."

Eleni nodded. "It was. And watching the sunset on a quiet beach was just what I needed."

"So what are your plans for today?" Maria asked.

"I thought I'd go into town. Maybe explore the area. It's been a long time, and I bet a lot has changed."

"It's changed some, but the soul of Kefalonia remains the same," Maria boasted.

Eleni smiled. She liked that idea. She'd had enough of change lately. "Well, has it changed enough that they have Uber now?"

"I don't know this Uber. You can take my car," Maria offered. "We'll be working in the tasting room all day and I won't need it."

"Oh, that's nice. How many days are you open to the public?" Eleni asked.

"Six. Tuesday through Sunday, when we have customers," Thalia replied somberly. "Some days are slower than others, though today we have a tourist group coming through."

"We don't get as many walk-ins as we'd like," Maria added. "Other local wineries are much larger than ours and have big advertising budgets, so they attract more tourists."

"Hmm." Eleni chewed on that for a moment. "What are the names of these other vineyards? Can you write them down for me?"

"Sure. Are you going to spy on the competition?" Thalia asked with a glint of mischief in her eyes.

"Possibly," Eleni said without further explanation. Her idea of exploration to reunite herself with the island had just taken on a new purpose. A plan was taking root in her mind. She wasn't ready to say anything yet, but once she made some inquiries, Eleni would share her ideas.

* * *

The most logical place for Eleni to begin exploring was Argostoli, the capital of Kefalonia. But Eleni didn't quite find what she'd hoped for. Although the main square was picturesque, the side street of Lithostroto catered mainly to tourists. Cafés and souvenir shops lined the vibrant alley instead of the unique shops of craftsmen's wares she had hoped for there.

As a teenager, she loved walking these streets. But her perspective had changed now. She was not frolicking aimlessly around with nothing to do but waste the day as she pleased. Eleni had a specific goal and needed to find what she was looking for elsewhere.

Before she returned to the car, Eleni couldn't resist ordering a frothy *frappé* from a café window and a bag of *mandoles*—almonds enrobed in deep red layers of hard-crack caramel—from a well-known candy store.

Feeling lighter than she had in days, Eleni drove from town to town, singing along to the songs on her nineties playlist. Boy bands and Britney Spears were the sounds of her youth, and aside from the Greek music she heard on the radio during her summers on the island, these songs reminded her of happier times.

But Eleni was an adult now, and her focus had changed. She viewed each town and every store she visited from a tourist's point of view. She was on a mission, and it kept her busy all afternoon. In Razata, she bought local thyme honey, a stunning hand-painted clay platter, and an artisan-crafted rose gold necklace for Angela as a thank-you for taking charge while she was away. In Assos, she stepped into a tiny shop where delicately embroidered linens were on display, and in Agia Effimia, Eleni couldn't resist purchasing fragrant bottles of herb-scented olive oil.

Satisfied with the day so far, she pulled a scrap of paper from her bag listing some of the other wineries on the island. Twenty minutes later, she pulled up to the one that apparently attracted the most visitors, according to her Google search.

Eleni parked outside and walked around to the entrance, observing the guests and staff. She had to admit, the place was quite impressive. Its rough stone walls had that old-world look, yet it also had an appealing modern flair.

Customers sipped their drinks while snacking on appetizers, and the servers seemed more than happy to chat while offering information on each variety of wine. Evidently, this was a larger operation than the Pangalos Varvos winery. Eleni needed to figure out how to make theirs distinguishable from the others, and this one was most probably their largest competition. She would likely be on the island for only another week or so, but perhaps she could make suggestions to lead them in the right direction, even if she wasn't there to execute them.

From there, she visited the other establishments that were more comparable in size to Pangalos Varvos. One was quaint, and the family-operated staff was friendly, but they only offered wine tastings, nothing more. A chalkboard sign suggested visitors bring their own picnic basket if desired. Eleni thought this was a wasted opportunity for additional revenue. Even if they didn't have kitchen facilities, at a minimum, they could offer cheese and crackers to pair with their wines.

Another place didn't seem bothered enough to even greet a customer, and Eleni wondered why it was recommended as a place to patronize. Pangalos Varvos was miles above them when it came to hospitality.

Finally, after visiting four different vineyards, Eleni felt she had all the information needed to develop a plan. The ideas were churning in her event-planning brain, and she couldn't wait to get back and map it all out.

CHAPTER 14

Eleni

Present Day

After Eleni had freshened up with a brief shower and a change of outfit, she opened her laptop, searching for information on the various festivals and events on the island. Indeed, there must be a way to capitalize on these occasions and bring further exposure to the vineyard. The aroma of herb-scented meats drifted in from the kitchen, making its way up to her room and luring her from her concentration. Her stomach grumbled in complaint. But Eleni wanted to answer an email from Angela before she closed her screen and descended the stairs to join the family for dinner.

"*Kalispera,*" she said, smiling in greeting as she found the only open seat at the table. It was next to Nikko's as if by coincidence, and Eleni wondered if that was by his design or his family's. Seeing how he avoided greeting her, she assumed it was the latter. Well, that was fine with her. She was hungry and was not inclined to figure out the reason for Nikko's mercurial mood.

An oval platter of fresh fish smothered in *skorthalia* took center stage on the table. So that was what she smelled—the irresistible lure of pungent garlic was one she could never resist.

Eleni's mouth watered at the sight of plump red tomatoes garnished

74

with fragrant basil; h*orta*, greens sautéed in olive oil and lemon juice accompanied by a mound of fried *kalamaria;* and skewered, marinated jumbo shrimp sitting on a bed of rice pilaf. She didn't know where to begin, but she wanted to sample all of it!

Eleni was anxious to share some new ideas for the vineyard and discuss what she'd observed at the other wineries. But right now, her mind was on filling her plate. Anyway, she figured everyone would be more receptive to her on a full stomach.

"That was the best meal I've had in years," Eleni complimented after all the food was devoured. "You should open a restaurant," she eagerly suggested to Maria and *Yiayiá* Thalia.

Maria laughed her off. "I'll leave that to Yanni. Cooking for the family is enough for me."

It was as if Maria had read her mind. But Eleni would keep that notion to herself until she learned how the family felt about the rest of her ideas.

Eleni set down her fork and cleared her throat. It wasn't her place to tell this family how to run their business, so she hoped they considered her suggestions in the spirit they were intended.

"Earlier, you mentioned that some of the other wineries had much more traffic than yours," she said, cautiously approaching the subject.

"It's never been our main priority," Stavros explained. "Maria and *Mamá* run the little store only because all the other vineyards have one. When my father and your *pappou*, God rest his soul, started the vineyard, they only cared about growing grapes and making good wine. They had little time for much else. They took side jobs in the off-season to supplement their income. When the first yield was finally ready for consumption, they had to figure out a way to market it."

"Did you know your grandfather worked in a taverna?" Thalia asked Eleni.

"My *pappou*? No."

"When he wasn't working at the vineyard, he was tending bar at the taverna to earn extra money," Thalia said.

Eleni turned to Thalia's husband, her *pappou's* old partner. "*Pappou* Kostas, did you also work in a taverna?"

"No, I worked on the ferry—the one that goes back and forth from Argostoli to Lixouri." He raised his glass of wine as if to make a toast. "My dear friend Andreas was the smart one," he admitted, his voice thick with emotion. "We made our first sale because of his connection with the taverna. One case of wine turned into two, and when patrons kept ordering our bottles, your *pappou* gained the confidence to branch out."

Eleni had never heard this story before. Why was that? Had she never thought to ask? She felt a flash of guilt. Maybe it was just that the vineyard had always been an entity in her life. One she'd taken for granted. She should swing back around to why she brought up the subject. Yet she was thirsting to know more.

"*Babá*," Maria addressed her father-in-law. "Eleni was trying to tell us something, and off you went telling one of your stories."

"No, please don't stop," Eleni urged. "I want to hear the whole thing from start to finish. Don't leave anything out. There's time to discuss what I needed to later."

"What you leave behind is not what is engraved in stone monuments, but what is woven into the lives of others." Pericles

CHAPTER 15

Kostas & Andreas

Kefalonia, Greece
1965

Kostas had hoped he was done with working on the island ferry for good. It wasn't the most exciting job, riding back and forth from Argostoli to Lixouri, the two largest towns in Kefalonia. He had been doing it since he was thirteen years old, and every day was the same. Tie up the boat, bring the plank down for the passengers to disembark and new ones to embark, remove the plank from the dock, untie the boat, and cross the island. It was repetitive and tedious, and he longed to do something more. Something to give him a sense of pride and accomplishment. And now that he was finally working toward his dream, it was easier for Kostas to show more enthusiasm as he completed his daily tasks.

Confident of an end in sight made the job more tolerable—a temporary situation to earn extra money until his new venture got off the ground. He and his friend, Andreas, had worked for years, saving every penny they earned to afford a piece of land to start their own vineyard. It seemed futile, merely a pipe dream between two young men until Andreas' father had passed away, leaving him eighty *stremmata* of forgotten, uncultivated land—the equivalent to almost twenty acres by U.S. measurements. They later learned that a modest house had stood on that property until 1953 when a devastating earthquake, which had measured 7.3 on the Richter scale, had leveled most of the island. Unbeknownst to his friend's dear father, he had provided the very miracle Andreas and Kostas had prayed for.

Work on the vineyard was never-ending, but surprisingly, summer required the least amount of their time. But once the harvest neared, all that changed; the labor was arduous and the days long. It took a few years, but their debut wines were finally ready to bottle and label. Now, their main focus was on finding a market for their wine. No small task with so many established vineyards already on the island. But that was where Thalia, Kostas' young wife, helped out. They had only been married a year, and although he'd initially wanted to wait until he had more money to support her, love had won out over sensibility.

As it turned out, the young woman's support was invaluable—not only for her cooking and housekeeping—she had ideas Kostas and Andreas hadn't the time or inclination to implement. Thalia asked the men to build a patio for guests to sit and savor their wine while enjoying the beautiful view. And then she'd come up with the notion of preparing a menu of *mezéthes* to pair with those wines. But Thalia needed to find a way for tourists to discover them. So she suggested Kostas hand out cards to ferry riders for a free tasting.

But it wasn't enough. Drawing visitors to the vineyard was vital, but they desperately needed to sell their bottles by the caseloads to survive.

* * *

After Kostas left for his shift, Andreas prepared to head to his own temporary position. When he was younger, he had worked at a seaside taverna, bussing tables and cleaning dishes. Now, he had returned as a bartender, pouring drinks to locals and tourists alike. But the little money Andreas was earning was not enough. He had to find another way to contribute to the vineyard's success. Then an idea came to him. So before he left for his shift, he went to the wine cellar and pulled several bottles off the rack.

The taverna was closed during *mesimera*, the sweltering afternoon hours when businesses shut down across the island. Andreas purposely arrived for his shift early, hoping to have a chance to speak to his boss. He had known the man for many years, and though he wasn't a warm person, Demos was usually fair.

Nervously, Andreas stepped into the owner's office, setting the bottles of wine in front of him. Demos was at his desk, his chair reclined, his round belly protruding over the belt of his pants.

"Demos, these are my wines," Andreas stated with an air of authority. But underneath his facade, anxiety clawed at his insides. He had a lot riding on this. "I'd like you to try them, and if you approve, I'd like to serve them tonight."

Demos leaned forward, stroking the scruff on his face. He stared at the bottles thrust before him, eyeing them blankly. He pulled a cigarette from a pack on his desk, lit it, and took a long drag. His expression gave nothing away. Andreas wasn't sure if he was contemplating or dismissing the idea.

Come on, come on, Andreas thought. *I just need a break—a chance.* But his stomach roiled with trepidation and self-doubt, certain Demos would turn him away.

"Bring me a glass," Demos finally ordered.

"Yes, sir," Andreas said, expelling the breath he didn't realize he was holding. He sprinted to the bar, and within seconds, he was back with a wine glass and a corkscrew.

"Robola first," Demos demanded gruffly.

Andreas nervously removed the cork, poured the golden liquid, and handed it to his employer, trying to stop his hand from shaking. He wondered if Demos even knew much about wines. He'd only ever seen him drink hard liquor.

After sniffing its citric notes and swirling the wine to appreciate the rich color, Demos downed the entire contents of the glass in one unsophisticated gulp. Then, without praise or critique, he motioned for Andreas to open the next bottle. Both the Muscat and Mavrodaphne were sweet wines, better consumed as an after-dinner drink or as a dessert wine. Andreas worried he wouldn't serve these varieties in his bar. There seemed less demand for them here amongst the rowdy patronage, though occasionally tourists ventured in for 'local atmosphere.' But the Robola had been his best bet, and now it seemed to have had little effect on his boss.

After trying all three, Demos lowered his glass with a loud thump. "You did okay, kid, for your first time out. I didn't think you had it in you."

"Thanks?" Not sure if that was an insult or a compliment, he asked, "So will you consider letting me serve them?"

"Tell you what I'll do. Serve out the rest of these bottles by the glass. If the response is good, I'll buy a case of each."

"Thank you! Thank you!" Andreas tried to contain his excitement, fervently hoping the patrons' response would be positive.

Demos cocked his head toward the door. "Go. Before you're late for your shift."

"Right away, sir." Andreas ducked through the door, juggling the open bottles before his boss changed his mind.

Within the hour, all three bottles were empty. Andreas surveyed the customers; the reviews had been more than favorable. Later, on his break, he showed the empties to Demos, hoping he'd keep his word.

"Gone in an hour, and everyone wanted more." Andreas beamed with pride.

Demos laughed, shaking his head. "A deal's a deal. Bring a case of each tomorrow."

Andreas could have hugged the man, but instead, he offered the firm handshake of a budding businessman. He was excited to tell his partner. But it was well after midnight when he finally finished his shift and cleaned the bar station. Kostas would be fast asleep by now, so the good news would have to wait.

The following day, Andreas found Kostas in the vineyards cutting back leaves so dense they could threaten to disease the grapes. It was difficult working part-time jobs and juggling the labor of the vineyard. He sidled beside his friend, pulled out his clippers, and began working. Excitement had him grinning from ear to ear.

"I have some news." Andreas cuffed his hand over Kostas' shoulder. "I took a few bottles of our wines to the taverna last night, hoping to get Demos to try them. I wasn't sure he'd even give me a chance, but he sampled them and agreed to let me serve the rest of the bottles."

Kostas dropped his shears in surprise, waiting to hear the outcome. "And?"

"And the empty bottles spoke for themselves! Not a drop left," he announced, a grin lighting up his face. "Demos ordered a case of each variety."

"Wonderful! Working at the taverna might just pay off after all," Kostas exclaimed.

It hadn't taken long for the busy seaside taverna to go through three cases of wine, even though the bar also carried labels from several other vineyards on the island. When Demos ordered several more cases, Andreas decided to branch out to other establishments. After all, if people enjoyed his wine here, why not elsewhere? Soon, he convinced nearly a dozen restaurants and tavernas to offer his wines on their menus. It had become clear to both men that they each had separate talents, and Andreas was far more of a businessman than a farmer. But it wouldn't be long until the harvest came, and their yield was their first priority. Until then, they would earn as much money as possible to bolster their savings, and Andreas would tap every resource on the island to expand their blossoming market.

Thalia proposed an idea as they sat down for an early meal during *mesimera*.

She had set out a fresh *horiatiki* salad garnished with the fragrant basil she grew in terracotta pots set out along the back walkway. It would pair well with the *kreatopita*, a hearty meat pie she had prepared for the main dish made with rice, herbs, and fresh tomatoes.

"I was thinking," Thalia started as she cut out pie triangles, set them on plates, and offered them to the men. "Have you considered reaching out to restaurants beyond Kefalonia, Andreas?"

Andreas sighed. "I've thought about it. If only there were more hours in the day."

Kostas set his fork down. Stroking his chin, he contemplated. "The way I see it, we have about two solid weeks before the first harvest. In the meantime, if we get someone to help out part-time, you could take that time to secure some more steady accounts."

"I can do that," Andreas agreed. "Can we afford part-time help?"

"For a few weeks, yes," Thalia said. She had been handling the expenses so the men could run the vineyard and hold down their second jobs. As it turned out, Thalia had a talent for numbers and economizing.

Andreas had to admit he enjoyed representing the winery, even when he didn't come out with a deal. He never grew discouraged. Instead, the rejection only fueled his incentive to land the next account.

"Where do you suggest I begin?"

"That's entirely up to you, my friend."

"If I may?" Thalia interjected.

Andreas nodded for her to continue.

"Maybe not one of the surrounding islands already riddled with their own vineyards. Perhaps Athens instead?"

"Athens? That's a big fish to fry," Kostas declared.

"Maybe not," Thalia disagreed. "I have an uncle there who owns two restaurants, and I'm sure he has other contacts he can introduce me to."

"Then Athens it is!"

* * *

At last, it was harvest, and Andreas came home after successfully garnering enough accounts to keep the vineyard funded for at least another year. Thalia's uncle was more than happy to stock their wines at both of his restaurants. And his contacts were also receptive; Andreas landed several of those accounts. But it wasn't as simple elsewhere. Andreas grew tired of going from one establishment to another, most unwilling to take a risk on an unknown label, but he pushed on. With his easy, personable manner, people were drawn to him, making it easier to get his foot in the door. He wasn't pushy or boisterous, and proprietors appreciated his integrity. In the end, he made more deals than he'd initially expected, and he felt satisfied that he had secured the vineyard financially, at least for a while.

One season rapidly rolled into the next, and while Kostas and Andreas were busy winemaking, Thalia's mind was churning with other ways to attract visitors.

Spring came, and Thalia begged her husband and Andreas to find the money to build a small tasting room, promising it would pay for itself in the long run. They agreed, erecting a structure no larger than a tiny cottage, promising to extend it if all went well. Thalia chose to paint the walls a pale shade of lavender to contrast with the dark-stained pine shelves that would stock the wine bottles. On the opposite side of the shelving, the bar, made from the same wood, stretched the entire length of the room.

But it was the entranceway she loved the most. An arched trellis, spilling with fuchsia bougainvillea, framed the doorway. A pathway made from the same stone led from the cottage to the patio. Thalia then drove ten-foot stakes into the four corners of the patio to support string lights, which she ran along the perimeter. She purchased new patio tables and chairs, replacing the mismatched ones she got by with, adding low-sitting vases of wildflowers to each table. And just like that, she had an inviting outdoor patio for visitors to enjoy.

Once again, the summer season allowed Kostas and Andreas to work their summer jobs, though finding the time had become more challenging now. Something had to be sacrificed, usually several hours of much-needed sleep. The vineyard was doing relatively well for a new establishment, but they remained fiscally conservative, setting aside enough money in reserves in case the unexpected struck. And it could happen. The men had picked the brains of more experienced vintners on the island. Anything from a bad sales year due to the economy to a bug infestation to a devastating storm could wipe out an entire year of income.

"If all goes as planned, one more season, and we should be solid," Kostas said. "After all her efforts, I need to steer more ferry riders into Thalia's tasting room, or I will have one very despondent wife."

Andreas smiled sadly. "At least you have a wife. I don't even have time to look for one."

"Ah, *file mou*, you won't have to look. Destiny will bring her to you," Kostas told his friend.

"Easy for you to say. You've been in love with Thalia since you were twelve years old," Andreas said with a laugh. "When did you become such a romantic?" he asked, playfully slapping him on the cheek. "Destiny!"

Little did Andreas know that Kostas' prophecy was about to come true. When he least expected it, he'd be stricken with an affliction to his heart that, up until now, had eluded him.

CHAPTER 16

Katerina

Kefalonia, Greece
1965

"Ticket, please," the young man who had just lowered the ferry plank asked.

Katerina handed it to him and walked onto the boat. She had just spent two weeks in Crete with her mother's parents. Now she would spend three weeks with her other *yiayiá* and *pappou* before returning to New York. Usually, her parents would make the trip with her, but the restaurant they owned in Astoria, Queens was down a cook, and they just couldn't leave.

The ride across the bay to Lixouri took only about thirty minutes. As she stood, taking in the scenery, she couldn't help but notice the man who'd taken her ticket. He had a bright smile accentuated by his sun-kissed skin. Once everyone was onboard, he circulated from person to person, handing out business cards.

When he came around to her, he asked in heavily accented English, "American tourist?"

"I'm visiting my grandparents, as I have every year since I was small," Katerina replied in fluent Greek.

"Ah, so not a tourist at all. *Ellinitha!*"

"Yes," she laughed. "And, no, I'm not a tourist, but I still like to explore like one," she admitted.

"Well then, I'd like to introduce you to a fairly new winery," he said, handing her one of his cards with a friendly wink.

Taking the proffered card, she quickly scanned it. "Coupons for a free wine tasting? So that was what you were handing out. I was wondering." She tilted her head to assess him. "So you perform two jobs at once? How do your employers feel about that?"

He pointed to the captain. "He's fine with it. And so is the vineyard owner." Kostas lifted a brow and grinned. "Let me introduce myself." He bowed formally, though Katerina sensed a twinge of jest in the gesture. "Kosta Varvos."

She eyed him suspiciously before flipping the card over. When she saw his name listed as one of the vineyard proprietors, the deepening crease between her eyebrows accented her confusion.

"But why do you work on the ferry if you have a vineyard to tend to?"

"It's the height of the tourist season!" Kostas exclaimed. "Do you know a better way to drum up business?"

"I suppose that's true," she mused, wondering if he was flirting or if this was just his way of bringing customers in.

"I'll tell you what," Kostas offered, pulling a pen from his back pocket. He took the card from her and scribbled something on it before returning it. "Instead of one glass of wine, you can try an entire flight on me. Just present the card to my wife, Thalia."

"That's very kind of you."

"I have to go; the boat is about to dock. But I expect we'll meet again soon."

What a curious man, Katerina thought after he'd hurried off. Not flirtatious then, as she had first suspected until he mentioned his wife, but certainly friendly and eager. Passionate. That's what it was. Passionate for success. It certainly made her curious. Perhaps she might visit after all.

* * *

The next afternoon, Katerina pulled up in front of a simple home flanked by grapevines. The rustic handcrafted sign reading Pangalos Varvos Vineyard indicated she was in the right place. A flagstone path led her past the house to a patio in front of a small building accented by a sweet-looking trellised entryway. Several patrons were seated on the patio, enjoying glasses of wine.

Katerina didn't know whether to wait to be seated or to find one herself. Then, she spotted a lovely dark-haired woman holding a tray of wine-filled glasses emerging from the floral entrance she admired. Not wanting to be rude, Katerina waited to be acknowledged. She watched as the woman served a party of six, happily snacking on *mezé*, before looking in her direction.

After setting down the glasses, she walked over to Katerina. "Welcome. Would you like a table?" she asked with a smile.

This must be Kostas' wife. She was stunning, wearing a simple floral A-line dress belted at the waist. Her eyes, the color of dark golden honey, were warm and inviting.

"Ah! You came," Kostas exclaimed as he joined his wife, wrapping his arm around her waist.

Katerina thought that was him when she noticed someone exiting a barn moments earlier. "Yes, you were very convincing." She smiled brightly at the couple.

"He has that way about him," Thalia said fondly, cupping her husband's cheek. "Let me seat you at a table. My name is Thalia."

"*Hárika.* I'm Katerina. It's very nice to meet you."

"It's a pity you're alone today. It would be nice to share the experience with a friend."

"I'm used to it," Katerina explained. "I'm visiting my grandparents and often wander off alone."

Just then, Katerina saw another man walk out of the same barn

Kostas had exited. From what she could tell, he was noticeably hand-some, even from a distance. Heading in their direction, he waved to Kostas and Thalia. She concluded he must be a fieldworker by the look of his worn-out work boots and grape-stained clothes. His tanned, muscled biceps were a further indication. But it was his strik-ing gray eyes that caught her attention as he approached. Her heart leaped when he smiled at her before addressing his friends, her skin prickling from the heat of his stare.

"Who do we have here?" Andreas asked.

"This is Katerina," Kostas said. "I met her on the ferry yesterday."

"Ah! One of Kostas' tourists," he said with a low chuckle.

But Katerina thought she detected a hint of disappointment in his tone.

"Katerina is visiting her grandparents," Thalia added.

"They live in Lixouri," Katerina told Andreas shyly.

"So then you'll be here for a while?" Andreas asked, gazing at her with interest.

Thalia elbowed her husband, raising an eyebrow to emphasize her point. "Katerina, this is my husband's partner, Andreas."

"Don't let her fool you," Andreas corrected. "We couldn't run this place without her."

"Which reminds me, I have tables to tend to," Thalia said. "Andreas, would you be so kind as to seat and serve Katerina for me? Maybe even show her around the vineyard, if she likes?"

"Give me ten minutes to change out of my work clothes." Andreas led Katerina to a table for two situated under a shaded area.

"I can wait," Katerina agreed. "It's a pretty spot to relax by."

It wasn't long before Andreas was back, freshly groomed in a pair of tan slacks and a white shirt with the sleeves rolled up just below his elbows. Again, her heart skipped a beat at the sight of him. She couldn't remember the last time she'd had this reaction to a man, if ever.

He took a seat across from her, their knees bumping.

"What would you like to drink?"

"I'll go with whatever you recommend," Katerina replied.

He lifted a finger. "I'll be back in a moment."

A few minutes later, Andreas returned with a flight of wines resting on a beautifully handcrafted olivewood tray and a platter of *mezéthes*. She noticed there was also a single glass of wine for himself.

They clinked glasses. "*Stin ygía mas!*" Andrea toasted. "Tell me about yourself."

"What would you like to know?" Katerina asked shyly. "There isn't much to tell." She shrugged. "I come from a typical tight-knit Greek family in New York. My parents own a couple of restaurants there. They urge me to finish my education but then, like most Greek parents, expect me to settle down and get married." Nervously, she wiped away the condensation frosting her wineglass.

Andreas stared at her intently. "You just told me about your family and what they expect of you. But I learned nothing about what you want."

Katerina's eyes met his as she considered that. He was right. She loved her family but had never considered stepping beyond what they wanted for her. Suddenly, his intense stare stripped her soul bare, and she felt an uncharacteristic urge to reveal her innermost thoughts to this stranger.

"I suppose that I'd like to have a little adventure first. I love New York. It's my home. But there's a lot of world out there."

"What kind of adventure are you looking for?"

Katerina felt a flush heat her face. "I don't know. I suppose anything that doesn't require me to follow a path my father set forth for me," she explained. "If it was up to him, I'd be married the second I finished my studies. With the husband of his choice, of course." Katerina sipped her wine, calming her nerves. "I don't know why I'm telling you this."

"I asked," Andreas replied. "You have no interest in marriage?" he asked.

"Sure, I suppose." Katerina shrugged. "In my own time and to someone of my choosing, after I've had a chance to travel on my own." She laughed. "Who am I kidding? My father will never let me do that."

"Have you ever considered living here?"

"Like, full-time?" Katerina questioned. She chewed on that for a moment before answering. "I feel as though this is my second home. I've been coming every summer for as long as I can remember. But no, I never thought about moving here permanently."

"Minds change when circumstances do," he said quietly, sipping his wine.

"I suppose that's true. My parents left Greece due to their circumstances."

"I have an evening job at a taverna. I have to leave in an hour. But I'm off tomorrow. If you're available, I'd like to take you out and show you around."

"On a date?" she asked, her eyes widening in surprise. The idea thrilled her, but it also scared her to death. This man unnerved her. Maybe it was the way he transfixed her with his gaze. Or perhaps she was just way too attracted to him. Or was it that she feared his expectations? He had to have women clamoring for him, and she was out of her depth, having barely dated at all.

He chuckled. "Yes, on a date."

"That would be nice," she agreed before she could give herself a chance to back out.

Katerina left the vineyard with nervous anticipation fluttering about her stomach, wondering how she would make it through the next day with her insides tied up in knots.

* * *

Katerina and Andreas spent every free moment with each other for the next two weeks. She even stopped wandering the island alone to spend more time with him. Instead, she helped Thalia serve the guests who came to sample wine. One afternoon, Katerina brought her grandparents to the vineyard to meet Andreas and show them where she had recently spent her days. Anxiety set in as she pulled up in the vineyard parking lot. If they didn't like Andreas for any reason, they would report back to her parents and likely forbid her from seeing him again. But, to her relief, they offered their full approval of the young man. For all the good it did. Katerina's time on the island was quickly coming to an end.

"Can't I convince you to stay?" Andreas pleaded the night before she was slated to leave.

"I have responsibilities. I have to go home," Katerina murmured regrettably, her eyes downcast, knowing she'd be leaving her heart behind. But she also had to remember that as much as Andreas had asked her over and over to stay, he never once said he loved her.

They were seated on a cushioned wicker loveseat on the front porch of the home Andreas had been sharing with Kostas and Thalia. The full moon illuminated the sky, thousands of stars twinkling a message. The world was infinite with possibilities. But was it really? Or was it riddled with duty and obligation? For the first time in her life, she found herself torn.

Andreas held her tightly, brushing his fingers up and down her arm. Turning, he faced her. "I know we haven't known each other long, but I love you, Katerina *mou*. I am in love with you," he confessed. "I'm not saying this now to make your decision to leave more difficult. But from the moment we met, I knew there was something undeniable between us. I've never felt this way about anyone before." Andreas lifted Katerina's chin and leaned in, kissing her tenderly. "I'm in love with you," he repeated.

A tear rolled down her cheek, and Andreas wiped it away with his thumb. "I feel the same. I love you too," she admitted. "More than I can express. But I don't know how we can make this work. My parents expect me to return home without question."

"We have one life. We need to make the most of it," he urged. "To do what we want, not what is expected of us."

"I wish it were that easy," she said as more tears fell. "I've never been as happy as these last three weeks."

"And that doesn't have to end," Andreas begged.

"I'll be back next summer," she said with resignation.

"That's an eternity. My heart won't survive."

Katerina hugged him, holding on for an impossibly long time. Her tears streamed down her face uncontrollably as she wiped them away, to no avail. After one last lingering kiss, she rose. "I have to go," she said with finality. She hurried down the porch, running to her car without looking back, afraid she would crumble if she did.

* * *

Katerina returned to New York in a miserable state. In her mind, her life had ended the moment she kissed Andreas goodbye. She confided in her mother, who, after seeing how distraught her daughter grew, went to Katerina's father, imploring him to reconsider the matter. Though sympathetic, he argued that living thousands of miles away from them was simply not an option.

She and Andreas wrote letters professing their love for one another, but the distance was unbearable. Katerina barely ate, her coursework began to suffer, and socializing for her was a thing of the past. She couldn't bring herself to act like her life could just resume as though Andreas had never existed. She just wasn't the exuberant girl her parents once knew.

One afternoon, she ran to the mailbox, anticipating a letter from Andreas, only to find that two had arrived instead. One was addressed to her, the other to her father. The envelopes dropped from Katerina's trembling hands. Her stomach roiled with anxiety. Merely bending to recover the letters made her ill. Katerina was tempted to open the one addressed to her father and read the contents. But deciding that was wrong, she ran to her bedroom instead and hid it in her dresser. Depending on what Andreas had to say and how he phrased it, it could change everything or nothing at all. More than likely, Katerina's father would hold firm on his position.

She opened the letter addressed to her and read every word twice. His proclamations of love made her miss him even more. Andreas made his intentions clear. He explained that his letter to her father was a plea, listing why a union between them benefited his daughter. Not only could he provide for her, but more importantly, he would love her eternally.

Oh, my Andreas, your determination will get you far in business, but not with my babá. But she loved him for trying.

After dinner, she handed the letter to her father. "Andreas wrote to me today, *Babá*. He wrote you a letter as well," she added, her voice trembling.

Her father eyed her with disdain. "Whatever the boy wants, the answer is a firm no!"

"I'll leave you alone to consider what he's written." Katerina left the room but stayed within earshot as her father read the letter out loud to her mother. Katerina was hopeful when Andreas professed his love and asked her father for her hand in marriage.

"The nerve! I don't even know this boy," her father bellowed. "I'm not sending her off to marry a stranger."

"Oh, for heaven's sake! He's not a stranger. He's from *your* island. I had a lengthy conversation with your *mamá*. She told me he's a nice, hardworking young man with a good future," her mother defended. "Your parents approve of the boy."

"I don't care."

"You don't care?" Her mother's voice was laced with anger. "Your daughter is unhappy. She's withering away. Is that what you want for her?"

"Why can't she find a nice Greek boy here?"

"Because she fell in love there. Is that so terrible? It's not enough for you that she met a Greek boy," his wife scolded him. "You want the circumstances to be exactly the ideal plan you have in your mind for her life to go. That's not how life works," she added, poking him in the chest. "It's not how raising children works. She's grown and should be allowed to make her own choices."

"Choices!" he grumbled. "Choices get girls into trouble."

"Your parents are over there. She has a family to fall back on if she ever needs it. And she always has us. You're her father and I know you want to protect her, but she needs to make the life she wants."

"*Vre, ynaíka,* leave me be so I can think about this," Katerina's father barked.

"I will leave you with *this,*" her mother said, glaring at him angrily. "You can't fight or control who Katerina falls in love with. If you plan to rule her life like a despot, you will be left with an unhappy, bitter daughter. And that is your choice, but it will never be mine," Katerina's mother snapped before leaving the room.

Katerina shrunk into the hallway when she heard the door loudly slam shut. Her mother stormed past her without notice.

It took a full day of brooding before Katerina's father sat her and his wife down at the kitchen table. He downed a shot of ouzo, poured himself another, and chugged down that one, too.

Katerina sat across from him, her eyes as big as saucers, waiting for him to speak. The tissue in her lap resembled a pipe cleaner after twisting it beyond recognition. Katerina's overanxious mind was reeling with trepidation, and when her father finally spoke, his words didn't register at first.

"I can't get away for several weeks. I'm not handing you over to a man I know nothing about," he groused. "If he meets my approval, I'll think about giving the two of you permission to marry. But this ... this boy better be everything your grandparents say he is, or we will be on a plane back home before you can wish him well."

Two months later, Katerina returned to Kefalonia with her parents. She hoped beyond all hope that her father approved of Andreas. If he didn't, she'd never see him again. But Katerina's father was impressed with the small vineyard and Andreas' ambition. He also couldn't deny that the couple was very much in love. Not only did he offer his full blessing on the marriage, but he also offered to add the Pangalos Varvos wines to both of his restaurant's wine lists. Little did Katerina's father know, but this agreement sparked an idea in Andreas' mind that would eventually bring his daughter back to him.

Just weeks after their arrival, a small village wedding took place. Shortly after, Katerina's parents had to return home. She would miss them terribly, but this was her life now, and her place was with her beloved husband.

CHAPTER 17

Eleni

Present Day

"Wow." Eleni listened with wide-eyed fascination, her elbows propped on the table, her hands fisted under her chin. "Over the years, I've heard bits and pieces but never the story in its entirety."

"And now you know how it all started," Kostas said proudly. "It's important to know where this all came from," he added, gesturing at the land surrounding them.

"This is your legacy!" *Yiayiá* Thalia accentuated. "Yours, Nikko's, and I pray someday, Yanni's," she said, rapidly crossing herself.

"Just remember, *kouklitsa*, none of this would have been possible without your great-grandfather's land," Stavros reminded Eleni.

"My son tells the truth," Kostas agreed. "We might never have found the money to buy land. The money we had was barely enough for planting and equipment. This land rightfully belongs to you."

"No," Eleni protested. "I know my *pappou* wouldn't agree with you on that."

"I believe Eleni had something she wanted to talk to us about before you bulldozed her with the past," Maria changed the subject, teasing her father-in-law.

"No, please, I'm glad you did," Eleni assured *Pappou* Kostas. "I wanted to hear every detail. It makes what I want to discuss even more important to me and to you."

Nikko watched Eleni curiously as he waited for her to explain.

"So even though I didn't know everything you just told me, I did know my grandparents met on this island, and my grandmother moved here to be with him. But from what I understand, even though my *yiayiá* loved the vineyard, she grew homesick after a while. She missed her family terribly, so they moved to New York."

"Andreas only cared for her happiness," *Yiayiá* Thalia explained. "At first, it was new and exciting, and Katerina was so in love. But later, she missed her parents and her life back in New York."

"Andreas couldn't stand to see her unhappy, so he and I devised a plan," *Pappou* Kostas interjected. "He suggested he move to the States to expand our sales territory while I stayed here to manage the vineyard."

"*Babá* always said that it turned out to be the perfect partnership," Stavros added. "We became far more profitable because of it."

"My Kostas had a talent for winemaking," *Yiayiá* Thalia explained. "But it was your *pappou* who had the head for business."

"Do you think we can swing back around to what Eleni has to say?" Nikko asked of his elders impatiently.

"It's fine, Nikko," Eleni said with a flash of irritation. "Thank you for taking me back in time with you," she continued, smiling affectionately at the rest of the family. "But I did want to talk to you about what you had touched upon with me earlier."

"And what was that?" Thalia questioned.

"About the vineyard not having as much exposure on the island as some others," Eleni explained. "And I can understand why you're more concerned than you were in the past."

A wave of grief ran through her at the thought of her grandfather and how his death affected the vineyard's future, but she reined it in, closing her eyes and drawing in a slow, deep breath.

Nikko reached for her hand under the table, offering support and comfort. He was a confusing man—definitely mercurial. Patting his hand in acknowledgment, she smiled softly in his direction before pulling away.

"My *pappou's* passing has left you without a wine distributor. I have my thoughts on that and will get back to it later. As you all know, I'm an event planner, and one of the things I do is to draw attention to all different types of businesses and establishments. I've developed an idea that could bring more traffic to the vineyard."

That got everyone's full attention. "We would love your expert opinion," Maria said.

"I spent the day wandering from town to town," Eleni started. "This island is rich with gifted artisans. I also went to several wineries to see what distinguished one from the other. Each catered to their guests in its own particular way: wine flights, appetizers, and an opportunity to buy wine by the bottle to bring home. Some establishments were more elaborate than others, but nothing was especially unique."

"What would you have us do then? Hire clowns to entertain?" Nikko said, smirking.

Eleni gave him a light slap on the arm. "Don't be snide. No. I think we should use the resources and talents of the island to our advantage. I'd like to speak to store owners about carrying their products here on consignment. Each store or product would have a designated spot in the tasting room. In addition, we could have a sampling of products at a kiosk by the patio as an enticement for guests to venture inside. Once they have, they'll be sure to make purchases, which will likely include several bottles of our wine."

"But that doesn't explain how we can get them here in the first place," Maria said.

"Well, working with the vendors would be sort of an agreement. We steer our customers to their stores, and in turn, they recommend our winery as a place to visit." Eleni looked in *Pappou* Kostas' direction. "And now your story has shown me how to take it one step further. Your brilliant idea that directed patrons here back then could work now," she added. "We could make up coupons for our artisan partners to hand out, offering a complimentary glass of wine."

Pappou Kostas smiled proudly at her.

"So, who do you expect to go to all these vendors and convince them to participate?" Nikko asked suspiciously.

"Don't worry, Mr. Busy Winemaker. Not you. Me."

"You? Don't you need to return to your big life in New York?"

Eleni detected more than a hint of bitterness in his tone.

"Nikko!" his mother warned.

"I already spoke to Angela. We have nothing pressing after the next event, on which she was already expected to take the lead. So I'm extending my stay to set this up."

"That's very nice of you." Nikko's expression softened slightly.

"Oh, and I only intend to carry locally handmade items or products unique to Kefalonia. I want to bring in *mandoles* from Voskopoula in Argostoli, thyme honey from Razata, and embroidered linens from a tiny shop I stumbled upon in Assos," Eleni explained enthusiastically. "I found unusual one-of-a-kind pieces of jewelry in several shops, and I have to refer back to my notes, but there was an olive oil shop that created soaps and creams infused with herbs and other botanicals." She was getting as excited now as when she had first walked into these stores. "Oh! And olivewood! Platters, bowls, and cutting boards. The natural grain of the wood is stunning."

"I like your idea. There should be no junk, none of those cheap trinkets that tourists can pick up on the street," *Yiayiá* Thalia added.

"And one more thing," Eleni said.

Nikko groaned.

"*What?*" Eleni splayed her hands out.

"It's great that you're setting this all in motion, but do you realize that once you leave, one of us has to pick up where you left off? *We'd* have to keep in touch with the vendors," Nikko emphasized, tapping his chest and pointing to his family. "It will fall solely on us to ensure they all get paid for their consignments, not to mention manage stock levels and run this retail leg of the tasting room." He leaned in and scowled at her. "We're winemakers, not shopkeepers."

"Nikko," Stavros said sternly. "We will work it out. These are solid ideas."

Eleni wondered what Nikko's problem was with her. He held her hand one minute to soothe her; the next, he shot down her ideas. She sucked in a deep breath, shooting daggers at him before deciding it was best to ignore him.

"As I was trying to say," Eleni continued, "I have one more thought. This island has so many festivals during the summer. It's energizing and exciting. I'm not suggesting we arrange a festival, but we could host themed evenings with a similar atmosphere, like a dinner and dancing night. Greek music with a special menu that, let's say, could be centered around one key ingredient. Everything made with pistachios, for example. Or another night centered around figs. Only ingredients indigenous to the island would be featured."

Eleni gave the family a lot to consider. "All of this doesn't have to be taken on at once, but there's a restaurant in New York that makes the most delicious braised short ribs cooked in Mavrodaphne wine. If we offered something similar and shared the recipe, your wine would sell out. We could even offer a cooking demonstration or a cooking class."

"Now you want us to hire a chef?" Nikko asked blankly.

"Stop being rude," his mother reprimanded. "Let the girl speak."

"Thank you, Maria," Eleni said. Ignoring Nikko, she addressed the rest of the family. "I emailed your son this afternoon." She turned and glared at Nikko. "Your *other* son. I laid out my plan, and he loved the idea."

"He did, did he?" Nikko crossed his arms. "He has no interest in the vineyard."

"That's not entirely true, Nikko," Eleni retorted, growing angry with his negative attitude. "Yanni told me he felt he had no place here because he had no interest in working the land or becoming a winemaker. He wants to be a chef. But he loves the island and his home, and this would allow him to contribute to the family business while still doing what he loves."

"Oh, okay." Nikko looked perplexed. "He never expressed that to me," he added quietly.

"Did you ever ask?" Eleni raised an eyebrow.

"Offering a full menu was never suggested as an option before," he admitted.

"I say we have Eleni put this idea in motion right away," Stavros said before tensions rose again. "And if my boy comes back home, even better."

"What about the U.S. distribution?" Nikko asked. You said you had an idea."

"Sort of. I'm still working on that. We can hire a sales representative to market to wine stores across the U.S., but dealing with restaurants is different and more personal. *Pappou* built relationships with Greek restaurant owners throughout the country. Whoever takes over that position will have to gain their trust. It takes networking. I'll make the initial rounds with *pappou's* replacement to ease the handover."

Everyone began talking at once, throwing ideas around and brainstorming the best way to maintain their clientele.

"Okay, enough business talk for tonight," Thalia ordered. She rose from the table and quickly returned with a platter of homemade pastries. That's all it took to quiet the room as they stuffed their mouths with creamy *galaktoboureko*, a unique custard encased in thin sheets of phyllo, drenched in orange-infused simple syrup.

But Eleni was still creating a list in her mind as she forked the pastry. Tomorrow, she would revisit the shops and come back with a solid plan. Getting this new idea off the ground was her immediate priority. Then she would tackle the other matter at hand—finding someone who could fill the shoes of her irreplaceable, greatly missed *pappou*.

GALAKTOBOUREKO

Custard
8 cups milk
1 ½ cups sugar
1 ½ cups semolina
6 eggs, beaten
3 tablespoons unsalted butter
1 tablespoon vanilla

Pastry
1 pound phyllo
1 cup unsalted butter, melted

Syrup
1 ½ cups water
1 ½ cups sugar
2 tablespoons fresh orange juice
2 strips of orange peel
2 cinnamon sticks

Preheat oven to 350°F

Method

Place milk, sugar, vanilla, and semolina into a large pot. Stir until mixed thoroughly. Add the beaten eggs and stir. Place over medium heat and simmer, constantly stirring until the custard thickens. When the custard has thickened, remove from the heat and add the butter. Mix through until the butter has melted. Place the custard in a bowl and cover with Saran wrap. Set aside to cool. Grease a 9x13-inch pan. Using half of the package of phyllo, butter each sheet with a pastry brush and place it in the pan. Keep layering the sheets until you have used up the first half of the phyllo. With a large spoon or ladle, add the custard over the phyllo. Layer and butter the remaining phyllo one sheet at a time, covering the custard. Brush the top layer with butter. Tuck in the edges of any overlapping phyllo. Score into squares with a sharp knife and bake at 350°F for 1 hour.

In the meantime, combine the water, sugar, orange juice, orange peel, and cinnamon sticks in a pot. Simmer for 20 minutes. Set aside to cool. Pour the cooled syrup over the warm pastry.

CHAPTER 18

Eleni

Present Day

Later that evening, after everyone had retired to their bedrooms, Eleni slipped out onto the front porch with her laptop. Settling comfortably on a wicker loveseat, she stretched out her legs and balanced the laptop on her thighs.

The gentle breeze whispering between the leaves was the only sound breaking the stillness of the night. Stars twinkled above as if winking their approval, urging Eleni on as she mapped out her strategy. Tapping away on the keyboard, she listed the items she hoped to carry while noting how to display them most advantageously.

Deep in thought, Eleni formulated a convincing pitch to approach vendors when Nikko startled her from her concentration.

"Can I sit?" he asked.

As if she had no control over her emotions, her heart fluttered at his mere proximity, though her mind protested her traitorous body. Eleni couldn't afford to let Nikko have this power over her. She was angry. No, that's not entirely true. She was beyond enraged and skittering dangerously into hurt, which she must avoid in order to stay emotionally disconnected. Cleary Nikko didn't want her here, much less sticking her nose into the vineyard's business. He hadn't supported a single idea of hers at dinner, even when the rest of the family was openly receptive.

"It's a free country." She shrugged noncommittally, swinging her outstretched legs off the cushion to allow Nikko to sit beside her. Instead of conversing, however, he cleared his throat and rested his elbows on his knees, hanging his head to stare at the wooden slats of the floor.

The silence was as heavy as the tension between them. Trying to ignore Nikko, Eleni began tapping haphazardly at her laptop, pulling up random websites irrelevant to her research.

"I didn't mean to upset you," Nikko finally said, facing her.

"I get it," Eleni said bitterly, her eyes still locked on her computer screen. "You're still angry with me. I left you and this beautiful place behind and never looked back. And now I am inserting myself where I no longer belong."

"No, you obviously don't get it," Nikko countered. "You've always belonged here. It's as much a part of you as it is of me. My grandfather's telling of your family history here proved that fact. But let's face it: You left then, and you'll leave again after you've made all these changes—changes we cannot manage independently."

And there it was—the brutal truth. Nikko didn't care if she stayed or left. He didn't care about her at all. His only concern was the project she had dumped on his family's lap to, in his mind, only create more work for them. Nikko's hot-one-minute, cold-one-minute attitude left her confused. But this revelation placed it all back into focus.

"This is what I do," Eleni emphasized, pushing her emotions aside. "I plan events that help businesses gain exposure and grow. I know how to attract attention and translate it into profits. I want to see the vineyard thrive. You might think I don't care, but I wholeheartedly do. What our grandfathers built meant everything to my *pappou*. This is how I'm able to honor his memory."

"You claim to care," he started. "But you know what else you do?

You leave," he accused. "And I also have a family to honor—or rather, protect. They love you like their own, and the longer you insert yourself, the greater the hope you'll stay. Are you willing to chance the emotional upheaval you'll cause?"

Detecting more hurt than anger in his tone, Eleni wasn't sure how to respond. Maybe she had him all wrong. She looked up to meet his brilliant sapphires, but distrust dulled them. Nikko's hostility was deeper than the concern for his family. Eleni recognized the lingering animosity coating his words.

Indeed, he couldn't be harboring a long-ago teenage heartbreak, could he? But why should she doubt that? The ache in her heart for the boy she once loved never left her, but it hid in the recesses of her being, wondering what might have been. Until she saw him. One glance and everything they'd shared sprung to the forefront of her mind. Eleni's pounding heart was proof of that. So wasn't it possible there were some residual feelings on his part, too? Even if it was unresolved resentment for the past and a broken promise of an unrealistic future?

But, despite her emotional turmoil, Nikko made a plausible argument. It wouldn't be right for her to initiate something this involved and then leave the family halfway through to manage it independently.

"What if I was to extend my stay even longer than I originally planned?" she threw out, holding his gaze.

Nikko's eyes flashed with a brief second of hope before he growled out a humorless laugh. "What about your company in New York?"

"I'll speak to Angela. She's perfectly capable of running it for now. And I'll tell her to hire another assistant."

"You would do that?" Nikko furrowed his brow warily. "And for how long?"

"Until I'm confident the retail space is organized and the details are set in place. Then I'll reevaluate my involvement once everything is running smoothly." Eleni laid her hand over his in assurance. "This is important to me. I want to see this through." Swiftly pulling her hand away, she apologized. "I'm sorry."

"Don't be," he said softly, reaching for her hand and threading his fingers through hers. "I believe you."

"Give me a chance to prove I can make a difference and contribute in some small way," Eleni pleaded.

"I have no doubt of your talents," Nikko said. "And I truly appreciate what you're trying to do. That's not the issue."

"Then what is, Nikko? Tell me so I can fix it."

Leaning back into the wicker settee, Nikko raked his hands through his hair. He remained silent for a beat before startling Eleni when his composure snapped.

"It's you and how God damned hard it is for me to have you here going about your days like we don't have a history. Like there was never anything between us all those years ago," he spewed, his chest heaving as the words spilled out. "It was so easy for you to erase me from your heart and entirely cut off communication. You destroyed me, and now you're back as if none of it mattered or had any effect on you."

Eleni covered her face with her hands, her fingers pressing into her eye sockets to keep the tears from spilling. When she finally attempted to speak, her throat clogged with emotion. She took hold of his chin and implored him to meet her red-rimmed gaze. "I have thought about you every day of my life," she confessed, her voice cracking. "Nothing was easy for me. Everything I loved was stolen away, including you." She held a hand up just as he was about to argue. "I know what you're going to say. It was my choice. But the choices I made were to ease both our heartaches. I was all my grandfather had. I wasn't about to leave him."

"Nothing was holding either of you in New York anymore," Nikko argued. "You could have moved here."

"You make it sound so simple, but you weren't in my shoes. You didn't lose your entire family on this island."

"People live, and they die." Nikko sighed. "I don't mean to sound unfeeling. But consider this. What if they had been killed in New York? Would you have fled the state? Or the country?"

"Probably not." Admittedly, Eleni had never contemplated it. Kefalonia had been a magical place for her, somewhere she imagined nothing could go wrong. It was six weeks of bliss out of every year, but when devastation careened onto its shores, her idyllic paradise was lost to her forever.

"If you loved me the way I loved you, then you would have come back to me once you came to terms with your grief."

"I'll let you know when that happens," Eleni sniffled.

"Eleni," Nikko whispered, taking her hand.

She dabbed at the corner of her eye. "I don't blame you for your anger or your resentment. I have no way to turn back the clock and change it. But I was a grieving teenager, and later, once the reality of it all settled in, I mourned not only for my family but also for what you and I would never have the chance to be. My whole life changed in an instant. One minute, we walked through your front door ecstatically happy, and the next, that joy was obliterated by immeasurable sorrow."

Eleni tenderly rubbed her thumb along the top of his hand. "Nikko, you were never far from my mind. I'm sorry I've made you feel that way. Make no mistake, you are who every man I've met has had to measure up to."

"How has that worked out for you?" Nikko joked.

"Do you really want to know?" Eleni bantered back.

"It depends on your answer."

"I think the idea of you has held me back," Eleni said honestly. "We were just kids. Who knows if we would have worked out in the end if all that happened didn't. But in my mind, you were an impossible standard to match, and I've never been able to feel for anyone what I felt for you."

It was more than Eleni wanted to reveal, but if this arrangement was to work, they had to come to a mutual understanding and finally let the past go.

"It's been the same for me," Nikko confessed.

She sucked in a gulp of air, breathing out slowly to steady her composure. Nikko's penetrating stare sent shivers skating up her spine. She smiled softly, resisting the urge to stroke his cheek or pull him in for a kiss. But it was no use. The space between them evaporated, the vapor heavy with electricity, attracting them like two magnets incapable of being repelled. All hesitation was forgotten when Eleni surrendered to Nikko's desperate, fevered kiss. Her mind lost the ability to reason as every cell in her body tingled with sublime recognition of what she'd been missing.

"Impossibly high standards to reach," Eleni breathed between kisses.

"To think that was just a kiss," he teased, wiggling his brows.

The implication wasn't lost on her. "That wasn't just a kiss. That was an invasion." She nervously laughed.

"I think I'd like to plunder further then," he said, claiming her mouth once more.

After a while, they sat silently, looking up at the ebony sky, a shooting star racing across the great expanse. Eleni took that as a sign—of what, she wasn't sure. Not to repeat history by leaving behind a trail of tears? Or simply to luxuriate in any modicum of happiness the universe allowed?

CHAPTER 19

Eleni

Thirteen years ago

Eleni's stomach fluttered like a kaleidoscope of butterflies breaking from their cocoons as her father drove through the familiar wrought-iron gates of the Pangalos Varvos Vineyard.

Once the families had customarily greeted each other with double-cheek kisses, Eleni's father pulled their suitcases from the trunk of his rented car. The women caught up, talking a mile a minute as they walked into the house. Peter snatched the soccer ball from Yanni's hand, and the boys began to kick it around on the front lawn. With everyone's attention elsewhere, Eleni and Nikko could reacquaint themselves without an audience.

Their back-and-forth letters and texts had run the gamut from playful and goofy to soulful and bordering on sensual. That kind of banter was easy from thousands of miles away. Now, everything they'd hinted might finally come to fruition. Eleni's stomach twisted in both anticipation and skittishness at the thought.

Taking her hand, Nikko led her away, and they quietly strolled down a row of grapevines, deep enough in to steal a moment alone. All it took was one kiss, his affectionate embrace, and a declaration of how much Nikko missed her to melt away her hesitation.

"What now?" Nikko asked after kissing her to distraction. "Should we disappear without worrying about anyone wondering where we went? Or should we stick it out and go inside to get you settled in first?"

"As much as I'd love to run off with you, I have a feeling your *mamá* and *Yiayiá* made a ton of food to welcome us."

"You have that right," Nikko laughed. Taking her by the hand once more, he led her toward the house.

"Besides, I'm starved," Eleni admitted.

"A bunch of friends are hanging out at the beach tonight. Are you up for it?" Nikko asked.

"Sounds like fun. Who will be there?"

"Some friends from school and town. Panos and Stefanos. Remember them? They came out on your *pappou's* boat last year with us."

"Sure, I remember."

"And some other people you don't know. A few girls. I think you'll like most of them." Nikko made a face. "Panos is after this one girl, but she doesn't seem interested. I don't know what he sees in her. She's annoying."

"Okay." Eleni shrugged, finding his opinion curious. "It takes a lot for you not to like someone. What's her name so I can be on the lookout for this so-called irritating person."

"Antonía. No need to search her out. She has a way of bringing attention to herself." Nikko shuddered like he needed to shake the girl off. "The only female I want on my mind is you," he said, leaning into her for another lingering kiss.

"Maybe running off is a good idea," Eleni murmured against his lips. "They might not even notice we're gone."

"Yes, they will," Nikko groaned, sliding his hands down the length of her body until he reached her ass. He squeezed it gently, saying, "To be continued."

Hand in hand, they walked back to the house. Eleni sighed as she took in her surroundings. The vines on either side of the long driveway, lush with full green leaves and hanging fruit fed by the golden sun and rich soil, made her smile. As they stepped onto the porch, rapid chatter and peals of laughter made Eleni feel at home. And so did the aroma of fresh basil and garlic that wafted in the air, her stomach rumbling in approval.

"I told you I was hungry!" Eleni laughed.

Later that evening, Nikko and Eleni arrived at the beach. By the looks of things, the party was well underway. Lively music disturbed the otherwise serene atmosphere. If they had been alone, the gentle waves splashing rocks and the soft breeze whistling between the trees would have been the only sounds invading their senses. Still, watching the crowd from above, dancing while bathed in moonlight and swimming under the stars was a whimsical sight. From where they were perched, Eleni thought the partygoers looked like mischievous fairies, communing with nature without a care in the world. Of course, this wasn't true. As they descended the bluff and drew closer, Eleni realized that her fanciful imaginings were just that.

"Let me introduce you around," Nikko offered as his friends approached. "Panos, Stefanos, you remember Eleni."

"Yes," Panos said. "From the boat last summer, right?"

"Yes." Eleni nodded. "Nice to see both of you again."

"And this is Kristos and Savvas," Nikko added.

"We've heard all about you. The girl from Brooklyn," Kristos said, punching Nikko's arm.

Eleni teasingly shot Nikko an admonishing stare.

"What?" he asked innocently. "No one has ever heard of Ast-or-ia," he dragged out.

"*Vre, Malaka*, everyone but you!" Savvas said. "I have cousins who live there."

"Me too," Stefanos interjected.

"Okay, I stand corrected." Nikko threw up his hands in surrender.

"But I'm not giving up the nickname," he whispered in Eleni's ear.

"There's beer and soft drinks in the cooler," Panos said, pointing to an area where a string of beach blankets carpeted the sand.

But before Eleni and Nikko could go, three girls linked arm-in-arm scampered over.

Ignoring the rest of the group, one of the girls came up beside Nikko, rested a hand on his bicep and leaned in to kiss him on the cheek, ignoring Eleni standing by his side.

Tall with a slim but shapely body, the bleached blonde was a little too close to Nikko for Eleni's liking. Nikko flinched and removed her hand from his arm, but the girl didn't take the hint.

"Hey, Nikko," she purred, raking him with her eyes from head to toe. "It's never a party until you get here."

Eleni tried to unclasp her hand from Nikko's, but he refused to let go.

"Antonía, this is Eleni." Nikko drew Eleni closer to his side, snaking his arm around her waist.

She should have guessed this was Antonía. Poor Panos. From what Nikko told her, he would love any amount of attention from her. Why, Eleni couldn't fathom.

"Right," Antonía said, assessing Eleni with a mocking glare. "You're that little girl that visits every summer."

"Let's grab a drink," Nikko said, whisking Eleni away.

What Nikko said earlier was true. The girl was annoying, and Eleni could add insulting and trashy, which, with her scrap of clothing, left nothing to the imagination, not to mention a few other not-so-polite adjectives, to the list.

But Eleni was a little hurt that Nikko only introduced her by name. Was it presumptuous of her to want him to add 'my girlfriend?' That would have put the little *strígla* in her place.

"Sorry about her. I warned you she wasn't very nice." Nikko held up a can of beer in one hand and a Coke in the other, offering Eleni a choice.

Eleni looked inside the cooler. "*Lemonatha*," she said, reaching for a bottle. "Well, she was very forward with you." She put the lemonade back in the cooler. "On second thought, I'll take the beer. You could have told her who I was to you instead of letting her call me your little houseguest."

"I don't have to explain anything to her. Antonía and the other two girls she hangs around are the biggest gossips. The less they know, the better," Nikko assured her.

"If you say so." Eleni popped open the can and walked away, heading toward the water.

"Eleni!" Nikko called, running to catch up with her. "This is why I told you about her before we came. The girl is a troublemaker."

"Maybe so, but she has her sights set on you."

"Don't be ridiculous. Antonía is like that with everyone."

"She didn't hang onto just *anyone*." Eleni spread her hands in wide exasperation, waiting for his response. "From what you said, Panos would do anything to get her attention, but I didn't see her pawing him."

"Pawing?" Nikko laughed. "Could we not fight? You just got here, and I'm not letting anything or anyone waste a moment of our time together."

"Sure," Eleni said with a sigh.

Nikko rested his arms over her shoulders and pulled her in for a kiss. That was all it took for Eleni to forget her surroundings but for the water splashing at their feet and the loud beating of her heart.

After a while, they joined the party, dancing and singing along to pop tunes. Some of the guys and a few of the girls split off to play glow-in-the-dark Frisbee and tug-of-war while many of the girls sat in a circle chatting.

"Go," Eleni said when she noticed Nikko watching them play. "I know you want to. It looks like fun."

"Join me."

"I'm fine here. Really," Eleni assured him.

Soon, Eleni found herself deep in conversation with a girl who wanted to pick her brain for information about the city. Arianna was interested in attending NYU next year and appreciated anything Eleni could share. Eleni found herself enjoying the girl's company when Antonía squeezed her way between them.

Annoyed, Eleni leaned back to continue talking without having her view blocked.

"Seriously, Antonía," Arianna snapped. "Can't you see we're in the middle of something?"

"I love girl talk," Antonía said. "Who are you talking about?"

"We're not talking about anyone," Arianna said, rolling her eyes.

"I was answering Arianna's questions about New York City," Eleni offered with a fake smile. "Anyway …the university is in a nice section of the city. You'll love it there. I'll give you my contact information, and if there's anything I can help you with, I'd be happy to."

"That would be great." Arianna rose from the blanket. "I'm going to grab a water. Can I get you one?"

"Sure, thanks," Eleni said.

"Bring me a beer while you're up," Antonía said. "So, Eleni, are you having fun?"

"Yes."

"Too bad Nikko has already ditched you for the guys."

"He didn't ditch me. It's a party—that occasion where you mingle with several people," Eleni said sarcastically.

"I'm aware. Nikko does a lot of …mingling."

This bitch was goading her. It took everything Eleni had not to react.

Antonía added, "Mingling with Nikko is something I look forward to every weekend."

"Funny, he told me he goes out of his way to avoid you."

Antonía laughed. "You really don't think he waits all year for *you*? All the girls want him, you know."

"Maybe, but you're the only one making it pathetically obvious,"

Eleni said flatly, rising. "Now, if you'll excuse me."

Insecurities that were never there before boiled to the surface because of that malicious girl. Eleni knew she should rise above it and not listen to the lies. She trusted Nikko, but was she being naive? She was only sixteen, and Eleni had no problem waiting to see him all year, but could she expect the same of him in return? Eleni's inclination at that moment was to run off alone to sulk. But she wouldn't let Antonía accomplish what she had set out to do. So, instead, she joined Arianna by the cooler.

"I was just about to come back. Here," Arianna said, handing Eleni a bottle of water.

"Thanks." Eleni's expression must have given her away.

Arianna eyed her. "What did she do?"

Eleni just shook her head, the lump in her throat constricting her voice.

Arianna linked arms with Eleni. "Let's take a walk."

Heading to the shoreline, they remained quiet until they were far from the crowd.

"At home, is there one person in your crowd or school who is barely tolerated?" Arianna asked.

"Isn't there always at least one?" Eleni scoffed.

"There sure is, and Antonía and her friends are those girls." Arianna angled her head in their direction. "They're what you call in the States 'mean girls' who dole out backhanded compliments, pit friends against one another, and try to control every situation."

"That sounds like a cry for attention," Eleni remarked.

"Whatever their reasons, you need to overlook anything Antonía says. The rest of us have."

"Why do you all hang out with them?" Eleni wondered.

"They just show up," Arianna explained, guiding Eleni to pivot around. "Let's head back. Our school isn't as big as I imagine yours is. They can be intimidating and seem to be able to wield power over some people. But the drama they provide is entertaining."

I could live without the drama," Eleni admitted. "Antonía implied that Nikko had been with her and other girls this past year."

Arianna laughed. "*Psémata*! Lies! I'm pretty good friends with Nikko. You're all he talks about. He told me you live in New York. How do you think I knew to approach you and ask you about it?"

"Really?"

"Don't let that girl weaken your faith in him," Arianna advised. "Trust me. More importantly, trust Nikko."

"Thank you," Eleni said, pulling her new friend in for a hug.

"I've been looking for you," Nikko said, jogging up beside the girls.

"Arianna and I have been getting acquainted."

"Kristos is looking for you," Nikko told Arianna.

"Thanks for the chat," Eleni said.

"Anytime. Nikko will give you my mobile. Let's get together soon."

When she left, Eleni cocked her head to one side, smiling. "Kristos? Friend or more?"

"They're dating."

"I really like her," Eleni said, refraining from offering her opinion on Antonía.

"I'm glad. We've been friends for as long as I can remember," Nikko said. "It's getting late. Let's head home."

CHAPTER 20

Nikko

Thirteen years ago

Waiting for Eleni to pull into the driveway was as drawn out as waiting for the first bud to bloom on a branch after a long winter. Nikko sat on the front steps of his home, anticipating her arrival. He'd strategically calculated the plane's landing, how long it took for luggage retrieval, and the time it took to drive from the airport to his home. A full hour had passed, and the only cars that had come through the gates were visitors to the vineyard.

Finally, a black sedan pulled up in front of the house instead of driving to the parking lot beyond. Peter jumped from the car first, quickly followed by Eleni.

"They're here!" Nikko shouted. In a split second, Nikko's mother and grandmother ran out to greet the Pangalos family.

"Finally," Nikko said with relief, lifting Eleni off the ground into a bear hug. "I thought you'd never get here."

Yanni emerged, soccer ball in hand, and greeted Peter, the two running off to kick the ball around. No one paid the two of them any mind as the women in the family had already struck up a conversation, heading inside the house. So Nikko took Eleni by the hand, and they disappeared between a row of lush grapevines. He took her into his arms, not wasting a second to kiss the lips he'd dreamed of whenever he closed his eyes at night. Ten months of waiting and longing. Ten months of written promises. After ten months of anticipation, the time had finally come. He wanted more than a kiss. More than an exploration of her mouth. More than the feel of her flesh as he inched his way up her skirt to find the globes of the ass he had so often admired. Nikko wanted it all, and he wasn't sure how long he could hold out to be with her in every way. But he also wanted the moment to be one they would remember for the rest of their lives.

After a family dinner reunion, Eleni and Nikko headed to the beach. Why he'd suggested spending the evening with a dozen friends was beyond him. Maybe they could slip away behind the cliffs or a large rock formation. But he wanted Eleni ingrained into his life so she'd consider staying once she was old enough to make her own choices. If she made friends, joined the community, and became invested, there might be more of a reason for her to live here than to just be with him. He wanted to be enough for her to take that leap, but even at her young age, Nikko knew Eleni needed more. She had goals and high expectations, and he'd expressed his own desire to find a life outside the island one day. But he hoped she'd want to take that journey with him wherever they ended up.

"Go," Eleni said, waving Nikko off. Some of his friends were engaged in a game of tug-of-war, while others caught Frisbees. I know you want to. It looks like fun."

"Join me."

"I'm fine here. Really," Eleni assured him.

Nikko grabbed the rope, tugging hard enough to help his side win a few rounds. Savvas whistled for him to join them at Frisbee. But Nikko's concentration wandered from the game when he spotted Antonía sitting with Eleni.

Whack! The Frisbee pelted Nikko in the head. "You did that intentionally," he shouted.

"Pay attention and that pretty face won't get hurt," Panos joked.

"If that girl is causing trouble for me …"

"You'll what?" Panos asked. "Leave her alone. She's really harmless."

Nikko smacked him in the chest. "You're too nice for your own good. Go find a sweet girl and forget about her."

"If I told you to forget Eleni, would you?"

"Never," Nikko said as he watched Eleni walk away from Antonía. He continued playing for a while before searching her out, only to find her by the shoreline with Arianna. He was glad they had hit it off and hoped it was a sign that Eleni would happily fit into his world.

CHAPTER 21

Eleni

Thirteen years ago

The next morning, Eleni awoke to a bright beam of sunshine blinding her. Groaning, she recalled falling into bed when she and Nikko returned from the beach. Jetlag had caught up with her. Exhausted, Eleni forgot to shut the blinds.

She looked at the clock on the nightstand announcing the early hour and dragged herself from the bed. "Just another hour or two won't matter," Eleni mumbled, pulling the strings to block the light. Then she tucked herself back under the lightweight quilt and fell fast asleep.

Eleni shot up with a start. It was ten o'clock. She had slept for three extra hours. It wasn't her intention to waste such a beautiful day. Rushing through her morning routine, she showered, coated her lashes with mascara, and dabbed gloss on her lips. Rummaging through her suitcase, Eleni found a tan crop top and a pair of khaki shorts and slipped them on.

The house was quiet when Eleni descended the stairs, calling out names to see who was home. No one was in the kitchen, not even *Yiayiá* Thalia, who usually wore out the floor by the stove. A platter of mouthwatering pastries was piled onto a ceramic platter on the island, though, and Eleni picked one off the top and bit into it as she went about her search. But no one was on the back patio either, so she meandered down to the cottage used as a tasting room for visitors, though she didn't expect to find anyone there either. The vineyard was closed to the public on Mondays.

Yet, there they were—her mother and Nikko's mother, Maria. Her Grandmother and *Yiayiá* Thalia, too.

"What are you all doing in here?" Eleni asked.

"She lives!" Eleni's *yiayiá* teased.

"There's much work to be done, even on the days the vineyard is closed," Maria explained.

"A little dusting and housecleaning before we restock the shelves," *Yiayiá* Thalia added.

"And I think I'm just in time," Nikko said, walking in with a case of wine.

Eleni's face lit up when she saw him. "I can help too."

Nikko set the case on the bar. "Sure. It would go faster and take fewer trips."

Once they were out of sight and had rounded the corner, Nikko pressed Eleni against the building, kissing her like he hadn't seen her in years.

"Mmm," she moaned against his mouth. "More of that. But for now, we have a job to do." Regretfully, she pulled away with a coy smile.

They took several trips back and forth from an old barn, which was used for every wine-making stage, from destemming and pressing to bottling and corking.

"I think I'm free for the rest of the day now," Nikko said.

"Have you been working a lot?"

"I have, and they've pulled Yanni in too. They want us to know the business."

"Do they know you don't want to make this your life?" Eleni was worried Nikko's dreams would be squashed by obligation.

"I've expressed my interests to them." Nikko twisted his lips in frustration. "They seem to think it's a frivolous, passing interest that will fade."

Eleni's brows nearly reached her hairline. "Wow! I think you're in for a challenge," she said as they returned to the house.

"What about you?" Nikko inquired.

"I don't know. I might major in business and decide later," Eleni pondered. "That way, I can either shadow my grandfather and take over when he retires, manage one of my father's restaurants, or not work for my family at all." She shrugged.

Nikko grew silent for a beat before asking what she wanted to do for the day.

"Can we hike up the mountain and search for unicorns?"

Nikko laughed. "You read too much mythology. There are wild horses, but I have to warn you, they're pretty elusive."

"All the more fun to search," Eleni said with a gleam in her eye.

"Okay. We'll take the truck as far as we can go, but be prepared to walk and climb a distance."

Eleni rubbed her hands together in delight. "I'll pack some supplies to take along."

Nikko wasn't joking. They set out on foot after leaving the truck by a monastery, which was apparently deemed the furthest a vehicle could go. Getting even that far was a strain, as an off-road vehicle was recommended. The hike was rocky and strenuous, but the view was ethereal once they reached the top. It was as if Eleni had reached the heavens and looked down upon a perfect God-created paradise.

"Now we wait," Nikko said.

"Have you been here before?" Eleni asked.

"Once," Nikko answered without elaboration.

They rested on a large rock, waiting, and Eleni wondered how long they would stay perched there before she was granted a glimpse of the glorious creatures.

"What if we sit here all day and they don't come?" Eleni worried.

"Then we come back tomorrow. But they'll come. This is their domain."

About twenty minutes later, a gentle beating rhythm pounded the earth as six horses came into view at once. Eleni jumped up, nearly squealing with excitement, but Nikko put his fingers to his lips, signaling silence. He pulled her into an embrace, her back to his front, and quietly, they observed the animals in their natural habitat.

Eleni had never seen anything so beautiful. She had seen many horses in Central Park pulling carriages or saddled up for riders. Others were used for racing, bets placed on them at the tracks. But this was life in its purest form—free to live without confinement, burden, or ulterior motives. With an air of regality, the majestic creatures trotted along, warmed by the sun, stopping to reap the fruits of this untainted landscape.

The air was arid, the terrain riddled with stones. The leaves on the trees were bare of the forbidden fruit of Eden, but to Eleni, that was what this place was, and she wanted it to be where Nikko made love to her for the first time. Led by a myriad of emotions, she had thought of nothing more all year. Caught up by the romance, she imagined Nikko as the hero in the kind of novels she loved to read, hoping to learn from them what to expect from this new experience. He wasn't a vampire who'd sparkle at the top of this mountain when the sun bathed his skin, but Nikko was who she swooned over. In her fantasies, she dreamed he'd whisk her away in seclusion—to a mystical place like this—where he would make her his.

But the other more pragmatic side of her was a bundle of nerves as she felt his arousal pressed against her. She'd also read that *other* book. The one everyone was talking about. The one she had to hide from her parents. And if *that* was how Nikko wanted sex, Eleni wasn't sure she was ready for it.

Eleni turned to face Nikko and looped her arms around his neck.

"Thank you for bringing me here." She raised up on her toes and gave him a deep kiss, but as she pressed closer to him, her eyes widened and her breath hitched.

Nikko further tempted her with his lopsided grin and heavy-lidded eyes.

"Nikko?"

As if he'd read her mind, he shook his head. "Not here."

"But it's secluded and romantic. There's no one to interrupt us."

"Except a dozen wild animals, maybe," Nikko pointed out. "No, I want our first time to be memorable."

"Isn't the girl supposed to be the dreamy one and the guy just wanting it under any circumstance?"

"Maybe. But not with us." Nikko pecked her forehead affectionately before taking her hand and guiding her back down the mountain.

By the time they arrived home, it was nearly dinnertime. Eleni helped set the table and carry out platters of food to the patio. The aroma of cinnamon, butter, and garlic made her stomach gurgle. It was a beautiful, warm, dry evening, not a cloud in the sky. Eleni enthusiastically shared their adventure with the families between forkfuls of food she devoured with zeal.

"Eleni," her father started. "Tomorrow, we're planning to visit Fotis and Soula Alexatos. They're also here for the summer, visiting family. Would you like to join us?"

"If you don't mind, I'd rather stay here and help out on the vineyard in the morning."

"We were thinking of going to the beach after," Nikko added.

"That's fine," Eleni's mother said. "Peter will come with us. They have a son his age."

"Is Yanni going with you, too?" Eleni asked. She looked around the table. "Where is he, by the way?"

"Yanni was helping me in the vineyard today, and his allergies got the best of him," Stavros said. "He's upstairs resting."

"Oh, that's too bad. I didn't know he suffered," Eleni said.

"He's always suffered a slight rash from the leaves but it's gotten a little worse each year," *Yiayiá* Thalia explained. "I'm going to keep my eye on him tomorrow."

After dinner, Eleni and Nikko sat on the steps of the front porch planning.

"Tomorrow is our day. My family will be occupied with the vineyard, and yours will be away. Even the boys won't be tagging along," Nikko said. "After we help out in the morning, we can change and head to the beach. I found the perfect spot."

"You did? At the beach?" Eleni asked, unsure, worrying her lip.

"Trust me?"

"Always."

"Good. Then leave it up to me. It's a day that neither of us will ever forget."

CHAPTER 22

Eleni

Thirteen years ago

At around eleven a.m. the next day, the black Mercedes Eleni's father had rented pulled up to the vineyard gates, braking when he noticed Eleni and Nikko heading in their direction.

They had spent the early hours helping to trim back dense vine leaves under the instruction of Nikko's father and grandfather on their acreage located on a higher elevation outside the estate gates. Once the men in the family permitted the teens to leave, Eleni and Nikko set out for home to clean up and change into their bathing suits.

Lowering his window, Eleni's father called out to them. "Don't forget the sunscreen. It's going to be a hot one today."

Eleni approached the car. "You say that every day." Eleni smirked, leaning in to kiss his cheek. "Have fun today, and say hello for me."

"We will," Eleni's mother said. "Be careful on the water, and no cliff diving!" she emphasized, wagging a finger.

"I won't. I promise," Eleni said, banging on the back window to get her brother's attention.

"What?" Peter asked innocently, lowering the glass.

Eleni made two fists and quickly bumped them together twice, an F-you gesture they had learned from the TV show *Friends* and often used on each other.

"I love you too," he laughed.

"Me, too, you little snitch. Do it again, and you won't hang out with us anymore if I have anything to say about it," Eleni threatened.

"That's enough of that," Eleni's mother ordered.

Eleni waved her family off, moving back a few steps as the car rolled forward.

"I heard you snickering," Eleni said, turning to face Nikko.

"I was just thinking that it's good we won't have to worry about prying eyes today."

Taking Eleni's hand, they strolled up the path leading to the house. Mud covered their shoes and hands, and their knees desperately needed scrubbing. They had ventured into the mountainous terrain where the Robola vines grew. Because of where they were situated, all labor had to be done manually. Machinery saved time and effort on the acreage of neatly curated rows closer to the estate home where the land was flatter. But on the steep hillsides, where Robola seemed to thrive almost haphazardly on rocky soil, old-fashioned manpower was the only option.

I'm going to take a quick shower, and then I'll put together a cooler with some snacks and drinks," Eleni said.

"And I'll find an extra beach blanket while you do that," Nikko said.

Eleni searched the pantry and refrigerator for items that wouldn't spoil in the heat of the day. By the time Nikko entered the kitchen, dragging a king-sized quilt over his shoulder, tomato salad, crusty bread, Mediterranean bean spread and crackers, olives, *dolmathes*, and a fresh fruit salad had been packed and placed in an insulated cooler.

"That's overkill," Eleni joked, gesturing to the quilt.

"You won't think so when you see how pebbly the sand is." Nikko peeked in the basket. "Just Coke and water?" He went to the fridge and took out a few beers, adding them to the cooler. "Ready?"

"As I'll ever be," she confessed.

"Hey," Nikko said, taking Eleni into his arms, "there's no pressure here. I love you. That's all that counts, and whatever happens or doesn't happen won't change how I feel about you."

"I love you, too," Eleni professed, looking deep into eyes as blue as the Ionian and as sincere as his promise.

Twenty minutes later, they arrived at a quiet beach that wasn't exactly desolate but wasn't nearly as crowded as their usual haunts. But Nikko led her further down the stretch, where the rocky cliffs led to large boulders near the shoreline. Eleni surmised that this area was too dangerous to attract divers and too shaded from overhanging trees that blocked much of the sun at this time of day for sun worshippers to bathe.

"Well, you're right. You found the most obscure spot on the beach. But someone could still stroll by," Eleni pointed out.

Nikko crooked a finger, beckoning for her to follow him.

Finally, when they reached their destination, Eleni was impressed. The naturally carved-out shelter at the bluff's base looked more like a small grotto. The ground was made from the same beach pebbles running the length of the shoreline, hence Nikko's idea to bring an extra-thick beach blanket.

"This is incredible." Eleni's face lit up. "How did you find it?"

"I stumbled upon it one day while walking around, miserably missing you," he admitted, dropping the items he'd been carrying to grab her waist. He pulled her in for a kiss, lacing his legs with hers.

"Hmm," Eleni purred. "You know what I did when I missed you?"

"What?"

"Daydreamed … of you. In class. At night. While watching TV. While hanging out with my friends."

"So all the time?"

"Pretty much," Eleni confessed.

"And now we're here," he whispered.

"We are," she breathed out a little nervously. Moving away, Eleni picked up the quilt and headed inside the grotto, folding it in half for more padding.

Nikko set the cooler and the beach bag to one side. "I think I'll have a beer. You?"

Eleni nodded. "Definitely." She took it from him and downed half the bottle in less than a minute.

"Whoa! Slow down," Nikko said, taking it away from her. "Brooklyn," he said in a calm voice. "It's me and you. It's just us. The way we've always been— comfortable and natural with each other." Taking her hand, Nikko guided her onto the blanket.

"I'm not sure this is how we've 'always been.' I don't remember feeling this way when we were eight," she joked.

"What way?" he asked, brushing his lips against hers.

Eleni tried to answer, but Nikko's trail of kisses on her face, throat, and down her shoulder distracted her.

"You know," she said shyly.

"Tell me. How do I make you feel?" Nikko carried on his ministrations, laying her down, inching his way back up to claim her mouth.

Eleni moaned. "Like that. You make me feel everything," she said breathlessly. "I never want you to stop kissing me."

"I want it all with you. I've thought about nothing else," he whispered. "I want your body, mind, and your beautiful heart."

Nikko untied the straps of her bikini top, the material falling away. The moment he palmed her breasts and ran his thumbs over the hardened nub of her nipples, Eleni felt pleasure shoot straight to her core. Her moan was a sign for Nikko to continue, and he took a nipple between his lips, teasing it with his tongue.

"You're so beautiful. I've dreamed of this for so long," Nikko murmured as he moved his mouth to her other breast.

Eleni floated in euphoria with her fingers roping through his hair until Nikko pulled the strings from her bottoms. She stiffened, her heart pounding wildly. The evidence of his arousal was pressed hard against her thigh, and although she wanted him, she was nervous.

"Like I promised, we stop the second you say so," Nikko assured her, pausing to look at her.

"No." Eleni wanted to please Nikko by making him feel the way he was making her feel. In a bold move, she cupped him, feeling his length and hardness. "I'm ready."

Nikko groaned as if it took all his willpower to control his need. "No, *agápi mou*, I'm ready. You're not. But you will be. Let me take care of you." He moved his hand downward, using his fingers to stimulate her.

"Nikko? Aren't you going to ...?"

"I'm getting there," he said sweetly. "I want to make this as painless as possible for you."

And suddenly, without even entering her, Nikko had full possession of Eleni's body—a nipple in his mouth and his fingers exploring her. A wonderful tension was blooming inside her, spreading, tightening, and elevating her until her blood heated, her insides exploded, and she cried out his name. "Nikko!"

Before she could fully float down from her celestial state, Nikko reached for a condom, rolling it on quickly. "*Now* you're ready," he panted. He positioned himself over her, lining up with her opening and carefully entering her.

There was pressure, and when Eleni winced at the slight pain, Nikko pulled back with concern. "No, I'm fine. I'll get used to it."

He slid into her again with gentle strokes, and once Eleni adjusted, they found a comfortable pace.

Soon, Nikko's rhythm became more intense and urgent, and suddenly, he quickened to faster, deeper thrusts. "I'm sorry, I'm sorry. I can't hold back."

"It's okay," Eleni said, wrapping her legs around him.

"Don't ... want ... to hurt ... you," Nikko struggled to say.

"I'm fine." Eleni wouldn't admit how much it hurt. Oddly, it was a tolerable and almost pleasurable pain once her body adapted.

Nikko moaned her name as he pulsated inside her until he came. Collapsing beside her, Nikko breathed heavily. "That was amazing." Lifting onto his elbow to face her, Nikko brushed the stray strands of hair from Eleni's face. "I love you. I will always love you. There will never be anyone I could ever love more."

Eleni's heart swelled with joy. "I can't imagine my life without you," she whispered. "I love you so much."

"I'm sorry if that hurt. It will be better for you next time."

"Well," she said playfully. "Can next time be now, then?"

Nikko raised an eyebrow. "As much as I'd love that, I think we should go for a swim and eat something first." He reached for her bathing suit and handed it to her. "Then …"

"Then what?" Eleni asked.

"Then try to stop me." He chuckled, stepping into his swimming trunks.

"How about if we skip the food for now and skinny dip instead," Eleni said, flinging her bathing suit top at him.

"Who are you, and what have you done with my Brooklyn?" Nikko asked with a laugh. "No, we can't go skinny-dipping. What if someone passes by?"

"I haven't seen a soul since we got here."

Nikko picked her suit top of the ground and tied the strings around her back and neck. "This isn't the time to be daring," Nikko muttered. Taking her by the hand, they exited their private shelter and walked to the shoreline.

Just as Eleni predicted, no one was within sight. "See, I told you," she said. Eleni pretended to pull at her bra strings.

"Keep that suit on," Nikko warned, splashing water in her direction. "I'll take it off later. One string at a time," he added. "That's a promise."

Eleni lunged toward him, jumping and crossing her legs around his waist. Nikko held on, supporting her bottom with his palms. He pressed his forehead to hers. "Keep this up, and I'll drag you back to our hideaway caveman style."

"What exactly do you mean by keeping it up?" Eleni giggled.

"Oh, Brooklyn, I think the Goddess Aphrodite might have wielded her powers of seduction on you from above."

"And here I thought it was *you* who bewitched me." Eleni untangled herself from his body. "So does that mean you're basically interchangeable with just about anyone?" she teased.

"Over my dead body!" Nikko declared, throwing Eleni over his shoulder and stomping over to their blanket.

"I was joking," she squealed, slapping his back so he'd put her down. "I want all my adventures with you."

After a round of playful banter, they sat on the blanket facing each other, their legs crisscrossed, their gazes heated yet frozen in place. Eleni swore she could read into the depths of those darkening pools and reach into the heart of his soul. And he must have seen the same thing reflected in hers—trust, desire, and love.

Just as he'd promised, Nikko untied the strings of Eleni's bathing suit. Chills raced up her spine as she bared her body to the boy she loved. Urging Nikko to do the same, she gestured for him to rise enough to shed himself from his swimming trunks.

Nikko pulled her onto his lap. "I want you this way. Face to face. Wrap your legs around me," he commanded.

Eleni complied and reached for a condom. He took it from her and sheathed himself. "Your pace. Your control," he reassured her.

Eleni moaned around a kiss as she lowered herself onto him. Nikko had been right. This time was easier … better, her sensations heightening as her body came alive with abandon. Soon, they found a rhythm, sweeping her away in undulating waves of pleasure. Their bodies were no longer separate beings but had become one in spirit, body, and soul. With one hand on his shoulder, the other cupping his cheek, Eleni stared lovingly into Nikko's heavy-lidded eyes until she reached her peak. Closing her eyes, she threw her head back, stiffening as she took him deep. Nikko rode out her climax with his own, stifling a desperate grunt when he buried his face in the crook of her neck.

When they came down from wherever their bodies had levitated to, Nikko and Eleni remained locked in place, panting, taking each other in … communicating wordlessly.

Nikko broke the silence first. "How will I ever be able to let you go?"

"Don't think about that now," Eleni said. "We still have a month, and maybe I can convince my parents to let me stay a little longer." She began plotting, running her hands along his biceps. "At least until right before school begins."

"Do that, and if you can't convince them, I'll have my *yiayiá* work on them," Nikko said. "She'll pull for me."

"She always does."

"But we need to think past that," he said, sliding his swimming trunks back on.

Eleni followed his lead and put on her bathing suit. "Now I'm hungry," she said, reaching inside the cooler. She was deflecting the subject. The thought of leaving him now was impossible, and the future seemed too far away.

"I'm going to move this stuff outside." Nikko gathered their belongings and spread the blanket out on the beach. The sun was still shining but soon would begin its nightly descent.

Eleni served out food on plates and handed one to Nikko.

"Even if you stay for the entire summer, there will still be almost ten months separating us."

"I know," Eleni agreed sadly. "But it's out of our control."

"But we can make a long-term plan, which will make it all more bearable," he suggested.

"I don't think being away from you will ever be easy now."

"You have two more years of school, and I only have one. I could apply to school in the States."

"Is that what you want, though? You have to think about what's best for your chosen career and decide where to go based on that."

"So you wouldn't want me to come?" Nikko's voice dropped to a disappointed whisper.

"Of course, I would," Eleni assured him. "But I love you too much to have you make decisions just so you can be with me. I want you to pursue your passions."

"Well, how about if I come to you for a year or two, and maybe you might think about studying abroad later?" He cocked his head in question.

"I would love for you to do that. And I would consider that as well. We can figure it all out as we go. I want to be wherever you are. Always," Eleni agreed, leaning in for a kiss.

"No one ever told me that grief felt so like fear." C.S. Lewis

CHAPTER 23

Eleni

Thirteen years ago

After Eleni and Nikko pulled up in the driveway, Nikko popped the trunk, removing the cooler and blanket. Eleni slung her beach bag over her shoulder, and the happy pair walked up to the house, dropping their belongings in the foyer when they stepped inside.

Eleni glanced at Nikko when a shiver crawled up her spine. For some irrational reason, a sense of unease suddenly took hold of her.

"What's wrong?" Nikko asked, his brows furrowing with concern when he saw Eleni's troubled expression.

"There's a weird vibe in here."

"A weird vibe?" Nikko questioned. "Since when are you all woo-woo?" He wiggled his fingers.

"I'm serious. Listen," Eleni insisted. It's dinnertime. Do you hear dishes clanking, pots and pans banging, or our grandmothers debating which herbs to add to the food?"

"Now that you mention it, no, but maybe they went out to eat?" Nikko shrugged before calling out to his family.

No sooner had he done that than his mother lumbered down the hallway, her eyes red-rimmed.

"*Mamá?*"

"*Pethiá*," Maria sobbed, pulling the teens in for an embrace.

Eleni's heart plummeted. She knew her instincts were correct. "Is it my pappou or Nikko's? Did something happen to one of them? Or one of the *yiayiás*?" As the family's oldest members, her mind immediately went to them. A heart attack or a stroke, perhaps.

But Maria dabbed her eyes with a tear-saturated Kleenex as she led them to the family room, where the mood was as grim and somber as a wake. Every person in the room looked as if the world had come to an end.

Eleni took note of who was present. Relieved to see both sets of grandparents, she was more perplexed than before. Her *yiayiá* and *pappou* stood unsteadily, crossing over to her, ashen-faced with grief. They grasped her in a desperate embrace, her *yiayiá* breaking out in uncontrollable sobs.

Eleni's head spun in confusion and fear. She pulled away from their clutches. "What's going on?" she asked, her voice trembling. "Where are my parents? And Peter? Are they still at the Alexatoses?"

Stavros intervened. "Sit down," he said, guiding Eleni to a chair.

"I don't want to sit. I want to know where my family is," she demanded, quivering.

"*Babá?*" Nikko questioned, but Stavros ignored his son, instead addressing Eleni.

"There's been an accident," he said solemnly.

"Are they in the hospital?" Eleni cried. "Please, take me to them." She looked around the room. "Why are they alone? *Yiayiá, Pappou,* why aren't you by their bedside?"

Maria came up beside her and stroked her hair. "They—" Nikko's mother choked on her words.

Yiayiá Thalia took over, kneeling before Eleni. "There is no easy way to tell you," she said, stroking Eleni's face affectionately.

The anguished expression in the older woman's eyes revealed the truth.

"No, no," Eleni whimpered. "No!" she screamed. "I just saw them a few hours ago. They were only going to the other side of the island. It has to be a mistake."

But the collective weeping around the room confirmed it wasn't. Her family was gone.

Nikko fell to his knees beside her, his grandmother stepping away so he could comfort her. But nothing or no one could ease her despair. Eleni couldn't fathom how her whole life could change in an instant. She had parents and a brother this morning when she waved them on their way, and now, without warning, they were gone. How was that even possible? She had been happy. Happier than she'd ever been. Now … She covered her face with her hands. Now, she felt nothing but agony searing her heart, branding it with a sorrow so deep it penetrated her soul.

"How did it happen?" she asked robotically.

"No!" Eleni heard her grandfather say. "Not tonight. We are all in shock. You've heard enough."

"I've heard nothing except that I no longer have a family," she stated bitterly. "I won't believe it until I hear what happened."

"Nikko, take Yanni out of the room," his mother ordered.

"No, I'm not leaving Eleni," Nikko argued.

"I will," Kostas offered, escorting the youngster out.

"The accident wasn't their fault," Stavros assured her. "It seems they were coming around a mountain bend when a speeding car lost control." He blew out a ragged breath and continued. "The angle of impact propelled the car over the edge."

Tears trickled down Eleni's face as she imagined her family's last moments, thoughts, and fatal realizations. They were really gone. "Rescue?" she managed to ask through the lump in her throat.

Stavros nodded. "Yes, but it was a recovery, not a rescue," he said wearily. "I'm so sorry."

Suddenly, the entire family surrounded her—Nikko, with his arms embracing her, Maria kneeling at her feet, the *Yiayiás* on each armrest, and her *pappou* and Stavros hovering above. Eleni had never been claustrophobic, but she couldn't breathe with everyone closing in. They meant well, she knew, but she wanted to be alone before they suffocated her with their good intentions.

"I'd like to go to bed," Eleni announced.

Maria rose to help Eleni off the chair, but Nikko stopped her. "No, I've got her."

Yiayiá Thalia glanced at her daughter-in-law, signaling for her to stay put.

"I can walk myself up," Eleni argued.

"Can and should are two different things," Nikko said firmly.

Once they were in Eleni's bedroom, Nikko pulled the blinds shut. She lay on the bed, unmoving, with no motivation to get under the covers.

Nikko went to the adjoining bathroom and ran water for a bath. When the tub was filled, he picked Eleni up into his arms and carried her inside.

"You need to wash the beach off you," he said.

"I don't care," she said softly.

"It will make you feel better," he said, stripping her out of her shorts and bathing suit.

She laughed humorlessly. "A bath? That will solve my problems?"

"No, but it can't hurt."

He helped her into the water, and though she didn't want to give in to its comfort, her body was soothed, though her heart and mind roiled with lament.

Nikko found her shampoo and proceeded to wash and rinse her hair. Then he soaped up a loofah and ran it over Eleni's body. He cared for her like a helpless child, but little did he know she felt as zombie-like as one of the Walking Dead.

After he wrapped her in a towel, Nikko searched her drawers for a nightshirt and slipped it over her head. Then he pulled back the quilt and helped her into bed. "Can I get you anything? Water? Something to eat?"

"I can't eat," Eleni mumbled. "I just want to be alone."

Nikko sighed. "Try to get some sleep. I'll check on you in a little while."

CHAPTER 24

Nikko

Thirteen years ago

Nikko sat on the floor outside Eleni's bedroom. She wanted space, and he'd give her what she thought she needed. But his place was by her side, and once she understood that, they would get through this together.

Leaning his head against the wall, he closed his eyes, thinking of how the day would be remembered. It was meant to be memorable—the first day of many happy days together, where he and Eleni cemented their love and planned for the future. Now, every precious moment they shared was overshadowed by tragedy and would be marked as the worst day of Eleni's life.

She had sensed something grave the minute they walked into the house, and he made fun of her. For as long as Nikko lived, he would never forget the abject devastation on her face when the tragic news was delivered. And he had felt it too, as if he'd lost half his own family. The Pangalos family may not have been blood, but they were bonded to his family in every way that counted.

That instant when his father told Eleni about the accident and she wouldn't accept it nearly destroyed Nikko. He fell to his knees beside her, distraught by his own grief, steeling strength he didn't know he had in order to comfort her. When his grandmother caught his eye and moved away to allow him to sit beside Eleni, he admired how his perceptive *yiayiá* missed nothing. She figured out immediately what Eleni meant to him with one look. And that's why she intervened with his mother, leaving Nikko to tend to the girl he cared for.

Maybe feeling a little hurt right now was selfish, but Nikko feared it would be easy for Eleni to shut him out completely. If only she understood the degree of his unwavering support and how determined he was to be by her side. Instead, he stood guard by her door in case she had a nightmare or suddenly called out for him.

Standing, Nikko paced the floor in frustration. He wasn't sure what the coming days would hold, but they wouldn't be pleasant. Turning the doorknob, he crept into her room to assure himself she was okay. But he needed her just as much as he hoped she still needed and wanted him.

Carefully, he climbed onto the bed so as to not disturb her sleep.

"I'm awake," Eleni whimpered.

Nikko exhaled. "I was hoping you were asleep. Now that I'm here, let me hold you." He laid down next to her and draped an arm over her body.

"This is all my fault," Eleni said.

"No, it's not. Why would you think that?"

"If I had gone with them like they asked or if I didn't stop to talk to them when they left, the chain of events would have been different."

"Eleni." Nikko sighed. This wasn't a time for flirty nicknames. "You can't possibly know if anything you did or didn't do would have changed it. This happened on the way home, so stopping to speak to them on their way over couldn't have had an effect."

"You don't know that," Eleni disagreed. It might have postponed their arrival, which would have affected how late they returned home."

"Are you looking to punish yourself? A five-minute chat with your parents wouldn't change a thing. And if you had gone with them, you might also have been ..." Nikko was about to say killed. "You might have been in the accident, too."

"And maybe I would have seen the car coming. Instead, I was doing ... stuff with you."

"Are you feeling guilty about that? Because I don't," Nikko said. "I wish this wasn't the memory that will be etched in our minds forever—that it happened on this of all days. But I don't regret it. Do you?"

"I don't know. Maybe."

And if Nikko wasn't grieving already, that answer gutted him. "It's been the worst ending to what I thought was the best day of my life up until tonight." He sat up. "Maybe I'd feel the same in your shoes. I don't know. I'll let you get some rest," he said, dejected, sliding off the bed and out the door.

CHAPTER 25

Eleni

Thirteen years ago

If one were to review the precipitation chart for the island of Kefalonia, one would learn that July was the month least likely for it to rain. The average days of rain were recorded at seven-tenths of a day—for the entire month, just to be precise. And the amount of rain accumulated averaged a mere four-tenths of an inch.

So when a downpour occurred on the day of Eleni's family's funeral that could rival a Southeast Asian monsoon, she took it as some sort of sign. Were the heavens crying for her loss? Or telling her to get off this God-forsaken island? Perhaps both. Eleni only knew two things for sure: she didn't know how she would make it through this day, and she wanted it over.

Escorted by her grandfather and Nikko on either side of her, Eleni walked to the church entrance. Stavros stood behind her, protecting her from the rain with an oversized black umbrella.

"I can't," Eleni gasped as she began to hyperventilate. Her fingers tingled, and her chest tightened. Her grandmother jumped in to help the men when her legs began to give out.

"We have her, Katerina," Eleni's grandfather assured her.

"I'm sorry," Eleni said, trying to calm her breathing. Her grandparents were grieving, too, and she didn't want to add to their burden.

Nikko opened the heavy, wooden door. "Let me take her in. I think she needs a little breathing room."

Eleni began to shake uncontrollably when they entered the narthex, her teeth chattering with dread. Greek Orthodox tradition didn't typically hold wakes since funerals were usually performed twenty-four hours after death. The caskets were open for mourners to view their loved ones inside the church during the service. This was just one of the many things escalating Eleni's anxiety.

Labored steps between deep breaths allowed Eleni to let Nikko lead her to the front of the church. Not a pin dropping could be heard as mourners watched Eleni approach the caskets. A guttural, bellowing wail ripping from the depths of her soul echoed off the walls. Eleni cried out their names, moving from one casket to another, shaking her head in disbelief—sobbing, gasping, weeping.

Gently, Nikko guided her to the front row, sitting next to her grandparents, Andreas and Katerina, who she needed to remember had lost their son, her father. Flashes of the service flickered in her mind like an out-of-body experience. Censers, prayers, chanting. Something about their memory being eternal. She went about the motions, following the caskets out onto the street.

Eleni had no recollection of how they arrived at the gravesite, but she recognized they were back on the vineyard property. The rain had slowed to a drizzle, but the clouds were as gray and lifeless as her soul.

After the funeral, dozens of people spilled into the house. This was the last thing Eleni wanted. Eating, drinking, and carrying on conversations as if the previous two days hadn't happened was unbearable. She was living a nightmare and needed to escape.

Eleni went to her room and stayed there. It didn't take long for Nikko to find her.

He knocked before entering. "Eleni?"

"Go away. I want to be alone."

"I just want to lay beside you and hold you. We need each other more than ever now," Nikko said, edging into the room.

"I can't do this now."

"Can't do what?"

"This! Us. Don't you understand that everything has changed?"

"And I want to stand by you through all of it."

"I'm sorry, Nikko, but I'm going to beg my grandparents to leave as soon as possible, and once we do, I'm never coming back."

"No, you're sad and not thinking straight," Nikko reasoned. "We had plans. We have a whole life ahead of us. That doesn't need to change."

"Everything has changed. Nothing will ever be the same again. The sooner you accept that, the easier it will be for both of us."

"Leave, if you must. But this doesn't end us," Nikko relented.

He left the room without another word. Eleni should have been relieved, but his acceptance of her impending and sudden departure only deepened her despair.

Ten minutes later, Eleni's grandmother entered the room with a plate of food.

"What's this I hear? You want to go home?" Her *yiayiá* brought a forkful of food to her mouth, which Eleni waved away.

"You have to eat."

"Did Nikko send you up here?"

"The boy worries about you." Her grandmother cupped her cheek.

Eleni ignored her assessment. "Can you ask *pappou* if we can go home right away?"

"I was hoping you would stay until the *mnimósyno*."

Eleni pouted. "The forty-day memorial? I'm not staying that long! Please. If you need to stay, I understand, but I feel like I will suffocate here. Maybe I can stay with Angela until you return to New York."

"No," she relented. "I'll speak to your grandfather. We only want to do what's best for you."

CHAPTER 26

Eleni

Present Day

One kiss. That was all it took to transport Eleni back in time. How could lips she hadn't touched for thirteen years feel so wonderfully familiar? The sexual and emotional awareness his kiss elicited was distinct to her and Nikko alone. No one after him or before him had made her feel … what? Cherished? At peace? Loved? Not her college boyfriend or any anticipatory first date kiss, and certainly not Gregory. That relationship was sensible and practical, not one born from romantic notions of mad, unconditional love.

But as Eleni lay restlessly in bed, she thought back, in vivid detail, to the summer that changed her life in every way. She permitted herself to remember what it felt like to make love to him, her skin tingling at the memory. It had been beautiful. She and Nikko had become one, body and soul, until the connection was severed along with their dreams.

Eleni had pushed Nikko away during her period of grief and never let him back into her life. She should have been able to rationalize that what happened to her family was separate from him. It was not his fault, and it wasn't the island's fault. But Eleni needed to lay blame, to lash out, and to escape. Nikko and the island became the scapegoats. It wasn't fair. Eleni saw that now, and that was on her.

Yet Nikko persisted. He had tried every means to get through to her. Oh, how he had tried, and in return, Eleni had been nothing but cold and merciless, fearful he'd penetrate the armor she had wrapped around her heart. But he was already inside, indelibly burrowed deep within. Eleni could protest and refuse to admit her love for him because it was easier to shut her emotions off, but she was only fooling herself. So when he finally gave up, it pierced her soul, though she knew it was for the best. Nikko had finally moved on.

Tread carefully, Eleni warned herself. It would be so easy to fall back into his arms. But she was older now and hopefully wiser. The last thing she wanted was for history to repeat itself. Eleni's time on the island was limited. Her life was in New York, and she wouldn't pretend otherwise. She had to keep a healthy distance from Nikko so they could remain friends.

"The pain of parting is nothing to the joy of meeting again."
Charles Dickens

CHAPTER 27

Nikko

Present Day

Nikko lay in bed, a hopeful smile on his face. He left his shade open to stare up at the same stars he and Eleni had admired earlier that evening. For the first time since she'd arrived, optimism overrode caution. Maybe it was how she seemed to wish upon a shooting star or animatedly spoke about her ideas to draw business to the vineyard. Or perhaps it was the kiss that he had longed for from the moment Eleni arrived. They were no longer a pair of inexperienced teenagers, yet he suddenly felt like one. Or was it the memory of how his lips recognized hers as if no time had passed?

Nikko's protective side thought better than to take too much stock in the brief dalliance. The situation could change at any given moment. But he and Eleni weren't children anymore, and their life's decisions were in their own hands. Nikko hung on by a thread of hope that Eleni felt as he did, and that now, she'd have the courage and will she'd lacked in her youth.

He replayed the moment on the porch repeatedly in his mind. Time stood still as he gazed into Eleni's eyes, his heart thundering in his chest, his skin tingling as he laced his fingers through hers. Nikko could feel the pounding of his heart as their mouths collided. He was a nomad who found water in an arid desert, a newborn taking his first breath, the first bud on a branch after a long winter. Eleni not only aroused his body; she awakened his spirit.

And at that moment, as soothing moonlight washed over them, Nikko decided he would invent a reason, any reason, to spend the next day with Eleni.

CHAPTER 28

Eleni

Present Day

Excited for what she hoped would be a productive day, Eleni awoke at the first sliver of light pushing its way through the slats of the window blinds. Though it would be hours before the shops opened, she quickly showered, dressed, and descended the stairs to enjoy an early breakfast.

"Good morning," Nikko said, smiling. "You're up early."

"I have quite a few people to speak to today."

Leaning against the kitchen counter, he said, "About that …"

"Please don't tell me you had a change of heart," she said, her face falling.

"No. Nothing like that. Actually, I've decided to come with you," Nikko explained. "As convincing as you can be, no one knows you here. Of course, not everyone knows me either, but they most likely know of the vineyard. It may help to have me as a representative along with you during the introductions."

Eleni crossed her arms over her chest and stared at him, trying to decide if he was up to something. Finally, she sighed, admonishing herself for her suspicions. Nikko wanted the best for the vineyard, and her plan was solid.

"You're right," Eleni agreed. "I would appreciate the help."

"The only thing is, we still have about three hours to kill before any shops open." Nikko raised a finger. "But I have an idea." He pulled out his mobile and tapped out a text.

"Who are you texting?" Eleni asked.

"I'll let you know if he answers." Nikko poured himself a coffee, sipping it silently until his phone signaled an incoming message. "Perfect!" He gulped down the remainder of his beverage and placed the mug in the sink. "Ready to go?"

"To where?"

"It's a surprise."

"Have I ever been there before?" Eleni asked.

"You have, but this time will be so much better."

She scrunched up her face in suspicion. "You're being very mysterious."

"Let's go," Nikko said with a chuckle.

* * *

"I know this place!" Eleni exclaimed. "The magical cave! But last time you brought me here, we had to wait in line for hours behind hundreds of people."

"It doesn't open to the public for another hour or so." Nikko took her by the hand. "Come. My friend manages the staff. He's letting us in for a private boat ride."

Crowded in a boat with strangers, Melissani Cave was an experience she had never forgotten. But the idea of having it all to herself was thrilling, even for only a few brief minutes.

Stefanos was waiting at the cave's entrance. The two men hugged, patting each other on the back heartily.

"This is Eleni," Nikko introduced them.

"Eleni," Stefanos said, eyeing her with a smile that made Eleni feel he had some secret information about her. "It's good to see you. You probably don't remember, but we've met before."

"Yes, I remember you from the beach, right?"

"And we had all gone on your grandfather's fishing boat once, too. I think we were around fourteen or so," Stefanos recalled. "I was sorry to hear about Andreas," he added somberly.

"Thank you," Eleni said. "I remember that day on the boat," she mused. "And you were a bit of a prankster if I remember," she laughed. "My *pappou* got rid of that boat so many years ago. I almost forgot about it."

"That sounds like me!" Stefanos confirmed. "With this guy as the instigator." He waved his thumb in Nikko's direction. "Are you ready for a private tour?"

"I can't wait!" Eleni exclaimed.

Stefanos escorted them through a narrow underground pathway leading to the cave. Rustic overhead fixtures dimly lit the passage to aid tourists. But once they reached their destination, the morning light shining down from a large hole in the cave's ceiling unveiled the extraordinary natural wonder she had remembered from years ago. Stefanos stepped into a rowboat tied up at the cave's edge and assisted Eleni and Nikko in boarding before freeing the small vessel.

As Eleni looked around in awe, a sense of tranquility came over her; any memories weighing on her soul evaporated at the magnificence surrounding her. Centuries before, the cave roof had collapsed, exposing the lake below. And what a phenomenon of nature it was to behold. It looked more like a giant well than a grotto, allowing the sun to filter in and illuminate the water. When the beams of light angled in a specific direction, a spectrum of light reflecting off the cave walls appeared in a rainbow of radiant color. Iridescent azure water glimmered around them, casting an otherworldly glow. Eleni had never seen anything so uniquely spectacular. The electric-blue shade of the lake's water was impossible to imagine except in books describing mythical lands.

When she glanced in Nikko's direction, Eleni caught him staring at her, his expression one of admiration and pride. He had made her happy this morning, and it pleased him. She could tell. She had seen that same look on his face so many years ago, but she had never forgotten it, nor had she forgotten the way her skin heated upon his stare.

Soon, it was time to leave, but Eleni wanted to stay and see if winged fairies might emerge. Or if a water nymph or two would rise from these mystical waters. Reluctantly, she disembarked, casting one last glance at the surreal view before she reluctantly walked away.

"I can't thank you enough for allowing us to enter before operating hours," Eleni said to Stefanos.

"It was my pleasure," he replied. "Maybe I will see you again soon?"

"I hope so," she assured him.

"I'm getting married in two weeks." Stefanos turned to Nikko, whispering conspiratorially. "Make sure you bring her."

"I'll do my best to make that happen," Nikko said with a smile.

"That was ... I have no words for what that was," Eleni said as they headed back to their car. "Thank you so much for arranging it."

"I'm glad you enjoyed it. Now, on to drum up some business!"

As they neared the parking lot, a line for the cave began to form. Eleni raised her brows. "I feel like we cheated the system," she laughed.

"It's all about who you know." Nikko shrugged.

"So Stefanos is getting married," Eleni stated. "Do you know the woman?"

"Yes. Theodora is lovely. You'll meet her if you agree to attend the wedding with me."

"I would like that very much." Eleni felt the heat of a flush rise on her face. *Seriously? A flush?*

They sat in the car, but before Nikko turned the ignition, he looked at Eleni's list, methodically plotting their route more efficiently than her random meandering from the day before.

"Agia Effimia is closest to here, so we'll start there," Nikko said. "Plus, I'm hungry, and there's a nice café by the dock I think you'll like."

"Hungry? We just ate breakfast."

"That was almost two hours ago. Then we'll head to Assos, then Razata, and maybe we'll discover a few other places for you to explore along the way. Sound good?" Nikko asked.

"Sounds good."

"We can finish in Argostoli because I'll be hungry again by then."

Eleni shook her head in astonishment. "Is your stomach all you think about?" she teased.

"Not all," he replied, meeting her gaze. "But it's in my top three."

They returned home satisfied with their day's efforts. Surprisingly, each proprietor they pitched to was open to the prospect of additional exposure and sales. Not one store owner or artisan declined. The day had proven to be more successful than she'd dreamed.

"I guess it was a good idea for you to come," Eleni said as she exited the car. "You charmed every woman from nineteen to ninety into accepting a deal."

"Do I hear a hint of jealousy in your tone?" Nikko asked with a smirk.

"No, no," Eleni protested. "Not at all."

"That's good. Because you had no problem flirting with George. 'Oh, George, I've never seen such beautiful craftsmanship. Oh, George, it's a true work of art.' Swoon, swoon."

Eleni shoved Nikko playfully. "I didn't say it like that. And I didn't swoon. Who's jealous now?"

Chuckling, Nikko threw his hands up in surrender and walked into the house.

Later, Eleni and Nikko shared the good news at the dinner table, and concrete plans were set to accommodate the merchandise.

"*Elenitsa mou*," Stavros addressed her. "I hate to bring this up after you've had such a pleasant day, but tomorrow is the reading of your *pappou's* will."

Eleni nodded solemnly. "I know."

"My father and I will accompany you there," Stavros reassured her.

"Andreas was like a brother to me," *Pappou* Kostas said. "And I love you like a granddaughter."

Eleni glanced at Nikko, sitting across from her. "What about you, Nikko? Will you be there?" she asked quietly.

"Not unless you want me to be?"

"Yes, I do," she said in a whisper.

"Of course, I will then." He smiled sadly at her, reaching over to touch her hand comfortingly.

She excused herself to her room soon after, suddenly feeling weary. Nothing in her grandfather's will could replace him or soothe her soul from the emptiness she felt at his loss. She would give anything to have him back, if only for a day.

CHAPTER 29

Eleni

Present Day

"My condolences on your grandfather's passing," Manolis Markatos offered, kissing Eleni on one cheek and then the other. "Andreas was an old friend, and I'll truly miss him. Please, take a seat," he addressed the group, gesturing to the chairs arranged in his spacious office.

"Thank you," Eleni said, exhaling a nervous breath. She wanted to get this over with. Something about discussing her grandfather's assets and possessions felt very wrong. As if this was all his life had amounted to. There wasn't a price tag high enough to equate to his worth or the love and support he had bestowed upon her all these years.

Nikko pulled the chair out for Eleni to sit, and then he, Stavros, and Kostas also took their seats, forming a semicircle around the attorney's desk.

After Manolis recited the standard legal jargon, he began to read her grandfather's wishes. "I, Andreas Pangalos, being of sound mind, bequeath all my monetary assets and possessions, including my apartment in New York, to my granddaughter, Eleni Pangalos. As for my share of the Pangalos Varvos Vineyard, I leave twenty percent of my half to Kostas Varvos. If he is not alive at the time of my death, it is to be passed to his beneficiaries, provided they are working members of the vineyard. Eleni Pangalos is to inherit the remaining thirty percent. If she chooses to sell her interest in the vineyard, it must be sold only to a member of the Varvos family. It is my hope and wish that the Pangalos Varvos Vineyard, created by me and Kostas Varvos, live on for generations to come."

Once Manolis finished, silence punctuated the somber atmosphere until he set down the document. "Andreas was plain in his wishes and wanted them simply stated," Manolis said. "Do you have any questions?"

Eleni blew her nose, tears clogging her throat. Naturally, she knew she would inherit his worldly assets as his only heir. But for some reason, it had never occurred to her that he'd leave her a share of the vineyard. The twenty percent he'd left Kostas ensured the Varvos family would have a controlling interest. As it should be. But now she truly needed to decide whether or not she'd become a working member of the establishment or sell her share to the Varvos family. Of course, she could step into her grandfather's shoes and become the wine representative for the vineyard. But juggling that position and her own company would be challenging. It was something she would need to consider logically.

"Anyone else?" Manolis asked. "Questions?"

"No," Kostas replied. "Andreas and I discussed this years ago. It's exactly as we had planned in the event of either of our deaths."

Eleni had been deep in thought, absorbing the details of her grandfather's will. Suddenly, she turned to Kostas. "So you're amenable to this?" she asked him quietly.

"Of course, *koukla mou.*"

Nikko gently laid his hand over Eleni's. "If there's nothing else, we can leave," he offered.

Manolis nodded when Nikko looked at him for confirmation.

"Oh, yes. I'm sorry," Eleni said, blinking the daze away. "It's a lot to digest."

"Nothing has to be decided right away," Nikko assured her.

Eleni stood as Manolis handed her his card. With a perfunctory smile, she thanked him politely before quietly departing, this new information weighing heavily on her mind.

* * *

Later that evening, Stavros and Kostas explained the details of the will to the rest of the family. Everyone remained quiet, shifting their food around their plates distractedly. They must have sensed that Eleni didn't need the added pressure of their opinions. She had to decide on her own what was best for her. But it was evident by the expressions on their faces that they were all bursting at the seams to spill their thoughts. It almost added some levity to the situation. It made her love them all the more for holding their tongues.

After dinner, Eleni walked around the vineyard, seeking solace in the serenity it brought. She needed to be alone with her thoughts. This was her vineyard too, now, she realized. But her roots had always been planted here in all the ways that counted most. If only the answers she needed fell from the sky. And, as if the universe heard her plea, the stars twinkled in what looked like a Morse code she couldn't decipher.

"Waiting for the gods to shine their wisdom down on you?"

Eleni jumped, a shriek escaping her lips. "You startled me!" she scolded Nikko. "Didn't your mother ever teach you not to sneak up on people?"

"Didn't anyone ever teach you it's unsafe to walk alone in the dark?"

"On private property?" She frowned. "What are you doing out here, anyway?"

"Looking for you." Nikko took her hands in his. "I tried so hard to stay away from you when you first arrived," he began, staring into her eyes. "When that became impossible, keeping you at a friendly distance seemed the best solution. But that didn't work either."

"What didn't work?" Eleni asked, puzzled as she held his gaze.

"Not falling for you again," he whispered as he closed the space between them. "Or, if I'm honest, there was no falling again. My feelings for you never changed. I locked them away, but they came to the surface as soon as I looked into your eyes."

"Nikko." She sighed, closing her eyes. What was she to say? Why start something that would only lead to heartache? They had been down that road before, but now it was apparent she wasn't the only one who hadn't really moved on. He'd always held a piece of her heart that no one else could touch.

"I haven't felt this alive in years," Nikko continued. "And watching everything you're doing for the vineyard—for the family—I think you feel the same."

"I'm doing what I'm good at and I'm happy to contribute."

Nikko took her by the shoulders, forcing her to look him in the eyes. "Please tell me it's more than that. Tell me you'll at least consider staying this time. That you could be happy here." His eyes implored her, and she could feel herself falling. Falling for him all over again. But had she fallen years ago and only pretended to pick herself up? She had no idea what to do, and the last thing she wanted was to hurt him again. Or herself, for that matter.

Eleni broke free from his hold. "My head is spinning from all that's happened," she said, her deep sigh signaling her anxiety. "I have a life in New York, Nikko. A business, an apartment, friends …"

"A man?" he asked, jealousy tripping over his tongue.

Eleni hesitated. She and Gregory were over. Nikko didn't need to worry about a change of heart regarding him. At least she knew that part of her life was over without any regrets. "There's no man."

Though only moonlight illuminated his face, she saw relief wash over Nikko at her confession. "There has to be a way to make it all work." He pulled her in gently at the waist. "Don't ask me to say goodbye again," he breathed, his lips brushing over hers.

Nikko's arms around Eleni were all that kept her knees from buckling. She felt so much for this man. Emotions she'd pushed aside for years to protect her heart. A heart that had been torn to shreds in so many ways, one that couldn't survive another loss. Allowing herself to feel would only open the door for more heartbreak when it was time to resume her life in New York.

But his touch rendered her powerless. The nearness of his lips and his breath tickling her neck sent goosebumps skating across her skin. Teasing her with a wisp of a kiss turned her bones to jelly. With a chuckle, Nikko held her tightly, aware of his effect on her. He kissed her again, but this time, it was deeper and more passionate, and Eleni responded with a moan.

"Nikko," she said, breaking the kiss. "I can't make any promises."

"I know. Just give your options serious thought." He looked down at his feet and shuffled, kicking up the dirt. "One thing New York doesn't have is me," he whispered pleadingly. "And no one there will ever love you like I do." He looked up to meet the uncertainty in her expression. She could see long-ago hurt lingering in the stormy depths of his crestfallen blue eyes.

Eleni drew in a sharp breath at his confession, knowing in her heart he spoke the truth. Reaching up, she cupped his cheek. Nikko took her hand and brought it to his lips, kissing the inside of her palm. She wanted to return those words, but the sentiment was lodged in her throat. Until she decided on her future, it wouldn't be fair to utter them, to express that hope, that chance of forever.

"There comes a time in your life when you have to choose to turn the page, write another book or simply close it." Shannon L. Alder

CHAPTER 30

Eleni

Present Day

"I'm so confused," Eleni told Angela during their FaceTime call. "I need more time to sort things out here."

"Sort *things* out? Or sort out your feelings for a particular wine-maker?" Angela challenged.

"I have a life in New York and a business I've left you solely responsible for. It's not fair to you."

"Don't worry about what's fair to me. Take all the time you need. I have it under control," Angela assured her. "I would miss you terribly if you decide to stay in Greece, but I want you to be happy. You have a lot to consider. And I don't want to see your chance for love slip through your fingers."

"I know," Eleni groaned. "It's just a lot. I can't upend my whole life."

Angela opened her mouth about to speak but hesitated.

"What is it? What are you not telling me?" Eleni asked.

"I saw Gregory. He came looking for you and was surprised you weren't back in town yet."

Eleni shrugged. "He's been leaving messages on my cellphone, so I guess that shouldn't surprise me, even though I made it clear we were over."

"He didn't seem to think so. He figured what with the arrangements for your grandfather 'out of the way,' as he phrased it, you'd come to your senses once your grieving period was over."

Eleni clenched her fist, her nails digging into the delicate skin of her palm. "What a little shit! Out of the way?" Gregory's insensitivity spiked her temper. "What gall! As if my *pappou's* death was nothing but an inconvenience." Eleni was even more irritated with herself. "Honestly, I don't know how I didn't see this side of his character sooner."

Angela bit her bottom lip as her face grew worried. "Don't be mad at me, but when I told him you were still overseas, I foolishly explained you were staying a while longer to manage the details of your inheritance," Angela said, cringing as she said it. "I'm so sorry. I feel like I gave away information he didn't need to be privy to."

"Whatever. Don't stress over it." Eleni didn't care. He was utterly inconsequential to her. She had done the right thing by breaking it off with him.

"His interest was piqued when I mentioned you had much to settle because the inheritance included the vineyard," Angela continued.

"That makes sense," Eleni mused. "Money was always at the top of his list of priorities, though he has nothing to gain here because we are o-v-e-r. When we first started dating, I thought it was a positive quality in wanting to secure the future. We never overtly discussed my grandfather's wealth, but he had an idea. And I'm beginning to wonder if that's why he's trying to hold on. Perhaps it's why he was drawn to me in the first place."

"Oh, Eleni, I don't think that could have been his only motive." Angela rolled her eyes. "I can't believe I'm about to say this because I never liked the guy, and I hate to defend him or give him the benefit of the doubt, but I think he cares for you. He just got lucky in finding an incredible woman with beauty, brains, and family wealth thrown in the bargain." She giggled.

"You're just saying that because you're my friend and you don't want me to think I wasted my time with someone who never truly cared for me," Eleni said. "But it's okay. I'll just chalk it up to one of my many relationship failures." She laughed, though it wasn't amusing. There were more important matters to focus on than Gregory and his pointless ulterior motives. "Well, if he happens to come around again, please tell him I have nothing more to say and that I'm not his concern."

"Will do," Angela promised. "In the meantime, everything else is running smoothly, so do what you have to with a clear mind."

When Eleni ended her chat with Angela, she knew one thing for sure. She had no desire to pursue anything with Gregory. She was utterly indifferent to him. The only man occupying her thoughts now was Nikko. Then, now, and always, if she was honest with herself. And maybe that was her problem all along. Her heart remembered what it felt like to be in love ...with him. Her skin recognized the electricity coursing through her veins when he was near. But was it merely the memory of that first unforgettable experience with love tugging at all her senses? Or had time and distance proven that their souls were truly and irrevocably bound together?

A knock on the door roused Eleni from her thoughts.

"Can I come in?" Nikko asked from the other side.

"Yes," she replied, striding across the room to open her bedroom door.

"I just wanted to remind you that tomorrow is Stefanos' wedding," Nikko said, not sounding like his usual confident self. "If you still want to go with me."

"Of course I do," she said with conviction, taking his hand in hers. But then, her own confidence wavered. "That is if *you* haven't changed your mind about wanting to take me?"

"No, I haven't," he said, emphatically. "Maybe tomorrow, instead of carefully tiptoeing around each other, we can dance together instead."

* * *

The next afternoon, Eleni, dressed for the occasion, met Nikko by his car.

Extending his hand to help her into her seat, Nikko raked her over from head to toe. "You really shouldn't outshine the bride, Brooklyn."

"Don't be silly." She laughed at the use of her old nickname. "The bride is always the star. I should know. I've organized more weddings than I can count."

"You look beautiful," he said, brushing his lips lightly over hers.

Eleni tugged at the lapels of his suit jacket. "And I may need to keep my eyes on you before one of the single girls at the wedding whisks you away!"

"Not a chance," he laughed.

They entered the car and were off, driving down the winding roads until he pulled off onto a narrow side street. "Why are you stopping?" Eleni asked.

"We're going to walk from here," Nikko replied. "You see, it's the custom for the bride and groom to be escorted on foot to the church by their parents, with their guests following behind. Then the couple meets outside the front of the church where the priest awaits them."

"What a lovely tradition." Eleni looked at the scenic path before her. Overhanging trees lined the street, but the road itself was not meant for walking in designer footwear. Crumbled cobblestones covered in dirt was an accident waiting to happen in stilettos.

"Nikko, I wish you had warned me. I'll never make it in these shoes."

Nikko leaned in, whispering in her ear. "I'll gladly carry you if it comes to it."

He took Eleni by the hand, and soon, they joined the guests' procession behind the groom. Lacing his fingers with hers, Nikko steadied her each time she faltered on the rough pavement in her four-inch heels.

Eleni thought they made a beautiful pair, if she said so herself—she in a fitted dress of rose petal pink, which accented her slim figure; Nikko in a gray suit with a necktie that enhanced the color of his blue eyes. But as handsome as he was standing before her now, Eleni loved the look he wore working in the field or wielding his magic to create rich blends. There was honesty in his mud-dried boots and wine-stained shirt. Raw and unpretentious, she could blissfully watch him in his element all day.

As the lively group neared the church, they sang a traditional upbeat wedding song, announcing that the groom was coming for his bride. Eleni turned her focus to Nikko. He knew all the words and sang them out loud as if he were belting out a proud rendition of the Greek national anthem. Smirking, she tilted her head to the side, meeting his eyes with a sparkle of surprise.

"What?" he asked with a laugh. "I've been to a lot of weddings."

Eleni shook her head in awe, smiling. "So many beautiful traditions." She had also been to many Greek Orthodox weddings in the States, but she'd never seen the bride and groom enter the church together in this manner.

She dabbed at her eyes when the priest placed the *stefana* on the couple's heads. The wreaths, made from silk flowers and tiny seed pearls, connected by a single satin ribbon, symbolized the couple's union.

Nikko squeezed her hand, echoing her emotion over the meaningful ritual. But Eleni couldn't contain her welling tears when the priest led the couple and their *koumbari* around the table for The Dance of Isaiah.

Nikko wrapped his arm around her. "It's the beginning of their life together." He smiled down at her, but she saw more than happiness for his friend reflected in his eyes. A cyclone of hope and possibilities swirled in those mesmerizing sea-blue orbs. It almost pained her to look at him. She had wounded him once before, and the last thing she wanted was a repeat of the past—for Nikko's sake ...and hers, but especially his. Eleni loved him too much to lead him on—to let him believe they had a future together. And there was her dilemma. She truly loved him and always had. Leaving him again would shred her heart beyond repair. But could she take the leap and turn the only existence she knew upside down?

* * *

Much later, when the stars had begun to dim from the hint of the sun rising over the horizon, Eleni and Nikko headed home, or so she thought.

"Where are you going?" Eleni asked when Nikko turned the car in the opposite direction of the house.

"It would be a shame to waste a sunrise," he answered matter-of-factly. "We're going to the beach."

"We're a little overdressed, but okay," Eleni agreed with a laugh. It had been a fabulous evening under the stars.

"I've never experienced a longer wedding reception in my life! Or one as lively," Eleni said, thinking of the endless courses of delicious food, money raining down on the wedding couple as they took to the dancefloor, and hours on her feet dancing to traditional Greek music and contemporary pop songs.

Nikko pulled up on the side of the road by a quiet beach.

"I'm not sure I can walk another step," Eleni complained. Discarding her shoes, she tossed them into the backseat of the car.

Nikko exited, dashing to her side to open her door. Then, without warning, he lifted Eleni out of her seat, picking her up.

"I was exaggerating!" she exclaimed with a yelp, winding her hands around his neck. She looked into his eyes, her breath hitching as she felt his heart hammering in beat with hers. Before Eleni thought the better of it, she ran her hands through his dark hair and took in his face; the cut of his jaw, and those full lips parting as he exhaled a shaky breath.

Without taking his eyes off her, Nikko carried Eleni to the shoreline and set her on her feet. "One second. Don't move," he commanded, his hands on her shoulders as if to cement her into place. "I forgot something."

Eleni threw up her hands. "Where would I go?" she called as he ran back to the car. When Nikko returned with a beach blanket, Eleni crossed her arms over her chest. "Did you plan this little rendezvous?"

"Not exactly, but I like to be prepared for anything."

"For anything?" she challenged. "I say that sounds a little too thought-out."

Nikko spread the blanket out on the sand. "If you don't like the idea of experiencing that," he offered, pointing to the colorful pageantry in the sky, "we can leave now."

"First the sunset, and now the sunrise," she murmured. If only this could be her life. But Eleni had obligations elsewhere in a place that wasn't fraught with grief.

"What did you say?" Nikko asked, sitting beside her.

"Just talking to myself. Admiring Mother Nature," Eleni said. "And feeling grateful to you for knowing I would love this."

Eleni detected a flash of disappointment wash over him, but Nikko immediately recovered. He inched closer to her, enough to grab Eleni by the ankles and slide her closer to him. It had taken her by surprise, and she squealed out a laugh, the sudden jerk making her fall onto her back.

Nikko took that opportunity to hover over her. "It's not your gratitude I'm seeking."

"What are you seeking?" Eleni asked, her heart jumping to her throat.

"Your mouth." Nikko proved it, pulling her in for a kiss, deep and hard—passionate and commanding. "Your heart." He trailed gentle kisses down her neck, past her collarbone, and to the swell of her breast. Pulling the straps of her dress off her shoulders, he added, "I want all of you."

"I don't know that this is a smart idea," she panted, already aroused. From the moment she saw Nikko looking blindingly handsome in his suit, Eleni's libido was on full alert. She should have expected it might culminate in this. Their dancing was an exercise in foreplay, his hands around her lower back heating her ever so intimately. Her body had been in a state all night, and now, her mind was seconds from losing the battle she raged between her body and heart.

"I say it's the smartest idea," Nikko disagreed. "Brilliant, in fact. But …" Nikko sighed, his lips refraining from continuing his exploration.

He removed his mouth from Eleni altogether, and she whimpered at the loss. Nikko rolled away into a sitting position, and Eleni didn't know if it was her heart shouting, 'idiot, moron, what's wrong with you?' Or if it was her girly bits pleading desperately for the euphoric satisfaction she'd only ever experienced with Nikko once before.

Before Eleni could find reason, she hooked her hand around Nikko's neck and pulled his face to hers. This time, she initiated the kiss, and the intensity of it told no lies. She wanted him. And if their tongues tangling didn't assure him, the unbuttoning of his dress shirt did. They took turns undressing one another— her back zipper, his trousers, his boxer briefs—until all that was left was Eleni's pale pink lace strapless bra and matching thong.

Nikko was gorgeous—every glorious bit of him. She had already seen his tanned chest and toned legs in his swimming trunks, but he looked like a god sitting before her naked under the golden-pink sun bleeding into the blue sky.

Nikko popped the hooks of her bra, letting the garment fall away. He moaned his appreciation and took both her breasts in his hands. Bending, he took a nipple in his mouth, sucking on the puckered nub.

Eleni moaned. Lost in the sensation of Nikko's tongue circling one breast and then the other and his hard length pressing against her while he pleasured her body, Eleni floated in a state of wondrous intoxication. She wasn't aware of anything but Nikko—not the birds chirping overhead, the waves splashing against the rocks, or the clacking of boat sails against the wind.

Nikko's mouth roamed down Eleni's ribcage to her navel. She shivered, her breath heaving as he teased, nipped, and licked at erogenous zones Eleni didn't know existed. When his fingers found their way to the edge of her panties, she moaned his name, her insides quaking with anticipation.

"Do you still think this is a bad idea?" Nikko murmured before continuing. His eyes smoldered with intent, but the slight smile twitching at the corners of his mouth let Eleni know Nikko was teasing her.

"Nikko, please," Eleni begged breathlessly.

"Please, what?"

He was intentionally torturing her just when she could detonate at any given moment. "Pull my panties off."

"Is that all?" he whispered, ripping the flimsy garment away and tossing it aside. "Then what?"

"Do you need me to spell it out?" Eleni asked urgently, her need growing desperate.

"Yes. I've waited so long for you," Nikko confessed. "I need to hear what you want of me from your own lips."

"You," she cried out. "Inside me." Skin against burning skin, Nikko taunted her entrance. He was steel, pressing into Eleni's most sensitive areas yet frustratingly not penetrating her. "I want you inside of me."

"I want that, too," Nikko panted. "I'm waiting."

"You're going to make me say it?"

Nikko looked into her eyes, his heated stare forcing the words from her. She thought he knew her better than asking her to say something so out of her character. But she couldn't wait another second. "Just fuck me already," she begged.

"You wound me, Brooklyn. Is that what you think I want?"

"I don't know what grownup Nikko wants," Eleni said, panting.

"I want you to want me to make love to you." Sincerity coated his words.

"I do. I want that," Eleni admitted. "But if you torture me one more second—"

"Grownup Eleni is very horny, it seems," Nikko teased as he reached for a condom.

"Maybe just for Greek winemakers who enjoy the sunrise."

"Better be for a singular winemaker," he warned, spreading her legs apart with his own. Nikko drew Eleni's arms over her head, lacing his fingers with hers. "Look into my eyes," he breathed as he entered her.

Their simultaneous moans muffled Eleni's pleas as Nikko moved inside her, his slow, sensual strokes growing deeper with each gentle thrust. Eleni felt worshiped as Nikko savored the feel of her heat, and she luxuriated in the pleasure he was offering. This was the love-making Nikko had longed for, and the feeling was exquisite, ethereal—otherworldly. But Eleni was close and desperately needed the release she sought. She grabbed onto Nikko's ass, pressing him into her harder.

"More. Nikko."

Nikko rolled over, taking Eleni with him, allowing her to control their pace. She rode him urgently, quickening her thrusts and taking him deeper each time. Framing his face, Eleni looked into his eyes as she came, and he fell over the edge with her. Nikko wrapped her in his arms, tightening his hold as he erupted inside her, drawing out every last pulse of his orgasm.

Sated, their bodies relaxed, Eleni collapsing over his toned chest. She remained quiet, reveling in a sense of joy she'd long forgotten. This is what it felt like to love—to feel treasured. She had buried the emotion in the darkest recesses of her mind for so long.

"Blame it on the wedding, or the dawn of a new day rising, or simply sharing it all with you … being here like this with you …

I don't want this to end," Nikko confessed, breaking their silence. "Death and circumstance pulled us apart. But we were young, and our choices weren't our own. That's all changed now. I don't want to imagine a future without you." Nikko sat up, coaxing Eleni onto his lap. "I want to walk around that table in church with you someday, taking our first important symbolic steps together."

Eleni brushed her fingers over his lips. He was declaring his love and offering her a future, but it was far too soon to entertain the possibility of a life with Nikko. There was so much to sort out first.

"I promised to be patient and to give you time, but I can't hold back how I feel."

"It's not that I don't love you. I do," Eleni vowed. "My love for you was never in question. It was never what kept us apart. But I asked for time because decisions that affect so many people need to be weighed. Your family, the vineyard, my employees in New York … Sometimes it's not about what we want but what's right overall."

Eleni was never one to throw caution to the wind and do whatever she wanted. She was all too aware of how her actions might impact others' lives. She wished she could in this case, though—how she wished she could. However, she was responsible for doing what was necessary and sensible rather than following her selfish desires.

"I won't bring it up again," Nikko said with a sigh. "You know what I want and where I stand. The rest is up to you." He stood suddenly, breaking their contact. "We should head home," he stated, sounding defeated.

"Nikko …" Eleni started.

"It's okay," Nikko said, collecting the blanket. "We're both tired. There's no need to say anything more."

The car ride home was uncomfortably silent. The tension between them was as thick as a dismal gray fog, barricading Nikko from her sight. When they arrived home, they went their separate ways— Nikko to his room without a word and Eleni to hers with a burdened heart.

CHAPTER 31

Nikko

Present Day

Grief, responsibility, and obligation overrode Eleni's desires. It frustrated and saddened Nikko that this second chance for them might be lost forever because of her sense of duty. It seemed everyone else's needs came before hers, and despite knowing it was selfish, it affected his happiness, too. He had never forgotten their time together or how he felt with her. Making love to her now wasn't a reminder of the past; it was proof his feelings had intensified. All his senses heightened in her presence, at the feel of her and the undeniable power of their bodies' surrender.

Nikko had dated many women on the island over the years. At first, it was in defiance, an angry rebound reaction, a way to punish Eleni, not that she knew what he was up to. Later, he honestly tried to move past his feelings for her. But no one even came close to stealing his heart the way Eleni had. He had tried everything to shake her from his mind, but it was no use. She had left an indelible mark on his soul, and Nikko had to learn to live with it. Someday, he might meet a woman who made him feel love so intensely again, but he certainly hadn't searched for it.

Just when Nikko finally came to terms with his single existence, carving out his career and throwing himself entirely into his work, Eleni returned to resurrect the feelings he'd prefer to suppress. Years of resentment and bitterness toward her resurfaced. Still, his resistance weakened, even with Eleni trying to show she wasn't affected by him. But Nikko knew her only too well; he didn't have to imagine the conflict running through her. It served to confirm what he felt all along. They were tethered and bound, and no amount of anger, time, or even the ocean separating them could sever their souls. But would her sense of obligation triumph over their own happiness?

* * *

The next day, Nikko stole glances at Eleni while she implemented her plan to help the vineyard gain exposure and revenue. With a faltering smile, she waved to him before continuing her work. Nikko watched with interest as Eleni moved about with a spring in her step, enthusiastically unpacking vendors' wares, arranging them on shelves and tables in the designated area of the tasting room, and showcasing each product with panache.

Later, while serving patrons, she offered to guide them through the newly renovated space, explaining where the products originated and how to find the store locations should they want to explore their wares further. Nikko could see from the number of customers leaving with gift bags that, so far, her idea was a success. Now, they needed the plan to go as well on the other end when the shop owners recommended that their patrons visit the winery.

Nikko admired Eleni. From his observations, it was clear that she enjoyed her work and had a talent for it.

"If you spend any more time staring at her, I might have to think about hiring someone to pick up the slack," Stavros chuckled, coming up behind his son.

"She's making a difference here," Nikko said, cuffing his father's shoulder.

"In more ways than one," Stavros agreed, lifting a knowing brow.

"*Babá.*" He shook his father off. "Her life is in New York. Eleni has made that clear."

"Maybe. But I see a happier girl today than when she first arrived," Stavros supplied with a knowing look. "Come on. Let's get back to work."

* * *

Each day, Nikko noticed the vineyard becoming more crowded. And every evening, the family enjoyed a sunset dinner together once they closed to the public for the day. After, if Nikko was lucky, he managed to steal an hour alone with Eleni, but things were not sitting right with him. Their exchanges had become awkward. He didn't know if Eleni was preoccupied with her never-ending ideas to improve the vineyard profits or concerned about leaving her business behind for too long, but he sensed she was avoiding him.

Nikko's insides felt like an overworked machine, the gears churning in his stomach in one direction while his heart twisted in another. It was the same feeling he had experienced many years ago. She was slowly distancing herself, and this could only mean one thing: her exit was imminent.

* * *

Guests were encouraged to explore the fringe areas of the vineyard without meandering too deep down the rows of vines. Across from the central patio was the tasting room that now doubled as a gift shop. The fermentation and bottling building was situated to the left side, back a little away from the visitors' grounds, almost hidden from view by lush foliage bearing clusters of grapes.

Nikko had spent the morning in the field, checking the soil's pH. Once done, he walked to the end of a row that led to the guest area. Brushing off the dirt from his trousers, he was about to head to the production room when he noticed a man at the far end of the path leading to the patio staring intently at Eleni. Usually, that alone wouldn't be disconcerting—she was a beautiful woman—but his demeanor struck a suspicious chord. With his arms crossed over his chest, his eyes narrowed, and a menacing look of disdain forming on his face, the man seemed threatening.

Nikko held off, waiting to see what this stranger was up to. When Eleni was free, he watched as the man strode purposely over to her. She knew him—this interloper sporting a bespoke suit on a sweltering summer day. Eleni's immediate recognition was evident in her perplexed expression. Nikko seethed as the man took her in his arms. But Eleni didn't respond in kind. Instead, she kept her arms stiffly to her sides until she relented and gave him a perfunctory pat on the back before putting some space between them. Nikko hoped that meant Eleni wasn't happy to see the man. Still, he wanted to stomp over and push the guy away from her. To warn him not to touch her without permission. But he had no claim on Eleni. She'd invited him into her body but not her heart or life. That was why it had been so strange between them these past few days. And that was why he had to avoid her. She was going to leave, just as she had before. And maybe this man would be the one to convince her to go.

CHAPTER 32

Eleni

Present Day

Eleni had just finished chatting with a table of four, sharing her suggestions on where to explore the island, when she stopped in her tracks. Stunned to hear a familiar but unwelcome voice call to her, Eleni turned and saw Gregory approaching. Even more disconcerting was the grimace on his face.

"What are you doing here?" Eleni asked, irritated and confused.

"The question is, what are *you* still doing here?" Gregory countered. He opened his arms, motioning for her to fall into his embrace, but when she didn't move, he took it upon himself to pull her in for a hug.

Eleni didn't appreciate the insinuation of his question or the assumption that he had the right to touch her. She had been crystal clear that their relationship was over before she left for Kefalonia to bury her grandfather. With infuriation clawing at her insides, Eleni couldn't bring herself to return the gesture, keeping her arms by her sides until relenting only enough to civilly pat him on the back before pushing him away.

"What I'm doing here is none of your business. And this place,"

Eleni said, swirling a finger to indicate the vineyard, "isn't either. So I'll ask you again," she challenged, cocking her head to one side. "Why are you here?"

Gregory pinched the bridge of his nose in frustration.

Really? Eleni thought when an exasperated sigh escaped his lips. She was furious. Here he was, in *her* family's vineyard, when she'd made it clear she didn't want him or his advice. And *he* had the audacity to act annoyed!

"Can we go someplace private to talk?" he asked.

"Private? No." Eleni pointed to an empty table on the furthest corner of the patio. "That table over there is about as private as I'll allow you. And you have ten minutes because this is the busiest time of day."

Gregory's mouth pressed into a hard line, but he nodded. He attempted to escort her by the small of her back, but she strode purposely ahead, out of reach.

"What would you like to drink?" she asked briskly.

"Whatever you recommend is fine."

Eleni stomped away. When she approached the bar inside the tasting room, she rested her hands against the countertop to steady herself. It hadn't escaped her that Nikko witnessed Gregory pulling her into an embrace. Oh, yes. She had felt his jealous stare from across the yard like flaming daggers. Eleni could only imagine the conclusion he'd jumped to.

"What is it, *péthi mou*?" Thalia asked, entering behind her and resting her hand on Eleni's back. "Who is that man I saw you speaking to?"

"Someone who doesn't belong here," Eleni replied.

She silently waited for Maria to pour a glass of wine for a woman standing at the bar. When she was done, Eleni asked for two glasses of Robola. "He hates this wine. Maybe he'll get the hint and leave," Eleni grumbled. As she filled the order, Maria listened with concern. "Do I need to have Stavros and Nikko remove him?"

"No." Eleni laughed in frustration. "I can handle it," she affirmed, taking the glasses from Maria with renewed determination.

Eleni set the wine on the table, pushing Gregory's drink before him. Before she could pull away, though, he rested his hand over hers.

"We're good together," he pleaded, but his expression showed insincerity and a touch of arrogance. For the life of her, she didn't know what he wanted.

"No, we're not," Eleni argued, yanking her hand away. "There isn't a single thing we agree upon or have in common. I don't know why I didn't see it sooner." She raised her palms skyward. "Our values don't align ...at all. You have to see that."

"That's not true. You've somehow got yourself caught up in"— Gregory scanned the surroundings— "this place. But it isn't you. Look at it," he urged, frowning his disapproval. "It doesn't even remotely measure up to the wineries we're accustomed to frequenting."

Eleni clasped her hands so tightly together that her knuckles turned white. Closing her eyes, she willed herself to keep her composure. "And therein lies the problem," Eleni confirmed with a cold stare. "The trappings of the new and shiny grab your attention. You look for perfection rather than the beauty in simplicity, history, and sentiment. My grandfather left me this vineyard, and I intend to ensure I do right by it."

"Exactly," Gregory agreed. "I can help you with that. The most fiscally wise decision is to sell your stake in it. Then, take the proceeds and invest your money. Return to New York with me. I can guide you through the entire process." Once again, he reached for her hand, but she snatched it away.

"You're not listening to me. When I said we were over, it was not a rash decision born from grief." Eleni's annoyance was growing by the second. "It was an epiphany. We could never work as a couple. I'm sorry."

Gregory opened his mouth to defend his position, but she shut him down. "I'd really like you to leave. After all, I wouldn't want to subject you to a shabby establishment so below your standards." She rose from her chair. "Now, I need to get back to work. As you can see by the crowd, others don't harbor the same ill will about this place as you."

Eleni waited, but Gregory didn't move. He rubbed his forehead, as he often did when frustrated.

"Go home, Gregory," Eleni demanded, punctuating each word with conviction. "*Kaló taxíthi*! *Bon voyage*! *Arrivederci*!" She faked a smile before turning her back on him to seat a group of arriving guests. Tension settled in Eleni's chest. She sensed Gregory's eyes boring into her. But since she had said her piece, Eleni decided he was inconsequential and ignored him. Yet, it wasn't until he finally left that she found the air to fully breathe again. He'd made her so mad. How did he have the audacity to think he had the right to decide her future? It was that right there, that overwhelming arrogance and his overall insensitivity, that infuriated her.

As the afternoon went on, she forgot about her ex-boyfriend. More visitors showed up each day for tastings, many leaving with purchases. Today was no exception. Eleni had been on the island for barely a month and felt proud that her contribution to her grandfather's legacy was impacting the business so soon.

All the occupied tables had been waited on, so Eleni sat down to rest her feet for a bit when she noticed a woman step onto the patio, bypassing the reception podium and seating herself at an empty table. It was a little rude, but she gave the woman the benefit of the doubt. She was alone, which wasn't usual, though most visitors came in pairs or groups.

As Eleni went over to greet the woman, her heart jumped when she recognized her. *Could this day get any worse?* Eleni wondered. *Who would show up next? Lucifer himself?*

"I heard you were back on the island," the woman sneered.

"Antonía," Eleni greeted coolly. She was still a bleached blonde, but the style was sleeker, the long strands shinier than years before.

Her breasts spilled out from the deep V of her low-cut minidress, not to mention, if she bent over, there would be more than just her lean legs on display.

"What can I get for you?" Eleni held to her professional manner, though she didn't offer her usual friendly hospitality.

"Whatever you suggest. I suspect we share the same taste. Especially in anything rich and …deep in flavor," Antonía purred, provoking Eleni with innuendo.

"You got it," Eleni said with a fake smile. *I will not let her get to me. I will not let her get to me.* She kept repeating these words in her mind as she headed inside the cottage.

Eleni returned quickly with a glass of red wine. "Let me know if there's anything else you need," she said, walking away.

"Not so fast, Eleni. Sit with me. We have a lot to catch up on."

Turning on her heels, Eleni fisted a hand on her hip. "Since we never were friends, I'd say we have nothing to discuss."

"You can't have him. He's mine," Antonía warned.

"If he were *yours*, there would be no need for you to stake your claim."

"You can't come here after all these years and ruin this for me."

"Ruin what?" Eleni leaned her hand on the table and glared at her. "There is nothing between you and Nikko. You're delusional."

"We've been sleeping together for years."

The woman was goading her, just as she had years ago. Still, the thought that Nikko might have lied and that his relationship with Antonía was more than he'd disclosed unsettled her.

"I don't know what fiction you dreamed up, but from what Nikko told me, it was one regrettable night," Eleni corrected Antonía. "But even if what you said was true, Nikko was free to date or have a sexual relationship with whomever he pleased. That doesn't mean there was love or any form of commitment behind it. It sounded like a drunken booty call to me. Now, if you'll excuse me."

Eleni walked away, disappearing out of sight from the public's view. She couldn't face anyone right now—not even Maria or Yiayiá Thalia—and she certainly couldn't bear to face Nikko. She fell directly into that woman's trap, and Eleni let jealousy overtake reason. But she was more ashamed of herself for stooping to Antonía's level. There was never an excuse to lash out and intentionally injure one's feelings, even if they instigated it.

Eleni dreaded confrontation, and her body trembled as a result. Calming herself by closing her eyes and breathing in and out slowly, the shaking eventually subsided. She determinedly walked back to the patio and over to Antonía's table with a renewed purpose.

"Maybe you were right. We should catch up or at least clear the air," Eleni suggested.

"Why? So you can continue to drill into me how unlovable I am or how I've allowed myself to be used for nothing but sex?" the woman sneered.

"No, I apologize for that." Eleni sighed. "I'm very aware of how you feel about me and that trying to upset or make me jealous gives you great satisfaction, but lashing back at you the way I did was inexcusable."

"You apologize?" Antonía repeated as if it were the most astonishing words to come from her mouth.

"Yes, for lowering myself to a level I never want to stoop to. I'm going to be completely honest with you," Eleni started. "I've never liked you either. You were nasty to me from the minute we were introduced. You hung all over Nikko, flirting with him in front of me and insinuating there was something between the two of you."

"Wow, great apology. I think we can be best friends now," Antonía said, raising a manicured brow.

"Let me ask you something. Did you honestly care for Nikko, or did you only want to conquer him because he was unobtainable?"

"Unobtainable." Antonia sniggered. "Unobtainable until he wasn't."

Eleni tried her best to keep her composure before she snapped again. "I wouldn't say a drunken one-night stand was 'obtaining' Nikko."

"You have some nerve. You drift on and off this island as you please, disrupting everyone's lives. Does it give you a sense of power to keep Nikko on a string? To throw him into turmoil every time you leave?" Antonía spat.

"It wasn't like that." Eleni resisted explaining herself to this woman. "You're making unfair assumptions."

"Am I? You wonder why I resent you so much?" Antonía leaned in, her eyes spitting venom. "It wasn't my name he uttered in my bed."

Eleni closed her eyes and massaged her temples. She needed a moment to articulate her thoughts carefully.

"I'm sorry. I really am—for you, for Nikko, and for me. It was a long time ago, and we were only teenagers—basically still children. What I did to Nikko was never intentional. I was drowning in grief. My mistake was to shut him out."

Antonía's expression softened. "I'm not sure I would have reacted differently under those circumstances."

"Thank you for that," Eleni said. "What happened between you and Nikko is between the two of you, but just as I so harshly stated before, one drunken night doesn't constitute a relationship. But because of Nikko's condition, his behavior or anything he said can't be taken to heart. He didn't purposely set out to hurt you. He was intoxicated."

"It still hurt," Antonía admitted. "Now, all these years later, I thought I finally had another shot with him, and here you are again."

Eleni laid a hand over Antonía's. "I'm not your enemy. Deep down, we want the same thing—to love and be loved. But it doesn't work the way you're going about it. Love can't be forced. It just happens—that unexplainable magic between two people. If Nikko fell in love with you, there wouldn't have been a damn thing I could have done about it."

Antonía nodded. "Just like I couldn't pull the two of you apart."

"Exactly. You're a beautiful woman, Antonía. Leave yourself open to finding the man meant for you."

Antonía kept her eyes trained on her wine glass. She ran her index finger around the rim, catching beads of red fluid on the tip of her finger. "You believe that, don't you?" Antonía asked.

"I do," Eleni said honestly. Eleni laughed inwardly. "I know we're a long way from sixteen, but I distinctly remember Nikko's friend, Panos, being crazy for you. You gave every boy attention except for the one that truly cared about you."

"I know," Antonía said. She ran her hair through her long tresses. "Looking back on it, I'm not proud of myself. I purposely threw other boys in his face. It made me feel like I had power over someone."

"We all had our insecurities in our teens; we just compensated in different ways. It was a long time ago. I saw Panos at Stefanos' wedding," Eleni said. "He's turned out quite handsome."

She shook her head. "We avoid each other. I haven't spoken to him in years." Antonía shrugged.

"If I were you, I would try to meet with him, even if only to say you're sorry."

"I don't know. I'll think about it."

Eleni rose. "I really need to get back to work." She noticed Antonía had drained her glass. "I'll bring you another."

"No, I should leave."

"Stay just a little longer. It's a beautiful day," Eleni suggested. "I'll be right back."

Eleni strode into the tasting room and pulled an open bottle of red wine from behind the bar.

"I saw you talking to Antonía," Maria said. "What trouble is she causing now?"

"None. We had a little chat, and I think we understand each other a little better now," Eleni explained, placing the wine and a small plate of *mezethes* on a tray.

Maria's brows lifted skeptically. "If you say so."

Eleni returned to Antonía, setting down the wine and *mezethes* before her. "For you. On the house. I can't have you driving home tipsy," Eleni said, smiling.

"Thank you. Really, Eleni, that's very nice of you."

"Enjoy." Eleni patted Antonía's shoulder before heading over to serve another table.

Eleni was grateful the business day was finally winding down. She was bone-tired but not so much physically as mentally wrung out from dealing with unwelcome surprise visitors. Someone must have given her the *máti* this morning because it sure felt like the evil eye had been cast upon her.

Eleni was wiping down a patio table when someone came up behind her and covered her eyes. Startled, she shrieked.

"Guess who?"

Turning, she peeled his hands off her and squealed in delight. "Yanni!" She threw her arms around him. "Finally, someone I'm happy to see today! Look at you!" she exclaimed, breaking the embrace to examine him. His spiky black hair prickled her fingers when they ran over the tips. Eleni giggled before letting out a small gasp. "Oh, your *mamá* is going to have something to say about this!" she teased, referring to the sleeve of ink running up his right arm.

"I'm hoping just seeing me after a year away will override any disappointment in my appearance," he replied sheepishly.

"Ha! That's one possibility," Eleni said with amusement. "Anyway, you're here!"

"Why so surprised?" Yanni asked. "I told you I would come."

"And I can't wait to get started!" Eleni was giddy with excitement. "Go settle in and see your family. Then come find me when you're ready to brainstorm."

Yanni kissed her on the cheek. "I'll be back soon. I want to get started right away."

CHAPTER 33

Nikko

Present Day

Lively chatter drowned out the evening sounds of summer. The entire family sat around the table on the back patio of the Varvos home, passing around platters of food, laughing, and sharing stories. The eagerness to regale Yanni with island news created a cacophony of competing voices relaying multiple tales simultaneously.

But it was Eleni who had his attention as they sat beside one another, whispering animatedly. Occasionally, Eleni would nod enthusiastically and type something into her phone. Nikko grimaced, feeling as if he'd been ostracized from an exclusive club. Or maybe it was just that he was just a little jealous she hadn't glanced his way all evening.

Nikko was delighted to see his brother, of course. They had always been close, though there were a few years when the relationship had grown strained. Yanni struggled to live up to their father's rigid standards and expectations. Nikko thrived in the vineyard, whereas Yanni felt stuck and unfulfilled. Even when Nikko secretly had other aspirations, he still enjoyed working the land, but his brother never had. For Yanni, the days dragged by, and he counted the hours until he could escape to the kitchen to help their *yiayiá* cook. That didn't bring favor with their father, and Yanni felt that Nikko was the anointed golden child, the one to make their father proud. Resentment set in, and Nikko didn't understand where it came from. It wasn't until their *yiayiá*, in her infinite wisdom, urged Yanni to speak to his father and share his dreams for the future, but he was afraid to approach the man.

Instead, Yanni confided in his brother first. And once he had, it all made sense. Now Nikko understood Yanni's moods and sudden envy of their father's approval. So together, upon Nikko's urging, Yanni finally spoke to their father. The judgment and rejection he feared were unwarranted. Stavros only wanted his sons to follow their dreams, so much to Yanni's disbelief he encouraged his son to do just that.

"So, *Agori mou*," Stavros addressed his younger son, "you and Eleni have put your heads together. Tell us what we can expect."

"I'm heading to the markets tomorrow to see what local fresh ingredients are available. We're moving into action right away," Yanni said enthusiastically. "Eleni will get the word out. Our first wine-pairing dinner is set for five days from now."

"That's ambitious," Maria said proudly.

"Harvest season is upon us. We must take advantage before the tourist season dwindles," Eleni explained. "Naturally, I'll work on building a local clientele too."

"I noticed you're selling the local thyme honey," Yanni observed. "That gave me the idea to make honey the themed ingredient for our debut dinner."

"And I asked Yanni if he would write the recipes on specially designed cards to offer each diner who purchases a jar of the honey that evening."

"What a wonderful idea," *Yiayiá* Thalia agreed.

"And who will choose the wine pairings?" *Pappou* Kostas asked.

"I thought I'd give Nikko the menu. But if you want to help us decide, I would appreciate your experience, *Pappou*."

"Nikko knows the wine. He doesn't need me." Kostas tipped his head to his grandson. "But I'm curious to see what he chooses." Then, the elderly man stood, lifting his wine glass. "A toast to my grandsons: Nikko, a fine winemaker, and to Yanni for contributing with his culinary talent to make Pangalos Varvos Winery an epicurean experience." Smiling, he turned to Eleni with affection. "And to *ī Elenitsa mas*. Your *pappou*, my dear friend, would be very proud of you. In a short time, you've increased foot traffic and exposure to our little vineyard. And you found a way to bring my grandson home. This is your home, too, now. Though it always has been."

Nikko saw the emotion swimming in Eleni's eyes as she stood to kiss his grandfather's cheek. Whether or not she believed it, this was her home. She had a stake in it—people who cared for her and loved her. But now it was up to her to decide what to do with that.

"Nikko!" Maria exclaimed. "I'm talking to you."

"Sorry, *Mamá*. My head is in a million places."

"I can see that," she scolded.

"Tomorrow begins the harvest," Nikko added, changing the subject.

"I'm aware. We plan on closing to the public to help you work the fields."

"That's not necessary. I hired extra hands so we wouldn't have to," Nikko said.

"I was hoping to help at least a little. I haven't picked grapes in years," Eleni put in.

"We start at daybreak. So come for a few hours before visitors begin to arrive if you like," Stavros offered.

Eleni turned to Nikko for approval. Shrugging, he kept his expression neutral. Staying detached was all he could do to protect his heart when she decided it was time to return home.

"After Yanni's dinner event, we'll be closed for two days for the Robola Wine Festival," Thalia said, interrupting her thoughts.

"Wine festival?" Eleni questioned. "Is that happening now?"

"Oh, that's right!" Thalia exclaimed. "You were never here for that.

Andreas always left the island right before it took place. Well, you are in for a treat!"

"But I'm confused. Why would you close?"

"Every vineyard has a designated space at the festival. We need to set up and run it," Stavros explained. "We've hired extra help, so we won't have to man it all weekend. It's the highlight of a winemaker's tourist season," he added.

"I look forward to it then!" Eleni rose from her chair. "If you'll excuse me," she said. "If I'm going to rise with the sun, I must go to bed now."

"It's going to be a long day for all of us," Nikko added. "It's time for me to say goodnight as well." Climbing the stairs, he caught up with Eleni. "Wait up."

Halting, she turned slowly to face him.

"I was just wondering who you were talking to today," Nikko asked uncomfortably.

She raised an eyebrow. "I spoke to many people. It was a busy day."

Nikko blew out a frustrated breath. "You know who I'm referring to."

Eleni rested a hand on his shoulder. "Trust me when I say he's no one you need to be concerned about."

Nikko picked at a knot in the wood of the stair railing. "It's just that you seemed surprised to see him and, if my instincts were right, a little annoyed."

"More than a little annoyed, but I suspect Gregory is on his way home by now."

"Gregory?" A jolt of jealousy shot through him even though Eleni had previously expressed no desire to resume a relationship with the man.

Eleni nodded. "Goodnight, Nikko." Turning, she strode away, offering no further information.

As he lay in bed, Nikko pondered how he'd work beside Eleni the following day. The tension between them was disconcerting. There was only one solution. He would send her off to the other end of the vineyard and let one of the hands show her what to do. Unfortunately, there was just no other way.

* * *

Stubborn woman. There was no avoiding her, even for his own self-preservation. Early the next morning, Nikko and Eleni harvested grapes on a rocky hillside. The terrain wasn't suitable for modern equipment, making the work laborious as everything was done by hand.

"Don't argue with me. If you want to help, you need to take direction," Nikko snapped. "Go with the crew to the south corner of the property. The land there is flatter and more manageable."

"But I want to pick Robola grapes," Eleni insisted.

"Listen, these vines aren't arranged in organized neat rows. They're planted in steep hills on rocky ground. It's tiring, especially in the heat of the day. Robola doesn't grow in the type of soil or conditions you're accustomed to."

"And that's exactly why I want to experience it," she argued.

Nikko threw his hands up in frustration. "Whatever. Have it your way." Exasperated, Nikko reluctantly demonstrated how to properly remove the grapes from the vines. He gave her a half hour before she changed her mind.

Lifting a brow, Eleni crossed her arms over her chest. "It's not brain surgery. I think I've got this."

"We'll see," he muttered under his breath.

She pinned him with a frosty glare. "You've made it clear you can't be bothered with me. Don't worry. Once I feel confident what I've put into place here is running smoothly, I'll be out of your hair."

What didn't she understand? He didn't resent that she was here. On the contrary, he resented the fact that she was leaving. He'd already told her he loved her. Why wasn't that enough?

Three hours later, Eleni was still picking grapes. He had to hand it to her; she wasn't a quitter. But the work was exhausting, and the vineyard would be open to the public in a few hours.

"Eleni, I think that's enough for today," Nikko said. "Go back to the house and get ready for the day."

Eleni smirked. "You didn't think I had staying power, did you?"

"To be honest? No."

With a mischievous smile, she flung the lemon-gold cluster of grapes she held in Nikko's direction, smacking him squarely on the chest.

"Oh, you're going to pay for that," he threatened. He reached into a tub of picked grapes and held up a cluster. Then, instead of flinging them, he charged toward her.

Eleni ran from him but tripped on a stone in her path. "Nikko! No!" She yelped when he hovered over her.

Laughing, he smashed the grapes in her face. "Retribution is fair play," he said.

Eleni squealed but grabbed a fistful of the fruit and pressed it against his cheek. In a test of wills, neither gave up. Their skin and clothing were covered in sticky drippings and peels. Their bodies linked as they rolled around on the rocky ground in a playful battle.

"Ouch, that hurts," Eleni complained.

Nikko lifted her off the ground, their eyes locking when he pulled her onto his lap. His breath hitched, thinking of how her naked skin had looked as the sun rose. And Nikko knew he couldn't resist Eleni any longer, no matter the price his heart would pay later. Leaning in, he kissed her. The sound of her sigh gave him intense satisfaction. "You're wrong," he confessed. "I don't resent you for staying." He pressed his forehead to hers. "I'm afraid of you leaving."

"Nikko," she said with a sigh, palming his cheek. "We will figure something out."

He wanted to believe that, but how could they make it work if she didn't choose to stay?

CHAPTER 34

Eleni

Present Day

The next several days sped by like a tornado whirling through an open plain. As fall ushered summer away, Nikko concentrated on the crucial steps to turn grapes into what the family hoped would be award-winning wine. He left the harvesting to the hired hands, supervised by his father and grandfather. Nikko spent long days crushing and pressing grapes. Then, the fermentation cycle officially began once all the initial steps were completed and the yeast added.

For Eleni's part, she was just as busy at the tasting room gift shop, restocking products made by the local artisans. Although her heart and mind were still at odds, the flow of new ideas excited her enough to quiet the indecision in her brain—at least for now.

Eleni went from shop to shop the following day, handing out invitations to the vineyard's debut dinner. By the afternoon, she made her last stop at a potter's workshop. A small storefront displayed her uniquely designed, one-of-a-kind pieces. Eleni called out to the artist.

"*Erhomaí*," Angeliki said as she appeared, wiping clay off her hands with a damp towel. "Eleni! I didn't expect to see you today."

"I came to give you this," Eleni said, handing the woman a handwritten invitation stamped with the vineyard logo. "It's our way of thanking you and allowing you to see how we display your pieces."

"Oh! I'd love to come," Angeliki said with a wink. "And I know who I want to bring as my plus-one. But honestly, this has worked out well for me too. It's almost like having a second store."

"A pop-up store," Eleni agreed, nodding.

Angeliki furrowed her brow in confusion.

Eleni smiled. "That's what we call them in the States. Sometimes, a company will briefly place a store in a town or city. It builds exposure and interest."

"Oh, I'd love a place at your vineyard for longer than a pop."

Eleni giggled at her misuse of the term. "Of course. We'd love that."

After Eleni had made her rounds, handing out all the invitations, she headed home to see what Yanni was doing in the kitchen.

"If this idea of yours takes off, we're going to need an industrial kitchen," Yanni said, pointing his wooden spoon at her.

"We haven't even had our first dinner service yet, and you're going all diva chef on me." Eleni laughed. "This kitchen is big enough for your mother and grandmother. I think you'll manage."

Yanni rolled his eyes. "Ha! You got me there." He waved her closer. "Come, try a taste." Eleni breathed in the wine-scented steam wafting from the spoon. She forked off a piece of tender short rib, taking a bite. "This is the best thing I've tasted in … I don't know how long," Eleni said with a moan. She removed a plate from the cabinet and handed it to Yanni. "I need more than a forkful. I can taste the sweetness of the wine, too. Mavrodaphne?"

Yanni nodded, looking pleased with her response.

"And you added honey as well?"

"No. Not in this dish."

"But we agreed, every dish must include the featured ingredient."

"I've already settled on this week's menu. I'm experimenting for next week's dinner when the common ingredient is Mavrodaphne," Yanni explained.

"Brilliant. You know what? If you keep this up, we might be able to afford that kitchen after all."

Dinner, as always, was a symphony of simultaneous conversations. It was impossible to follow one, much less all of them, so Eleni let her mind wander. Angela had called earlier. Her business calendar was filling up with the fall wedding season underway, alongside their many other bookings for corporate events. The assistant Angela had hired was working out well, too, but with Eleni in Greece, there was still a lot for her friend to manage.

She'd given Angela the go-ahead to hire an additional assistant, but she worried she had dumped all her company's responsibilities on her friend's shoulders.

Eleni was still musing over this as she sat on the front porch, falling into a trance while staring at the twinkling stars. If she left the vineyard now, she would do so with only half her goals accomplished, and she didn't want to do that to the family. But if she stayed, she'd abandon what she had worked so hard for in New York. And then there was Nikko and her feelings for him to consider. What to do? What to do?

"What's weighing on you?" *Yiayiá* Thalia asked as she joined Eleni. She sat beside her, giving Eleni's hand an affectionate pat.

Tears clogged Eleni's throat, but for the one that managed to escape, which streaked her cheek. She wiped it away, shaking her head.

Thalia let the silence fall between them for a few beats before she broke it.

"What you've done here is remarkable. You're a talented young woman. You've made a difference, and we'll hold to your changes and improvements even after you're gone."

Eleni looked into the older woman's eyes, searching for approval.

"I know you have a life in New York, a business, friends. Staying here would mean leaving all that behind. Now you need to ask yourself whether leaving all this behind will be just as difficult," she said, gesturing to the land before them. "Or will it be even harder than what you've already let go of this past month?"

"That's what makes this so difficult. I lose either way," Eleni said, sniffling.

"Instead of torturing yourself with the conflict of what you should do, stop and breathe. Close your eyes and picture what you want your life to look like. And most of all, listen to what *this* is telling you." She pointed to Eleni's heart. "It will never fail you."

"I wish it were that easy."

"And what does your heart do when you see Nikko? You love him, no?"

"I'm trying to think logically and keep him out of the equation until I decide what to do."

"*Elenistsa mou*, love is the answer to every equation." Thalia took Eleni's face in her hands. "I will leave you to your thoughts."

Eleni sighed. There was so much to look forward to over the next week—the vineyard dinner and the wine festival—but her heart felt heavy. She knew that once it was all over, she would have to decide one way or another.

MAVRODAPHNE SHORT RIBS

Ingredients
6 beef short ribs
8 tablespoons unsalted butter
1-750 ml bottle of Mavrodaphne wine
48 ounces of beef broth
3 cinnamon sticks
2 bay leaves
Salt and pepper to taste
2 large Vidalia onions, sliced
8 ounces sliced baby Bella mushrooms
¼ cup cornstarch

Method
You can make this dish in a slow cooker or a Dutch oven. Melt four tablespoons of butter in a large skillet or the Dutch oven. Brown the short ribs on all sides.

Melt the remaining four tablespoons of butter in another large skillet and sauté the mushrooms and onions.

Add the onion/mushroom mixture to the Dutch oven. Alternatively, transfer the short ribs and the onion mixture to the slow cooker. Add the wine, broth, cinnamon sticks, bay leaves, salt, and pepper.

Set the slow cooker for 4 hours. If using the Dutch oven, bring the liquid to a boil and then lower the temperature to a simmer for around 3 hours or until the meat begins to fall off the bone.

Whisk the cornstarch with a small amount of water to smooth out any lumps. Ten minutes before serving, add the cornstarch mixture to the pot, allowing the fluid to thicken as it simmers.

CHAPTER 35

Eleni

Present Day

The Robola Wine Festival was absolute pandemonium. In the best possible way. Lively. Fun. Joyous. Like water on a scorching hot day, wine and food samples were offered to the masses. Women dressed in traditional costumes danced in choreographed circles while men drew attention from the crowd while dancing the *Zeibekiko,* each trying to top the other's performance. Who could leap higher? Who could rotate in flight? Who could limbo to his knees while balancing a shot of ouzo on his head?

It was similar to the Greek festivals she'd attended in New York, sponsored by the local churches. The difference here was the magnitude of the event.

Eleni and Nikko had just finished a long shift at the Pangalos Varvos booth, finally relieved by auxiliary staff. They searched for the rest of the family among the throngs of people, but Stavros spotted them first and waved them over. Nikko held Eleni's hand firmly as he led the way, squeezing through the overcrowded maze of tables and chairs. The irrepressible current running between their joined hands almost made her pull away protectively. But she didn't. She couldn't.

A thrilling sense of comfort washed over her each time he held her. Those feelings gave Eleni a confusing perception of belonging, as if her body understood she was precisely where she was meant to be. And those same feelings caused her mind to be at war with her heart over what to do.

"How did you get a table so close to the band?" Eleni asked with a smile. The entire family was seated together, platters of food and several bottles of wine set before them.

"Connections." Stavros winked.

They had barely sat down when Stavros stood. "It's time for *Zeibekiko*. Come." He summoned his father and two sons.

Reluctantly, Nikko rose.

"Go," Eleni said, giving him a playful shove. She laughed as they joined a group of lively men already in motion.

She watched as these men she'd come to love as her family moved with the sound of the *bouzouki*. This dance was an expression of art, an interpretation of their emotions, a soul-baring confession of everything the dancer felt within him. It was stunning to behold.

With Stavros, regality and pride exuded from his every move, each spin and brush of his fingers dragging purposely across the floor. Kostas was a sight to behold, a jubilant patriarch holding his own, and though his movements were slower, they were no less mesmerizing.

But in Nikko, she saw something entirely different. Elegance. Confidence. But there was also a contradictory shield no one but she could detect. As he spun in slow, deliberate circles, his arms outstretched, his head bent down, Eleni wondered what his soul was trying to conceal. Then, raising his head, he pinned her with a stare, and she knew. The sadness in his eyes said it all. He was guarding himself against her choices. And her heart felt as though the life was being squeezed from it.

CHAPTER 36

Nikko

Present Day

"Are you ready to get out of here?" Nikko asked Eleni. They had eaten to their stomachs' content, sampled wines from several competing vineyards, and conversed with the many locals with whom Eleni had recently become acquainted.

As they wound down, slowly dancing to a classic Greek ballad, Nikko was ready to spend time alone with Eleni. He suspected their time was ending; she was being careful to hold back her usual signs of affection. She avoided meeting his gaze or stroking her fingertips over his bicep as she usually did when he was by her side. Instead, she treated him like the rest of his family, with affection but not the kind he hoped for.

Eleni finally smiled at Nikko.

"Sure, if that's what you want."

Against his better judgment, that's precisely what Nikko wanted. "The house will be empty for hours."

By the uncertainty in her expression, Eleni knew what he was implying; Nikko was sure of it.

Eleni answered by tightening her linked arms around his neck and pulling him to her height for a kiss. "Then we shouldn't waste a minute," Eleni whispered in his ear.

Their lovemaking was passionate—urgent—and carnal. Nikko tore Eleni's sundress, the remnants of the thin material falling to the floor, and pushed her exposed body against the wall of his bedroom. He devoured her mouth and breasts like a savage, supporting the globes of her bottom with his palms as she wrapped her legs around him. Nikko's thrusts were punishing, deep, desperate—until he exploded inside her.

"I'm sorry," Nikko panted, setting her on her feet. "So sorry." Eleni hadn't yet fallen over into bliss, but he wasn't done with her yet.

"Don't apologize. You didn't hurt me," Eleni assured him. "And … I wouldn't mind a repeat performance," she whispered, her eyes heavy-lidded.

"I'm apologizing for not taking care of you first. I would have preferred to worship and savor your body, making you come over and over again," Nikko murmured. In one fluid motion, Nikko lifted her and carried Eleni to his bed. "And I didn't use a condom," he groaned. "I don't know what came over me. I couldn't wait another second to be with you."

"And that felt magnificent," Eleni said, lacing her fingers with his. "I'm on the pill, so don't worry."

"Maybe if I knocked you up, you'd have a reason to stay here with me," he joked, wiggling his brows.

"Nikko, that's not how it should go," Eleni said solemnly. Her brown eyes, which had sparkled moments ago, dimmed, and Nikko wondered what had suddenly changed.

"You're right. You shouldn't be forced into a decision."

He began to slide off the bed, but Eleni pulled him back. "Don't use words like 'forced.' You seem to think our relationship isn't recip-rocal, but believe me, it is," Eleni promised. She sighed. "I need to share something with you."

"You can tell me anything." But the look on her face worried him.

"After my family's funeral, when we returned home, I was so distraught. I wasn't eating, and I barely left my bedroom. Two months passed, and I realized I hadn't had my cycle in almost three months."

"Go on," Nikko said cautiously, narrowing his eyes suspiciously. "Wait! Were you pregnant? With my baby?" His mind was reeling. Before she had a chance to answer, Nikko fired questions at her. "Why didn't you tell me? Did you get rid of it or put it up for adoption?"

"Nikko!" Eleni stopped him. "I wasn't pregnant. I thought I was, and that escalated my anxiety. It was another reason I couldn't bring myself to speak to you. I was beside myself."

"If you had been, we would have gotten through it together," he said, relieved.

"I know that would have been your intention, but we were teenagers. We hadn't even graduated from school. My mental state and grief at the time had apparently affected my periods," Eleni explained. "It happens."

"I was swallowed up by my own heartache. I didn't stop to really consider how life-changing the events of that summer were for you," Nikko admitted. "It was selfish, I know that, but I wanted us to be together."

"I'm not telling you this to make you feel bad. I only wanted to make you understand that I was going through more than you possibly knew."

Eleni entwined her legs with Nikko's. Nuzzling closer, she erased what little space there was between them, kissing the worry wrinkles forming on his brow. "I can't predict the future, but we have today—right now—and we should cherish it. I know I will for as long as I live."

That almost sounded like the beginning of a goodbye, Nikko feared, but the sight of Eleni naked on his bed made him throw caution to the wind.

Eleni held his gaze as she pulled his Vineyard logo T-shirt over his head. "It's only fair that I get to admire every inch of you."

"I'm yours," Nikko vowed.

"Remember the first time we made love? Or the second time, actually. You wanted me to look into your eyes as you moved inside me."

"I remember," Nikko said. "I have lived every minute of that over and over in my mind."

"That's how I want you now—face to face, me on your lap, so you can see the truth in my eyes. I will always love you," Eleni murmured. "No matter what happens."

Eleni braced her legs around Nikko's waist, seating herself onto him, sighing in pleasure as she took him deep. They were skin to skin, joined as one body with no beginning or end, and Nikko reveled in the rapture of her heat. He held her gaze just as she commanded. Nikko indeed saw love in the depths of her eyes, but uncertainty and regret were also reflected in their expression, and he sensed their end was near.

"There are far, far better things ahead than any we leave behind."
C.S. Lewis

CHAPTER 37

Eleni

Present Day

Eleni pulled open the window shade, but sunshine didn't filter into the room. Instead, ominous greenish-gray clouds dulled the atmosphere, indicating a storm was brewing. After weeks of glorious weather during the happiest times she could remember in a long while, it had suddenly turned grim, mirroring her current mood.

Sighing, Eleni pulled clothing out from the guestroom closet. She could no longer ignore the commitments she'd left behind. It wasn't fair for Angela to shoulder the burden of a company for which Eleni was responsible. It was time to go home. With a heavy heart, she arranged for a car to take her to the airport that afternoon. Was she taking the coward's way out by not telling the family beforehand? Yes, but it was easier for everyone this way. Dragging out a goodbye for days was more than she could bear. Eleni loved each and every member of this wonderful family. And as for Nikko—what could she ever say to him to make him understand why she had to go?

Once she finished packing, Eleni descended the staircase with her bags. On the last step, she lost her footing, and one of her suitcases fell with a loud thump.

Maria scurried down the hall toward the source of the noise.

"*Pethi mou?*" she questioned, hurt swimming in her brown eyes when she found Eleni by the front door with her luggage.

"I have to leave this afternoon, Maria. I'm so sorry," Eleni apologized. "I was about to look for you and *Yiayiá* Thalia. I have business in New York that can't wait any longer. I couldn't bring myself to say anything sooner because I'll miss all of you terribly," Eleni quavered as tears rolled down her cheeks.

"I understand," Maria said solemnly, pulling Eleni into her arms. "It's okay, *Elenitsa mou.* But I'm going to miss you more than you know."

"*Mamá,*" Maria called out. "Come say goodbye to Eleni."

Thalia shuffled down the hallway. "Eleni?" the older woman questioned.

"Please don't look at me that way, *Yiayiá,*" Eleni begged. "I have responsibilities in New York."

"I know, I know," she said, affectionately patting her face. "You always have a family here. We love you. Remember that."

"I will," Eleni said, embracing both women. "You all mean the world to me. I'm going to find *Pappou* Kostas, Stavros, and Yanni to say goodbye."

"And Nikko?" Maria's eyes swam with concern.

"And Nikko." Eleni closed her eyes, inhaling nervously before exhaling a shaky breath.

Eleni found Stavros and Kostas in the fields. She thanked them for everything they had done for her, especially helping her through her grief over her grandfather's death. It was another tearful goodbye that made leaving even more difficult. When she asked where Yanni was, they said he was at the markets, buying fresh produce, so she texted him, apologizing for departing before she could talk to him.

With her heart galloping at the pace of wild horses speeding through an open plain, Eleni anxiously entered Nikko's workspace. "Nikko?" she addressed him, her voice trembling.

Turning, Nikko stared at her, their eyes locking. He knew. She could tell by his defensive stance and the firm grip on the beaker he held all too tightly.

"You're leaving?"

Eleni didn't respond—the words she wanted to say were lodged in her throat.

"Answer me," he demanded.

"How did you know?"

"I've sensed it for days," Nikko said with resignation.

"You know ... I couldn't ... stay forever," she managed to say before bursting out in sobs. "Work ... Angela ... respons—"

"Fuck!" Nikko shouted, throwing the beaker against the wall.

Startled, Eleni covered her mouth to stifle her shriek. Blood-red liquid dripped down the wall as shattered glass splattered to the floor, just like the remnants of her heart.

"Just go!"

The contempt in Nikko's voice almost overshadowed the hurt. Almost. But it was there in the undertones, and there wasn't anything she could say to make this easier for either of them.

Eleni trudged back to the house. She was leaving the island just as she came—grief-stricken, but for very different reasons. She wanted to tell Nikko what he meant to her, but he didn't give her the chance. Eleni couldn't blame him. Still, she couldn't leave without an explanation. So she sat at her desk, drafting note after note until she'd written what she needed as best she could.

Dear Nikko,

Leaving is the hardest decision I've ever had to make. I want nothing more than to fall into your arms day after day, night after night. But I have responsibilities that I've ignored for far too long. I will never forget these past two months. They will remain in my heart and dreams forever. Each day with you was a blessing I'm eternally grateful for.

All my love,
Eleni

Quietly, she walked to Nikko's bedroom, hesitating as she turned the sealed envelope nervously over in her hands. Eleni hoped her words would heal her absence. She had to make him understand that obligation was the only thing pulling her away—nothing or no one else could. Resolving herself, she slipped it under the door.

Eleni glanced at her watch. The taxi would be here any minute. She wandered about one last time, not surprised to find *Yiayiá* Thalia by the stove.

"It's time," Eleni said sadly.

Thalia pulled her into her embrace. "I'm going to miss you. Just promise me you will always follow your heart. It will lead you to where you belong." She winked.

Eleni nodded, wiping away her tears. "I'll try."

A horn honked, and Maria called Eleni's name.

"I'm coming."

Maria and Thalia kissed and hugged Eleni repeatedly, whispering endearments in her ear.

"I love you both so much. Thank you for treating me as one of your own."

"You are and always will be," Maria cried. "*Kaló taxíthi.*"

Eleni didn't look back as she entered the backseat of the taxi, but once inside, she couldn't control the steady stream of tears rolling down her cheeks. Maria was sad to see her go, but Eleni knew she was more concerned about her son and how her leaving would affect him. A mother's eyes held nothing back, and Eleni was racked with guilt.

The last thing she wanted was to hurt any member of that family.

Later, as her mind wandered during the plane ride home, she reminisced about the past months. Aside from enduring her grandfather's funeral, she had not spent happier or more fulfilling days in years. This was a very different scenario from her last two trips to Greece. Her thoughts drifted back to her previous departures and how history had a habit of repeating itself. No matter how hard she tried, it always ended with loss and deep heartache. Pulling a Kleenex from her bag, she wiped at her tears. Nikko would never forgive her this time, and the memories of him would haunt Eleni until her dying day.

CHAPTER 38

Eleni

Thirteen years ago

"Stay," Nikko begged Eleni. "We have each other. That's all that matters."

But Eleni was numb. She had just buried her parents and brother only days before. There were no words to adequately express how much she wanted off this island. And she had pleaded with her grandparents to make the arrangements right away.

"Look at me, Eleni." Nikko held her face in her hands. "I loved them, too, and I know that doesn't compare to your loss. But you can lean on me."

"We already had this conversation. I need to go home," Eleni finally answered, but her tone was flat, emotionless. "Tomorrow."

"Tomorrow! No!" Raking his hands through his hair, Nikko blew out a frustrated breath. "You need me now more than ever. And I need you," he pleaded desperately.

"The arrangements have already been made." She spoke as if a robot had hijacked her body. She was dead inside, and she may as well have been made of metal and wires. But that emotionless feeling was better than giving in to the kind of pain only humans endured and allowing it to overwhelm or torment her. No, it was better to feel nothing at all.

Rising from where they were sitting on the front porch steps, she began to walk away. "I have to pack."

Nikko circled her wrist, pulling her back to him. Standing, he wound an arm around her waist. "I love you," he declared. Sincerity and concern were reflected in his eyes as he implored her. "I love you," he repeated. "Don't leave me."

"There is nothing left here for me but bad memories now," Eleni confessed. "Once I leave, I'm never coming back." She broke from his embrace, disappearing into the house.

* * *

The ride home to New York was met with silence. Her grandparents had lost their son, daughter-in-law, and grandson. Eleni sat between them on the plane, each holding her hand for comfort. Her grandmother sometimes stroked her cheek or lifted her hand to plant a kiss there. They were worried about her state of mind, but Eleni wondered if it was more than that. She felt their overprotective nature would go into overdrive now, afraid to let anything happen to her, too. And that was understandable. Eleni was all they had left in the world.

Once they landed and she switched her phone back from airplane mode, a string of texts from Nikko came rushing through.

Nikko: You left me. I love you and you left me.
Nikko: I'm sorry. I know you're grieving.
Nikko: I know you're sad now, but don't say you won't come back.
Nikko: You have to come back.
Nikko: I love you.
Nikko: I'll wait for you. 10 months and 4 days. You'll be back.
Nikko: Please answer me.
Nikko: Are you home yet?

Nikko: You have to be home by now. I want to help you get through this. Talk to me.
Nikko: It's always been you. I love you.
Nikko: I'm calling you. Pick up.
Nikko: Don't shut me out. Please. I love you.

Eleni didn't return any of his texts. Yet Nikko continued to plead for her to return next summer or at least answer him now. He promised he'd wait, hoping she'd change her mind. Text after text, he professed his love, even suggesting she move to the island and attend school in Greece so they could be together.

Eleni hated to cause Nikko such heartache, but it couldn't be avoided.

She didn't have the capacity to deal with her own broken spirit. How could she heal his? Even if her family hadn't been killed, what future did they realistically have? They were teenagers with a whole world yet to be discovered. Who they were at sixteen might not work for them as a pair in years to come. And there was also the matter of geography. Eleni had to convince herself of this. It was the only thing she could do under the circumstances. She could only deal with one loss at a time—one heartache at a time, but it was of little consolation.

As soon as Eleni arrived home, she shut herself in her room. Nikko's barrage of texts broke through the armor she had wrapped around her heart to keep her sorrow from consuming her. Drowning in her own tears, he only made her decision more difficult. Though she loved him, returning to the island that had taken everything from her was inconceivable.

CHAPTER 39

Eleni

Ten years ago

"Answer the boy," Andreas ordered, dropping an envelope into her lap. "Ignoring him is wrong."

Just like he had after her family was killed, Nikko texted, emailed, and sent letter after letter through the mail in the weeks following Eleni's grandmother's funeral. Each one went unread, stacked haphazardly in a pile on her bedroom desk.

"I can't answer what I haven't read."

"Eleni *mou*," he censured. "I was in deep grief but still recognized what was happening before me. Nikko made every attempt to get your attention—to console you. But you wanted no part of it. And I understand you're mourning the loss of my Katerina, but why not take comfort from an old friend?"

"Because he isn't just an old friend. He wants more, and I can't give it to him."

"Don't you think I know what you meant to each other? You're nineteen years old. You can make your own choices," he reminded her. "You can live in Greece if you choose to and be with the man you love."

"I can't live there. Not after what happened."

Andreas took a seat in an upholstered chair by the window. "What is really holding you back? Is it really being on the island, or is it a sense of responsibility to me?" her grandfather asked. "Because if you think for one second that I would want to hold you back from being with the boy you love, you're wrong. I know true love and nothing would make me happier than to see you experience it."

"My place is here with you," Eleni confirmed. "We only have each other now, thanks to that place that stole everyone I love."

"Unless the ground opened up and swallowed them, the island didn't take them from us. It was an accident—one that could have happened anywhere," he pointed out. "At some point, you have to make peace with it and live the life you want with the person you want."

"How can I make peace with it? Do you expect me to go on and be happy when my parents are gone and my little brother died before he was old enough to figure out his hopes for the future?"

"Is this about returning to the island or more about punishing yourself for not dying along with them?" Andreas' tone remained compassionate but firm as he tried to illuminate some insight into his granddaughter.

"The island," Eleni responded right away. After a moment, she added, "Both, maybe."

"I suspect it's more about the guilt—unwarranted as it is. So why would you avoid a place that has given you years of wonderful memories."

"Because I can." Eleni looked away from her grandfather's penetrating stare. There was some validity to what he suggested, but it was too hard for her to deal with right now. "It's just easier this way."

"Is it, though? You look quite unhappy." He stood, resting a hand on her shoulder. "I'll leave you to think it over."

Eleni stared at the letters for nearly an hour before putting them in date order. She read every single one through the tears blurring her vision. But it was the last letter that was her undoing. It was the short-est one of all, but each word was punctuated with anger and defeat: *You win. I give up. I hope you find whatever it is you're looking for.*

It was what she wanted, wasn't it? She had pushed him away, and now she wouldn't be bothered with his influx of pleas. So, if that was what she'd hoped for, why did it feel like her entire world had just come to an end?

CHAPTER 40

Eleni

Present Day

Eleni was wrung out. She drifted in and out of sleep, but her dreams were haunted by an abyss of grief of her own making.

Once the plane touched down at Kennedy Airport, instead of feeling a sense of relief to be home, an emptiness settled in the pit of her stomach. Eleni began to question her judgment and her handling of personal affairs. In business, she was confident and always knew what to say and how to solve problems. She was a person who made sensible choices, and now she needed to shake everything else weighing on her mind and get back to what she did best.

* * *

"Good morning, Angela." Eleni walked into her office, handing her friend a Starbucks coffee. "Latte?"

Jumping from the desk, Angela shrieked excitedly, her dark ringlets bouncing about her shoulders. "I can't believe you're here! I wasn't expecting you until next week," she said, throwing her arms around Eleni in a tight embrace.

"I saddled you with all the responsibility for far too long," Eleni said with a wan smile, returning the hug.

"It was fine. I enjoyed taking the reins, even when I had to juggle multiple events at once," Angela admitted. "But, Eleni, where does this leave you and Nikko?"

"Cut to the chase, why don't you?" Eleni shrugged. "It leaves us where it always does—an ocean apart." She tried to ignore the melancholy squeezing her heart. "It's history repeating itself, I suppose."

Angela placed her hands on Eleni's shoulders. "Not by his choice, from what you've told me. It's always been yours. It's up to you to break that cycle."

Angela released her, stepping away. Then, looking over her shoulder as she walked back to her desk, she added, "Unless he just doesn't mean that much to you."

Eleni glanced at her in irritation. "I know what you're trying to do, but it won't work."

"I'm not trying to do anything. Okay, maybe I am," Angela admitted. "Have you even spoken to him since you left?"

Eleni rubbed circles into her temples. "Leaving wasn't an easy choice, but it was the one I had to make. It was time to return to my real life and everything I built here." Eleni gestured for Angela to sit at her desk. "Now, can we just change the subject so you can fill me in on what we have on the schedule for the next few weeks?" she asked, sitting across from her.

"I just have one more thing to say, and then I'll drop the subject," Angela promised. "I wish I had recorded our FaceTime chats while you were away so you could see what you looked like. Every time you spoke about what you did on the vineyard, your face lit up. And when I'd ask you about Nikko, you became even more radiant. You were happy."

Eleni sighed loudly. "Are you finished?" she asked, pulling her laptop from her tote bag.

"Eleni …"

"Angela," Eleni said in warning. "You know how much I love you and respect your opinions. But what's done is done, and I doubt Nikko will ever speak to me again after this. End of story."

Eleni was grateful Angela didn't bring up Nikko for the rest of the week. Still, he was constantly on her mind. And her friend's lecture hadn't helped. Usually, mapping out ideas for an upcoming event gave her a thrill. Walking from her apartment to the office usually invigorated her as she anticipated the day ahead. The city she loved so much now seemed confining compared to Kefalonia, where she could walk for miles, breathe in the fresh air, and listen to the sounds of nature. Even her apartment felt claustrophobic. Eleni dragged herself through her days. Nothing felt as it had before, even after a week of settling back into her routine. Since everything in New York was exactly as she'd left it, there was only one conclusion: she had changed.

That evening, Eleni changed into comfortable yoga pants and a loose t-shirt. Pulling a notepad out of her tote bag, she began to form a to-do list, devising a new plan. The first order of business was to fill the vineyard's sales representative position previously held by her grandfather.

An idea took root in her mind, and Eleni wondered why she hadn't thought of it sooner. She checked the time on her iPhone. With the time zone difference, she decided it was safe to make a call. Timewise anyway. But how she'd be received was another matter. She had kept in contact with Maria and *Yiayiá* through email, answering their questions regarding restocking inventory. They also updated her with island news, but there was radio silence where Nikko was concerned. Eleni hesitated to bring him up in conversation, and they didn't offer any information.

She pulled up Yanni's number from her list of contacts. She hadn't spoken to him either since she left the vineyard. Staring at the phone, Eleni hesitated, her finger hovering over the send button. Nikko was his brother. Was he as angry with her as Nikko was?

She sucked in a deep breath. *Nothing in life worth having comes easily*, she told herself.

"Hi, Yanni. It's Eleni."

"I'm aware. Your name came up on my screen," he said. "What do you want, Eleni?"

The reception was even colder than she'd expected, but Eleni pressed on. "If you're willing, I'd like to discuss a few things with you."

"Why do you think I wouldn't be willing?" Yanni asked sardonically. "Because you broke my brother's heart? Again?"

"I deserve that. But if it makes you feel any better, my heart is shattered too. I'm miserable," Eleni admitted.

"Then why did you leave in the first place? And with barely any warning! Then, to make it worse, you left him a letter spilling out your feelings. What were you thinking?" Yanni berated her. "You would have been better off saying you felt nothing at all. At least then he'd be able to move on once and for all."

"Yanni, please. There's nothing you can say that will make me feel worse than I already do. I made a huge mistake, and that's one of two reasons why I called you," Eleni explained. "I'm not happy here anymore. I'm in love with your brother and need to be wherever he is. I want to return to the vineyard, and I hope you'll help pave the way for me."

"I don't know. You can't keep doing this to him. Nikko isn't in the best state of mind. He's shut everyone out," Yanni supplied. "He won't survive another blow if you return for a while only to leave again."

"I'm returning for good," Eleni said resolutely.

"Seriously? You're going to uproot your entire life? Abandon the business you said you *had* to go back to?"

Yanni's doubt in her was warranted. Before Eleni had a chance to respond, however, he lashed out at her.

"What happens if he's done this time and isn't interested in picking up with you again?"

Eleni gasped in response. The thought frightened her to no end, knowing it was a possibility. She regretted leaving the island and putting Nikko through this. Yet, doing so cemented in her heart and mind what she truly wanted and how she envisioned her life going forward. Not only regarding her relationship with Nikko, but also her change in career and lifestyle. The past week left her with no doubt that New York no longer felt like home. Home was with the Varvos family and the vineyard. Home was with Nikko.

Finally, Eleni broke the silence. "I'm committed to the vineyard. It's where I belong, even if Nikko wants nothing to do with me—even if he never forgives me, though I desperately hope he does."

"You're serious," he uttered in surprise. "Well, I can't wait for you to return. Everyone misses you, and Nikko is ...well, let's just say there's no living with him."

"So you're not angry with me anymore?"

"You know I've always had a soft spot for you. I was never able to stay mad at you for too long," Yanni admitted. "But if you hurt my brother again, you'll have to answer to me, and I won't be so forgiving."

"Noted. But I fear you might have to pick up the last shreds of *my* heart off the floor, not Nikko's, if he doesn't give me another chance."

"I hope the two of you settle this drama. I just want to create culinary masterpieces, not dish out relationship advice."

Eleni couldn't help but laugh. "Talking about settling issues brings me to another matter," Eleni said. "I want you to take my grandfather's position."

"But how? Why me?" he asked, perplexed.

"Who better than a family member? The restaurant owners will love you, and I can teach you what you need to know," Eleni offered. "We can work up a schedule so vineyard dinner events don't conflict with your travels."

"I'm surprisingly interested," he said thoughtfully. "We can discuss it further when you arrive."

"Yanni?" She wasn't sure if he'd understand what she was about to ask of him. "Do me a favor. Don't let Nikko know I'm coming back. Maybe just soften him up so he doesn't hate me so much when I return. But I'd like to approach him on my own terms."

"That's a hard no," Yanni said. "If you want my help, we're doing it my way. I'm not letting you blindside him."

"I'm not looking to do that!" Eleni exclaimed. "I just don't want him questioning my motives before I've had a chance to speak to him."

"It's still a no. I'll casually mention you're returning, but best I can do is I won't say why. At least he'll have a heads-up."

"If you think that's best," Eleni said, resigned.

"If you want my advice, I suggest you call him before you arrive."

"What if he won't pick up?"

"Showing up doesn't guarantee he'll speak to you either," Yanni said.

"Okay," Eleni groaned, painfully aware it was a likely possibility. After promising to send Yanni her flight information, she ended the call.

Rising from the couch, Eleni walked to the large window facing the street below. She'd always loved the late-night vibrancy of the city, but after spending a couple of peaceful months on the island, her perception had changed. Tall buildings and flood lights diminished the illumination twinkling from the constellations above. Fume-emitting, screeching cars, horns blasting, and loud sirens never bothered her before, but now Eleni found herself grimacing at the noise. She missed quiet nights, sitting on the front porch with merely the buzzing of cicadas and the gentle whisper of an Ionian breeze rustling through the leaves on the trees to interrupt her inner thoughts. But most of all, she missed Nikko.

For the second time that night, her finger hovered over the send button on her phone. But when she finally pressed it, the call went to voicemail and Eleni hung up. After a few moments of contemplation, she called back. Again, it went to voicemail, but she braved leaving a message this time.

"Nikko, it's Eleni. Please don't delete this message before listening. I … would like a chance to speak to you … and apologize. I have something I need to say." Eleni's words caught in her throat, emotion overtaking her. "It's too important to leave on a message." Eleni exhaled nervously. "Anyway, that's it for now, but you'll hear from me again soon."

Eleni had just made the biggest decision of her life, and for better or worse, everything was about to change. She clutched the gold Byzantine cross around her neck and prayed that it all worked out as she hoped.

* * *

"Good morning, Angela," Eleni said brightly, walking in with a bounce.

Angela's eyes widened. "You're in a good mood. Did something happen that I should know about?"

"Yes! Absolutely! Have a seat," Eleni suggested. "You were right."

"I'm right about a lot of things," Angela laughed. What in particular are you referring to?"

"Everything you said about Nikko, and the vineyard, and … Nikko."

"You said Nikko already," Angela stated, raising an eyebrow.

"I know." Eleni lifted her palms skyward. "He deserved another mention. I miss him so much."

"Are you going back to Greece?"

"If I can tie up all the loose ends here," Eleni confirmed. "As you know, my grandfather left me thirty percent of his half of the vineyard. But you might not know that he also left me monetarily comfortable."

"You mean rich," Angela said bluntly.

"I wouldn't go that far, but enough to make some changes that I might not have been able to otherwise," Eleni explained. "Angela, you've put as much into Eleni's Affairs to Remember as I have. And during these past two months, it would have crumbled without you. So, if you're interested, I'd like to hand the business over to you."

"To run for you?"

"Not exactly. I'm giving it to you," Eleni said.

Angela's mouth went agape. Stunned, she replied vehemently, "What? No! You can't just hand over your business. Maybe I can buy it from you," Angela mused, biting her lower lip. "If you can hold a note for me, that is. It's not like I have that kind of capital."

"No. That's not what I want," Eleni said. "You worked for this. Even before I left for Greece, you'd become more of a partner than an employee, working countless hours alongside me."

Nibbling on her thumbnail, Angela thought for a moment. "Then that's how it should stay. You remain on as a silent partner. This is your company. You deserve to profit from what you've built."

Eleni steepled her hands, her elbows propped on the desk. "Okay, under one condition. Your half is earned free and clear as a bonus for all the work you've put into it."

Angela groaned. "I don't know. That doesn't seem fair."

"It is. Trust me. I won't be here to pull my weight. Besides, that's my final offer," Eleni stated firmly. "Unless you'd like me to sell it to someone else," she challenged.

Angela broke out in a grin. "You drive a hard bargain. Deal!" She popped out of her chair and hugged her friend. "So, you're going back to get your man?"

Eleni grinned widely. "I sure am." Then, with her confidence deflating, she murmured, "But there's no guarantee he'll want to have anything to do with me. However it turns out for us, though, I have a stake in the vineyard and want to contribute to its success." Again, she fingered the cross dangling from her neck. She needed all the prayers in heaven to win Nikko back.

CHAPTER 41

Nikko

Present Day

The weeks after harvest were one of the busiest times of the year. This turned out to be advantageous for Nikko. Immersing himself in work kept his mind off Eleni. Or did it? The ever-present scowl on his face might tell a different story. And the mutterings under his breath as he ran grapes through the presser only confirmed it. More than upset, he was furious with himself for repeatedly opening his heart to her, only for it to end in the same result every single time.

The difference this time was that Eleni had also left her mark on his corner of the world. What Nikko considered his sanctuary was now littered with constant reminders of her. So he avoided the guest areas of the vineyard. He couldn't bear to see the retail space in the tasting room thriving because of her stroke of genius. Nikko glowered at the gift bags visitors carried, stamped with the very logo Eleni had explicitly designed for his family's vineyard. It was all too much.

Even his brother's return was her brainchild, and Nikko couldn't bring himself to participate in the themed dinners Eleni had orchestrated. So, instead, he often found himself at the local bar; at least there, he didn't have to face his family's sympathetic looks.

Four shots of ouzo had numbed the ache in Nikko's chest until Yanni entered the bar and sat beside him.

"I think you've had enough," Yanni attested, snatching the shot glass from Nikko before he chugged yet another.

"*Gamísou*! Fuck off!" Nikko cursed. "I'll be the judge of that."

Raising his brows at the collection of empties lined up before Nikko, Yanni declared, "You're done."

"What are you doing here anyway? Shouldn't you be cooking up five courses of pistachio-accented food or something?" Nikko asked with a hint of resentment in his tone.

"Well, at least you're not so pissed that you can't remember the menu," Yanni said. "One point for you. It's almost midnight, though. I've been finished for a while."

Yanni motioned for the bartender. "A shot of *ouzo* for me and a tall glass of water for my brother." When the bartender served their drinks, Yanni pushed the glass before Nikko, urging him to drink it. "You can't go on this way, working yourself to the bone by day and cloistering yourself from everyone by night."

"She left me a letter," Nikko mumbled half-drunkenly. "A fucking letter! She breaks off our relationship and then leaves me a goddamned letter to say she loves me. Who does that?" Nikko scrubbed his hands over his face. "That's what I get for ignoring my intuition."

"I love you, brother, but you're an idiot. Hey!" Yanni snapped when Nikko dropped his head onto the cool surface of the bar. "Pick yourself up and look at me!" he demanded. "Don't you think it was as hard for her to write that letter as it was for you to read it? She loves you. That's a fact, not something I'm just dreaming up to lessen your pain."

"Lessen my pain?" Nikko laughed humorlessly. "How does that lessen my pain? I'm alone! Her love for me obviously wasn't strong enough to keep her here, was it? Or at least, I wasn't. Love doesn't solve anything when real life gets in the way. It just makes everything messier."

Yanni slapped his brother's cheek affectionately. "You're wrong. If it's true, honest love, you can get through anything. But relationships take effort and work. And maybe that's the test—how much you're willing to fight for it. Did you even ask her to stay? Did you try to look at her side of it? Did you go after her? Tell her what she meant to you?" Yanni asked with conviction.

"I told her I loved her so many times, and that my biggest fear was that she'd leave again," Nikko admitted. "What more could I do or say?"

"That's not enough." Yanni laughed snidely. "It doesn't sound like you gave her a reason to upend her entire life to stay here with you," he said, shaking his head. "Did you offer to leave everything you worked for here to be with her in New York?"

Nikko shook his head. "No. I ... that wouldn't make sense."

"Why? Because your life is here? Your work is here?" Yanni asked with a pointed glare. "The same goes for Eleni, yet you expected her to give up everything for you without offering to do the same for her." Yanni raised his eyebrows, waiting for a response.

Nikko leaned back on the barstool, closing his eyes as he raked his hands through his hair. His brother was tormenting him with facts he didn't want to admit he should have considered.

"Telling Eleni 'I'm afraid of you leaving,'" Yanni imitated in a crybaby voice, "isn't enough to make her commit to a life with you."

"Enough!" Nikko barked. "Enough. I get it. I messed up. Why are you doing this to me?"

"Because I love you. And there might be a chance to fix this. You messed up, but so did Eleni," Yanni admitted, cuffing his brother's shoulder. "I don't mean to be insensitive or hard on you. But I can't sit here and watch you like this for another day. And trust me, Eleni got a small dose of what I just gave you, too. But one of you has to make the first move and spell out how you feel without reservation."

"I can't do that. I'm too angry and not setting myself up for rejection yet again. Not when I know damn well Eleni won't be running back. She made her choice clear. The subject is closed."

"A lot you know! It's far from closed."

"What are you saying?" Nikko asked.

"She's on her way back," Yanni said, helping his brother off the barstool. "So let's get you home and sobered up."

"Is that what she called to tell me?" He waved his question off. "It doesn't matter," Nikko slurred. "She'll do whatever she came for and then leave again. Like she always does."

"Don't be so sure about that."

"I'm not sure about anything. I didn't answer her call," Nikko rambled as Yanni helped him out the taverna door. "That'll show her."

Yanni snickered and said, "*Ne, maláka,* you showed her."

CHAPTER 42

Eleni

Present Day

During a few chaotic days, Eleni listed her apartment with a real estate agent for rent, had her attorney draft a partnership agreement for Eleni's Affairs to Remember, and hired a moving company to store her belongings. There was still much to iron out, but she could do most of it through video conference calls and emails.

The red-eye flight should have afforded Eleni a night's sleep, but she was too wound up. Her mind raced anxiously on how to approach Nikko and what reaction to expect.

Now, as she stood waving to Yanni when she saw the blue pickup truck pull up to the arrival lane at the airport, butterflies fluttered frantically in her belly, colliding in a myriad of emotions she couldn't begin to describe. She was both excited for and terrified of what might come to pass.

"It's good to have you back," Yanni said, pulling Eleni into a hug. "It hasn't been the same here without you." He opened the passenger door for her.

"I hardly think my absence could have made much of a difference," Eleni said once they had settled into their seats.

Yanni chuckled. "You don't know! My *mamá* is doing her best to keep up with the inventory, but the vendors keep asking for you. She was okay with reordering the same items you had initially stocked, but when they suggested something different, she couldn't decide. I don't think she was confident in her judgment."

"Oh, that might be my fault," Eleni admitted. "I left her with a detailed handbook to follow. But it was only meant to be a guide." Eleni wanted Maria and Thalia to trust their instincts and not follow her instructions like the rule of law.

"We hired another server, at least until the season dies down," Yanni continued.

"How would you feel if the season didn't die down?" Eleni asked with a gleam in her eye. "The off-season might not be as busy, but what if we could draw in more locals during the winter?"

"I'm listening," Yanni said, his interest piqued.

"Since I own part of the vineyard, I want to invest in it. How would you like that industrial kitchen?" Eleni held up her hand before Yanni could get too excited. "Nothing too extravagant, but efficient enough for commercial use."

"Amazing, of course," he said, taking his eyes off the road to glance at her appreciatively. "But where am I feeding these people off-season during the colder months? *Mamá's* dining room?"

"Of course not." Eleni chuckled. "I don't want to overstep, so I need to talk to the family first. But I want to build an adequate-sized venue to continue the themed dinners during the winter, host private parties, and maybe even hold intimate weddings. Nothing too elaborate. Do you think they'd consider it?" Eleni asked nervously.

"I think it's a great idea," Yanni said. "Propose it to them and see what they say. But how will this work if you want me to take over your grandfather's position? If I cook for events year-round, traveling as the vineyard wine rep will be challenging."

"If your parents agree, we can discuss the logistics later. But we can mark events off the calendar for the weeks you'll be away."

"You make it sound so simple."

"It will take planning and coordination, but that's what I do. We can make it work. You'll see." *If only everything were that easy.* "What about Nikko?" Eleni asked hesitantly. "How do you think he'll feel?"

"About you or your ideas?"

"Both," Eleni said, fidgeting with the strap on her handbag.

The familiar crunch of gravel beneath the tires announced they had arrived at the vineyard. Before Yanni answered, they both shook their heads in amusement, watching the front door swing open with a flourish.

"I think you're going to have to work hard for this one," Yanni warned.

She wanted to prod him for more information, but Maria and Thalia were already pulling her from the car. And although she was weary, a surge of energy ran through her as they affectionately greeted her, both women peppering her with kisses.

"I'm so happy you came back!" Maria exclaimed. "I need you!"

Eleni laughed. "I'm sure you're doing perfectly fine, but I'm happy to be back too."

"*Éla! Éla mesa,*" Maria insisted, ushering Eleni into the house. She had barely reached the door when *Yiayiá* Thalia took her by the wrist, dragging her into the kitchen. The elderly woman placed a hearty bowl of *stifado*, a Kefalonian beef stew, in front of her, urging Eleni to eat.

Her stomach grumbled the moment the aromatic steam hit her nostrils. Without argument, Eleni forked a tender chunk of meat. "This is incredible," she said with a moan.

"Now!" *Yiayiá* Thalia started as she and Maria sat across from her. "When you emailed to say you planned to return, we had no idea you meant for good until Yanni told us."

"An answer to our prayers," Maria said, crossing herself three times in rapid succession. "And Nikko? You've spoken to him?"

Eleni put her fork down, sighing. "No. He wouldn't answer my call."

"That explains why his sour mood hasn't changed," *Yiayiá* Thalia said.

"I'm not sure he's as enthusiastic about my return as the rest of you." She fiddled nervously with the food in her bowl. "Regardless, I'm here to stay. I want to be involved in the vineyard, contributing to its success. After I got back to New York, nothing was the same. I realized my time here was the happiest I'd been in a long while." She reached across the table, taking hold of the women's hands. "Thinking back, this is where I've always been the happiest ...before all the loss I had to endure."

"Oh, *glyki mou*," Maria cooed with tenderness. "It's the times of grief that make the moments of joy all the more precious. Ones not to be taken for granted or to let slip by when offered up like a priceless gift."

"I know that now," Eleni whispered, a single tear escaping from the corner of her eye.

"As for Nikko, I know my son, and he loves you. But he's been very moody. *Po, po, po!*" Maria gestured the exclamation with an exaggerated roll of her hand. "We've let him keep to himself because he hasn't been our good-natured Nikko since you left."

"So, tread lightly?" Eleni asked.

"What does this 'tread lightly' mean?" *Yiayiá* Thalia asked.

Eleni giggled, thinking how silly the expression must sound to her. But most Greek idioms made no sense either when you took them literally. "It means 'be careful what I say and do around him.'"

"No! You go to that boy and tell him you love him. Knock some sense into him," *Yiayiá* Thalia argued, fists clenched like she was preparing for a boxing match.

"He could argue *he* tried to knock sense into me, and I left anyway."

"But you're back now," Maria said with warmth. "Don't let his stubbornness ... or yours ... keep you from what was always intended."

"Always intended?" Eleni questioned.

"You'll understand what I mean in time," *Yiayiá* Thalia said. "Go now. Take a nap. You must be exhausted after the long flight."

"No, I'm not that tired, really. But I'd like to shower and freshen up first. Then I'll find my courage and seek out Nikko."

* * *

Eleni took her time meandering the sections of the property open to the public. She might have been procrastinating, but she also wanted to see how her small changes fared while she was away. While less crowded than in the summer months, the stream of visitors was still greater than before she had implemented her ideas, which pleased Eleni greatly. Wandering into the tasting room, she waved to Maria, who was working behind the bar.

"It looks like you've kept up with the inventory just fine," Eleni told Maria. "What were you so worried about?"

"It was a lot to keep organized. But I hired someone to help me." Maria gestured to the young woman by the cash register. "That's Flora. She's wonderful with the customers."

A pang of jealousy shot through Eleni. The young woman was stunning. Light brown streaked with golden strands ran the length of her long mane. She had full, pouty lips, large, doe-shaped eyes, and the figure of a 1950s starlet.

"She's beautiful." Eleni almost swallowed her question—almost—but she had to know. "Is she dating Nikko?"

"No!" Maria laughed as though the question was absurd. "What would make you think such a thing? She's his cousin. A distant cousin, but still family."

"How come I've never met her before?"

"I'm sure you did years ago, but she's much younger than you. Only nineteen," Maria said.

"Wow! I didn't look like that when I was a teenager."

"Don't worry, *koukla*. My Nikko only has eyes for you. Go find him."

Eleni tried to calm her heightening nerves as she walked to the fermentation building, but her heart was beating so hard it could have bruised her ribs.

Tiptoeing inside, Eleni quietly made her way to where she assumed he'd be. Smiling, she took in the sight of him, engrossed in his work. She watched as he drew out a wine sample for testing. For what, she wasn't sure. But if she had to guess, Eleni mused it was to check for sugar content. Keeping a healthy distance, Eleni waited for Nikko to notice her. When he finally turned, his surprise stopped him dead in his tracks.

They both stood in place, their eyes locking briefly until the steel in his expression made her look away. Eleni had repeatedly practiced what she would say in her mind during the flight, but facing him now, she was suddenly tongue-tied. She imagined Nikko running through so many emotions at that very moment. With uncertainty, Eleni took a few steps closer to him. She could see the conflict swimming in his expressive sapphire pools. Affection. Hurt. Anger. Oh, the anger. A chill ran up Eleni's spine. She knew penetrating the wall he had built around himself was probably impossible.

Eleni wanted to turn and run away. Fighting the urge took every-thing she had, but no, she was done running. "Hi," Eleni breathed.

Nikko shook his head. "I can't do this again."

"I know, and I'm so sorry, but it's different this time."

"And every time I believe that it ends up the same. You tear out of here as fast as you can," Nikko said bitterly. "Do whatever you came back to do before you run off again, but stay out of my way in the meantime."

"Okay," Eleni said softly, resigned. "But you should know—"

"I don't want to know anything. Your business is not my concern."

Eleni nodded. Turning, she walked to the door, but once she was out of his sight, she fled, tears streaming down her cheeks. Eleni didn't stop until she arrived at her bedroom. Yanni had warned her she had a challenge ahead. And on some level, Nikko's reaction was not only what she'd expected but also what she deserved. But facing his hostility was more painful than she had imagined. Still, Eleni wouldn't give up. Somehow, she had to find a way to break through his barriers. He had to hear her out. After everything she'd been through and everything that had kept her from the island and Nikko in the past, it couldn't end like this.

CHAPTER 43

Eleni

Twenty-two years ago

Eleni's mother repeated the exact words each morning: 'Don't go beyond the vineyard gates.' Eleni never did, though, nor did she have any desire to. She only ever wanted to find Nikko. At his age, he didn't work hard labor in the fields, but his father had begun teaching him in the hopes that he would be ready to take over when he came of age.

"Are you looking for Nikko?" Kostas asked as she wandered past.

"I am. Is he here?" Eleni asked Nikko's *pappou*.

"Three rows down," he answered, thumbing in the right direction.

Eleni skipped as she went, brushing her fingers along the edges of the grape leaves. "Nikko," she sang out.

"I'm here," he said, waving his hands to catch her attention with an ear-splitting smile on his face.

"You can go," his father said from beside him, winking. "I think that's enough for today."

Grinning, Nikko took Eleni by the hand, and off they went. They played hide-and-seek and catch-me-if-you-can. After a while, they found a blanket and sat by the front entrance, watching visitors meander their way through the open wrought-iron gate.

"I don't want you to leave next week," Nikko said quietly.

"I don't want to go either. But I'll be back next year."

Nikko reached for a potted bougainvillea plant, nipping off a magenta flower. "For you," he offered.

Eleni sidled up next to Nikko. "Someday, I'm going to come back and stay forever." She nodded her assurance as though it were decided. "And when we grow up, I'm going to marry you," she whispered in his ear.

He smiled shyly. "That's a long time away."

"It doesn't matter," Eleni said. "You'll always be my best friend in the whole world."

"The way I see it, if you want the rainbow, you gotta put up with the rain."
Dolly Parton

CHAPTER 44

Eleni

Present Day

When Eleni didn't come down for dinner that evening, Maria knocked on her door.

"It's me. Maria. I have a tray of food for you."

Eleni went to the door and opened it. "That's very sweet. Thank you."

Maria looked at Eleni's tear-stained face with compassion. "May I sit with you for a while?"

"Sure, but I don't think I'll make very good company."

Nikko's mother set the tray on the desk. Then, lifting the plate of grilled lamb chops, she sat on the bed beside Eleni, bringing it close enough for the aroma to entice her. *Païdákia*," Maria chimed. "I know you love them."

She was right. Usually, Eleni would eat lamb chops every day, given a choice. But her churning, anxiety-ridden stomach rejected even the thought of food.

Maria squeezed lemon over a chop and handed it to Eleni. "Just one bite."

Eleni reluctantly complied. But that one taste was all her taste buds needed to overrule her rebelling belly. "Delicious," she said with a sniff before taking another bite. The blend of herbs and garlic, married with the lemon and olive oil, created an explosion of flavor in her mouth, and without coaxing, she reached for a second chop.

"I hope you don't mind, but I got the sense that Nikko wasn't very receptive when you approached him today, so we filled him in at the dinner table on what you plan to do here," Maria said.

Eleni looked at Maria in confusion. "I was going to discuss that with you tonight. How—"

"Yanni explained it to us last night." Maria smiled. "He was very enthusiastic. And then, when you didn't come down for dinner tonight, we shared your ideas with Nikko."

"I'm sure he disagreed with all of it," Eleni said. "He wants me to disappear; the sooner, the better."

"That's not true." Maria stroked Eleni's hair. "He's hurt and understandably protecting himself. You need to give him a little time." She took Eleni's chin between her fingers. "And you need to show him that you're here for good. You and I both know you're not back simply for your interest in the vineyard."

"I'm afraid it might be too late," Eleni said, resigned.

Maria waited for a beat. Then, taking on a serious expression, she continued, "It's never too late to come home. And home isn't always where you were born or lived most of your life. Home doesn't have to be a place at all. Sometimes, it's a person who fills every corner of your being. You want to be with them because they fill your heart and feed your soul." Maria took Eleni's face in her hands. "Nikko is your home, and you are his. I've known this since you were young. Give him time. He loves you." Maria rose and headed to the door.

Eleni had to know. "Maria? What did Nikko think of my new ideas?"

Maria grinned. "He didn't want to admit they were solid, but trust me, he was pleased," she said, leaving the room.

* * *

The following morning, Eleni decided she would afford herself one day to mope. After that, she would begin implementing her latest plan. There were contractors to call and red tape to sift through, especially if construction here was anything like it was in the States. She would have to figure it all out.

Eleni roamed the island, particularly the spots where she and Nikko had gone together over the years. She parked her car at a cliff's edge and looked down at the nearly empty beach. The weather had cooled to sixty-eight degrees Fahrenheit. There were a few stray sunbathers, but most people walked barefoot along the shoreline, taking in the last remnants of the summer. At the height of the season, this spot was usually saturated with beachgoers, all claiming their place in the sand while accompanied by a colorful array of umbrellas. Teens would line up by a protruding rock reaching out from the cliff, waiting their turn to take a deep, brave plunge into the crystal-blue water. But not today.

Next, Eleni drove to the entrance of Ainos National Park. She remembered hiking the mountain with Nikko when they were teenagers. She'd been determined to see the mystical, elusive wild horses that inhabited the mountain. It took some doing, but they eventually found the ethereal creatures. Now, recalling the laborious trek—winding, rocky roads leading uphill in a car that wasn't equipped, plus the long hike—Eleni thought it best not to attempt it alone.

From there, she continued to the monastery of Agios Gerasimos, the island's patron saint. The echo of Eleni's steps on the marble floor publicized her entrance into this holy place. Worshipers silently lit candles while others knelt by the gold encasement containing the incorrupt relics of the saint. Eleni took a seat and meditated on the inspiration and beauty of the vibrant jewel-toned floor-to-ceiling icons dominating every structure's surface. The enormous spherical gold chandeliers suspended from the three-story ceiling created the illusion of where Earth ended and Heaven began. She felt a sense of serenity here, as if the air's molecules consisted solely of celestial angels wrapping their wings around her in a protective blanket.

Among the faithful, Eleni found the courage to face her future, whatever that might bring. All the changes her life had undergone these last few months, both by a stroke of fate and by her own choices, had brought her to this moment, to this corner of the world. They led her here, where home was meant to be.

GRILLED LAMB CHOPS

Ingredients

8-10 lamb chops, rib or round bone
1/3 cup olive oil
2 tablespoons dried oregano or ¼ cup loosely packed fresh, snipped
2 tablespoons dried basil or ½ cup fresh, shredded
4-5 mint leaves, shredded
2-3 cloves of garlic, crushed
½ teaspoon each of salt and pepper
Juice and zest from 2 lemons

Method

Mix all the ingredients (minus the lamb) in a bowl. Rub the herb mixture onto each lamb chop. Place the chops in a marinating bag or container and add the remaining marinade into the bag. Marinate for several hours or overnight. Grill or broil.

CHAPTER 45

Nikko

Present Day

The whole day had passed, and Nikko had not even caught a glimpse of Eleni anywhere. He couldn't blame her for skipping dinner the night before. He had been stone-cold rude. But when his family shared her reason for returning, his heart couldn't help but thaw just a little. If nothing else, Eleni had proven she was committed to filling the void her grandfather had left, contributing to the vineyard's success in ways her talents allowed.

But where did that leave Nikko? Would Eleni return to the States once the event venue was complete and everything running smoothly? No one seemed capable of answering the one thing he wanted to know. How long was she staying this time? Now that he thought of it, every family member seemed to evade the question, which told him she wasn't planning to stay.

"Your avoidance of answering my questions tells me everything I need to know," Nikko groused, rising from the table and throwing his napkin down.

"Before you jump to conclusions," Nikko's mother said, grabbing his arm before he walked away, "speak to Eleni. The answers need to come directly from her, not us."

Nikko wrenched his arm from Maria's hold and left the room without another word.

* * *

Nikko couldn't get his mind off Eleni as he went through his daily routine. It was focused on her while he clipped back vines, preparing for the upcoming winter. It was on her while he tested the sugar levels in the fermenting tanks. And it was on her while blending grapes in hopes of creating a complex and unique wine. Where was she? Nikko guessed he couldn't blame Eleni for staying clear out of his path. He, indeed, didn't roll out the welcome mat for her when she stunned him with her presence. Okay, so he shouldn't have been too surprised. Yanni had mentioned she was returning. But he didn't say it would be this soon, though anything his brother told him that night was lost in a fog of intoxication.

Nikko's emotions ricocheted like a silver ball bouncing around a pinball machine. Yet it didn't prevent his heart from nearly leaping from his chest when he found her suddenly standing before him. Nikko recovered quickly enough, though, his anger simmering. Confusion over her motives dominated his guarded heart. His anger was his shield. Their eyes met briefly, his cold stare evidently rattling her when she lowered her eyes in response. Then Eleni disappeared, fleeing from his workspace and out among the vines. Eleni had vanished like vapor evaporating into the atmosphere, and he wondered if he had only imagined her.

Nikko ended his workday early. Walking through the back entrance of their home, he expected to find his mother, grandmother, and Eleni with their heads together, catching up on island news or whipping up the evening's dinner. But she was nowhere in sight.

"Oh, Nikko *mou*," *Yiayiá* Thalia greeted. She lifted the wooden spoon from the pot on the stove and pointed it at him. "Have you seen Eleni today?"

"No," Nikko answered gruffly. "Why? Did she flee the country again?"

"Don't be smart. You're not too old for this!" Then, raising a threatening brow, she waved the wooden spoon at him. "*Tha fas xýlo.*"

Nikko had to chuckle. He and Yanni had run as fast as their feet would take them when she swung the *koutali* in their direction. "She's probably out making deals with shop owners," he guessed, relaxing slightly with a shrug.

"She's been gone all day," Maria added. "We didn't even see her at breakfast. I don't know who's more stubborn. But the two of you can't avoid each other forever."

"Kostas!" *Yiayiá* Thalia called. "It's time," she told her husband when he entered the room.

Kostas looked from Nikko to his wife, from his wife to his son and daughter-in-law, and finally back to Nikko. He nodded. "*Éla*, Nikko. It's time we had a talk."

Kostas gestured for Nikko to follow him into a sitting room where the family sometimes watched television at night. With a perplexed expression, Nikko hesitantly complied.

"Have a seat," his *pappou* ordered, the rest trailing in behind.

"Why do I have the feeling I'm going to hear something I don't want to know?"

"That all depends." Kostas sat in his favorite recliner, facing the flat screen mounted to the wall. Swiveling to face Nikko on the couch adjacent to him, he sighed. "When you and Eleni were small, you were inseparable. She followed you everywhere, and you didn't seem to mind. You all but forgot about your other friends when she was on the island."

"Is this going to be a lecture on the importance of old friendships?" Nikko asked darkly.

"Nikko!" his mother barked a warning.

"My old friend, Andreas, and I watched the two of you year after year, and we dreamed of a future."

"A future?" Nikko asked, frowning in confusion.

"A future when he and I might be long gone. A future for the vineyard that the two of you would carry on. Together." Kostas lifted his hand to halt Nikko's tirade. "Before you say anything, it was our hope that both of you would be interested in making this your life. Your father and I were happy you made that decision without pressure from us. But once tragedy struck, Eleni wanted a life far away from here and the painful memories this place brought her."

"We lost all hope she would return. Although, I prayed for it," *Yiayiá* Thalia said, making the sign of the cross. "Andreas would be so happy Eleni has become invested once more in the vineyard."

"So what is your point, *pappou*?" Nikko asked, his patience wearing thin. "That I need to make peace with Eleni so we can function as a team?"

"That, too, yes," Kostas admitted. "But there's more. And maybe an old pact or, in this case, a *proxenió* might no longer matter, but I think you have the right to know."

"*Proxenió*?" Nikko asked, his brow creasing with confusion until his expression was replaced by one of horrifying alarm. "Wait … Are you telling me—" Nikko rose and began to pace the room like a caged animal once the astonishment of what his grandfather had said struck him. "Are you telling me there was an arrangement between you and Andreas for Eleni and me to marry? Who does this in this day and age?" He tugged at his hair, trying to grasp this crazy, insane concept. Finally, he turned to his parents and *Yiayiá*, sitting quietly on the sofa. "How could all of you decide my life in this way?"

Nikko's grandmother spoke up. "You're not bound by it. Of course, you have the right to say no, but we thought it was time you knew."

"Damn right, I can say no. Who arranges a marriage nowadays?" he asked, his voice rising in anger.

"It happens to this day and more often than you think," his *Yiayiá* said.

"It was only two men dreaming of a way to unite our families," Kostas assured him. "It was no secret that you and Eleni had a close bond from a young age. We touched on the subject as a mere wish, but after everything that happened, Andreas brought it up more seriously, fearing that Eleni would be alone once he passed away."

"Does she know?" Nikko asked.

"Not yet," Stavros interjected. "But at some point, she should be told as well."

"If you say it's not binding, then why did you feel the need to tell me?"

"Because of this." Kostas handed Nikko a black velvet box.

Nikko looked at his grandfather suspiciously. When he opened the package, he cursed under his breath. Inside were two wedding bands and an emerald-cut diamond ring.

"Did you buy these when I was ten years old to make your wedding arrangement official?" Nikko asked sardonically.

"No. They belonged to Eleni's parents," Kostas explained patiently. "After the accident …their death, Andreas asked me to place them in the safe for a future date when Eleni could take possession of them. Or preferably, for you to present them to her upon your engagement."

Nikko laughed bitterly. "You had my whole life mapped out for me without my knowledge. I don't even get to choose my bride or the ring to propose with."

"We thought this had sentimental meaning for Eleni and that she would one day want her parents' rings," Maria explained calmly.

"Then you should have given them to her years ago," Nikko said. "As for whatever you think will happen between Eleni and me now, put it out of your minds. For all you know, once the venue building is complete, she'll return to the States, just as she did after setting up the retail space." Nikko was done with this conversation. "It's what she does," he stated emphatically. "And even if she doesn't, I don't need anyone choosing a wife for me." Nikko dropped the ring box onto his grandfather's palm and stormed out of the room.

CHAPTER 46

Eleni

Present Day

Eleni spent the next two days meeting with architects and contractors. In between, she worked with Yanni, reviewing what he needed to know about distributing their wine in the States.

"We'll make the rounds together for your first time out," Eleni assured him. "That way, I can introduce you to the contacts who already know me through my grandfather. As a vineyard family member, you have an advantage over an outsider replacing the position, so I believe you'll be received warmly."

"When is the best time of year for client appointments, and how often do you recommend I contact them?" Yanni asked.

"*Pappou* contacted each restaurant and wine store at least every four months. It's a lot of ground to cover, so once you've established a solid relationship, some of this can be done remotely."

"I think I'll mesh with the restauranteurs easily and win them over," Yanni stated confidently. "I'm looking forward to it."

"I've been on the phone setting up appointments. But, unfortunately, I can only make the rounds with you for two weeks, so I've given the clients you'll meet on your own a full rundown on your background."

Yanni cocked his head to one side, examining Eleni. "You've completely changed your life to dedicate yourself to the family business," he stated. "But not all of it has gone as you hoped. What's going to happen when we get to New York? Do you think you might have a change of heart?"

It seemed Nikko wasn't the only one Eleni had to prove her intentions to. Yanni's concern for his brother wasn't misplaced. Trust had to be earned. Still, she'd be lying if she didn't admit she was a little hurt.

Shaking her head, Eleni looked directly into his eyes. "I have no regrets about my decision. I'm committed and excited for what's to come. But I am looking forward to seeing Angela. I already miss my friend."

* * *

The night before their flight to New York, Eleni wrapped herself in a cozy sweater and sat on the front porch writing in her notepad. There was a definite chill in the air, although the thousands of twinkling stars set on a backdrop of indigo sky warmed her insides.

As much as she loved spending time with the close-knit family who lived here, she appreciated these quiet moments of solitude when she could grab them. Alone with her thoughts, she found herself planning and formulating another one of her to-do lists to keep her busy for the next several weeks.

The creak of the front door roused her from her reverie. *Yiayiá* Thalia and Maria were suddenly by her side.

"It's a beautiful night," Maria said.

"Hmm," Eleni agreed, sighing.

"We need to talk to you about something," *Yiayiá* Thalia said carefully.

"Is everything okay?" Eleni asked. The women's faces had taken on a serious expression.

"It's about you and Nikko," Maria said.

Eleni exhaled her exasperation. "Look, I know you mean well, but there's nothing to be done. I tried speaking to him. He made it clear he wants nothing to do with me, and he's done a good job at avoiding me so far. I don't know what else I can say to convince him otherwise."

"And you've avoided him as well," Maria pointed out.

"To make it easier for everyone involved," Eleni argued.

"But it's not easier." *Yiayiá* Thalia took Eleni's hand. "This isn't how it was meant to be."

Eleni laughed. "And who decides how it's meant to be?"

"Fate, destiny … your family?"

Eleni narrowed her eyes suspiciously. She detected some significant meddling was about to take place.

Yiayiá Thalia removed a worn, velvet box from her apron pocket. "Your grandfather wanted you to have this in case one day you might want to wear them during your own marriage." She handed the box to Eleni.

Her eyes widened when she saw the contents. "My mother's engagement ring!" she gasped.

"And your parents' wedding rings," Maria added.

"I always assumed my parents were buried with them."

"No. Your *pappou* wanted you to have them. Andreas and Kostas had hoped that you and Nikko would choose to wear them one day," *Yiayiá* Thalia began. "They made a *proxenió* of sorts."

Eleni's jaw went slack. She stared at the women as if they had just told her they had proof that the world was flat after all. Speechless, she sputtered, "Of …of sorts? What exactly does that mean?" Eleni shuddered. "A *proxenió*? You can't be serious?"

"It wasn't a formal binding. It was more like a hope and dream between two best friends and business partners. It was also an agreement meant to protect you when Andreas was gone. Neither of you is obligated to uphold it, of course," *Yiayiá* Thalia explained.

"Even if it were binding in some archaic way, I'm not sure you could make two people get married if they had no interest in doing so," Eleni said.

Thalia ignored Eleni's comments and pressed the jewelry box into her lap. "This belongs to you, regardless. Do with it what you want, but please examine your heart. If the love is there, it doesn't matter who makes the next move." She rose and began to head indoors.

"My boy loves you, and you, him," Maria said, stroking Eleni's hair. "It only takes one look at both of you to know this is true." And with that, she, too, rose and followed her mother-in-law inside.

Once alone, Eleni exhaled a slow, deep breath to calm the budding anxiety growing within her. She rubbed her thumb over the fading velvet encasement. It made sense her grandfather would want her to have her parents' most important possessions. He was a sentimental man. But this other revelation blew her away. Had she actually been promised to Nikko years ago? And had Nikko known this all along? Or did he just find out recently? Either way, it might add yet another layer to his resentment of her.

Eleni had to compartmentalize and force this from her mind for now. Focusing on Yanni and the wine distribution was her priority. This latest development in her tumultuous personal life would have to be dealt with later. Wrapping her head around the idea of an arranged marriage, even to Nikko, was too much to absorb, and it was beyond her comprehension that her grandfather would do this without her knowledge. This business trip was the distraction she so desperately needed right now.

CHAPTER 47

Eleni

Present Day

Two weeks later, Eleni returned to the vineyard confident she'd made the right choice in Yanni for her *pappou's* replacement. He won over every restauranteur with his culinary expertise and wine-pairing knowledge, not to mention his irresistible Varvos charm. The wine shop owners were also receptive to him. She had no qualms at all about leaving him to his own devices.

Once Eleni had settled in and unpacked, she opened the top drawer of her dresser. Under a layer of camisoles sat the faded velvet box containing her parents' rings. She removed the diamond engagement ring that had once adorned her mother's finger, tempted to try it on. She had once, a long time ago, after begging her mother. But no, she would not slip the ring on now. Not unless Nikko had a change of heart and one day forgave her. But even if he did, it might not necessarily mean he'd want that kind of a relationship, much less marry her, for that matter. Adrenaline surged through her veins, causing her heart to jump. What if he were already involved with someone else? Is that why he'd been so cold? His mother claimed otherwise, but maybe she wasn't privy to his personal life. Eleni could say without a doubt she was in love with Nikko, and it had absolutely nothing to do with their families wishing for it, arranging it, or pushing them toward the altar. She wanted him with every fiber of her being. Eleni now understood she had always felt this way, even when she didn't dare to face it.

During her trip to the States, she had time to think long and hard about how this so-called arrangement affected her future. It didn't—not in the least. *Proxenió* or not, she was in love with Nikko and wanted to spend the rest of her life with him. The question was, how did Nikko see it? And would he eventually come to the same conclusion—that their grandfathers, with their infinite wisdom and insight, knew Eleni and Nikko were meant for each other?

Eleni rummaged through her closet until she found the outfit she was searching for. The weather had cooled, so the sundresses she had worn the month prior were no longer appropriate. Instead, Eleni shimmied into a tan body-hugging, long-sleeve wrap dress and slid her feet into a pair of leather knee-high boots. After brushing her hair and touching up her makeup, she descended the stairs, determined to find Nikko, praying he wouldn't turn her away this time before she could say what she should have long ago.

Finding Nikko shouldn't be difficult; Eleni had his routine down and knew exactly where to look for him. She marched with determination to the building where he spent a good part of his day, her heart beating at double rhythm in her chest. But she had to be the one to make the effort. She was the one at fault—the one who had walked away when, this time, she should have made another choice.

"Nikko," Eleni determinedly said as she entered, mustering her courage. He was sitting at a corner desk. When he heard her voice, Nikko swung his chair around.

"Back so soon?" Nikko muttered indifferently. "You must be building up a load of air miles with all your indecision."

"When I said I was here to stay, I meant it," Eleni declared. She wasn't about to let him push her away—not this time. "Look, you may want nothing to do with me, but somehow, we have to make this work—at least for the vineyard's sake. And for your family. It's unfair to place them in the middle of our tension. Besides, avoiding each other will be nearly impossible."

"Fine," he agreed begrudgingly. "Are you done now?"

Frustrated, Eleni hesitated, about to say yes and make her exit. But no. She wasn't done. And even if she had to prove it by leaving every last shred of her heart on this cold, concrete floor, she'd lay it down for him to stomp on like his precious grapes, if that's what he chose.

"No, I'm not." She fisted her hands at her sides. "I'm sorry my parents died and that returning here was too traumatic for me. And I'm sorry the result meant cutting you off and never seeing you again. And I'm sorry I made the choice I did this time, too. If you think that was easy for me, you're wrong."

Nikko sat with his arms folded, his expression unreadable.

"I know I made mistakes. I'm not perfect. And I felt bound by an obligation to everything and everyone but myself and what I truly wanted. But I've come to terms with that, so I'm here to stay. For the vineyard …and for you." Eleni sucked in a quivering breath. "Because I love you. Just as I always have." She shook her head, correcting herself. "No, that's not true. I love you even more now, so much more."

Nikko stared at Eleni stony-faced. She didn't know if he was weighing the enormity of her words or simply didn't care, but Nikko's apparent indifference gutted her. *He didn't care. Her heartfelt confession meant nothing to him.* Eleni forced back tears as a feeling of abject mortification swallowed her, and she wished she could disappear into the ether like the mountaintops on a foggy day. Eleni had to get out of there. Turning, she fled, ignoring Nikko even when she heard him call out her name in exasperation.

"I can't," Eleni stuttered, refusing to face him. "I can't," she muttered, bolting from his sight.

CHAPTER 48

Nikko

Present Day

It was never a question of whether Eleni loved him. They had always had an undeniable connection. Anyone in the same room with them would have to be near death not to feel the electrical charge in the air. But Nikko feared that he had always loved her just a little bit more than she did him. He would have sacrificed anything to be with her. But Eleni shut him down time and time again, until, eventually, he had no choice but to do the same.

How many times would she dare test his resolve? Nikko couldn't allow her to play with his heart—to let him believe this time would be different. But Nikko stood planted in the one spot, paralyzed by the revelation that Eleni had given up her life in New York, including her company, not only for the vineyard but more so for him. For him! She had seriously done it this time. She had chosen him over everything else. So why was he frozen in place like a moron instead of running after her?

"Eleni!" Nikko called out again, finally chasing after her. "Wait!" he pleaded, catching up with her.

"Please, Nikko. I've humiliated myself enough for one day."

Laying his hands on her shoulders, Nikko turned her to face him. "I love you. I do. So much it hurts and …that frightens me." He sighed. "I just need time."

"Time," Eleni repeated, sounding unconvinced. "For what? To test me? To make sure I mean it this time?" she asked through a sob. "To make sure I stay," she muttered as if talking to herself.

"Yes."

"So you need some sort of proof or reassurance?" Eleni shrugged his hands off her. "You don't trust me," she said, looking up at Nikko with sad, glistening eyes.

"I need to know you won't leave me again," he corrected, although he presumed it all did boil down to trust in the end.

Eleni looked into Nikko's eyes. "All it takes is faith. I'll figure out a way for you to restore your faith in me." She cupped his cheek affectionately before walking away. "I can promise you that."

Nikko watched her as she headed down the path. The last thing he wanted was to cause her anxiety or pain. But he had to protect his heart, too. One more stab from this woman and the damage would be unrepairable.

"Step out of the history that is holding you back. Step into the new story you are willing to create." Oprah Winfrey

CHAPTER 49

Eleni

Present Day

Eleni was restless. She didn't know what to do with herself. Her concentration was lost between the pillows of clouds above and the dark bottom of the mysterious sea. How could she make Nikko believe she was in this for the long haul? Staring at her computer was proving unproductive. One thing was clear: nothing on her to-do list was getting accomplished today. Eleni grabbed her bag off the back of her desk chair, making a snap decision to take a drive.

She had no destination in mind but wasn't in the frame of mind to stop and visit shop owners with whom the vineyard had collaborated. So she drove aimlessly, letting her mind wander until, after a few hours, she found herself parked in front of a church. As if by fate, it carried the same name as her beloved grandfather. Agios Andreas was an old Byzantine monastery, partly ruined in the earthquake of 1953. A new church, cared for by an order of nuns, was built and consecrated from its ruins.

It was now the middle of the afternoon; evening vigil services wouldn't begin until after sundown, and there wasn't a soul in sight. This was the second time Eleni had sought comfort from above in a matter of weeks. A sense of tranquility came over her upon entering the church, the solitude instantly calming her. The smell of fragrant incense and melting candle wax soothed her soul. There were no pews or any kind of seating in the nave except around the church's perimeter, meant for the elderly or disabled. Eleni lit an amber bees-wax candle before moving from one icon to the next, venerating each of them by crossing herself and respectfully kissing the holy images.

She was unaware of anyone's presence until a gentle hand cupped her shoulder. Turning, Eleni came face to face with the kind expression of a middle-aged nun dressed head to toe in a flowing black garment.

"*Paraklasis* is not for another three hours," the sister said, referring to the nightly prayers.

"Thank you. I'm only staying a few minutes," Eleni explained.

"I see. I am Sister Fotiní." The woman took Eleni's hands in hers.

"I'm Eleni," she offered, bowing to show her reverence.

"Ah! You are named after one of our greatest saints. Now, what is troubling you, my child?"

"What makes you think I'm troubled?" Eleni asked.

"The eyes are the window to the soul, and I see turmoil reflected there." She gestured to a pair of chairs set against the wall. "Come, sit. Unburden yourself."

For the next fifteen minutes, Eleni found solace in the sympathetic nun. She shared the history of her relationship with Nikko and all that had transpired to separate them. With undivided attention, Sister Fotiní listened, occasionally patting Eleni's back or stroking her hair.

"This is not a dilemma at all," she declared, grasping the large cross dangling from her neck. "You are both adults now and finally living in the same place. And you say you're here to stay. Proving your love is simple. Do you want this young man in your life forever?"

"Yes, of course." Eleni drew a tissue from her handbag to pat dry her tear-stained eyes. "I really do," she sniffled.

"Then declaring your commitment is all it will take."

"But I already told him how I felt, and it wasn't enough."

"Show him," she emphasized. "Show him before God."

"Are you asking me to …" Eleni hadn't finished her thought before Sister Fotiní nodded.

"Go. Don't waste another moment." The sister hurried her along, smiling. "You'll be in my prayers this evening."

* * *

Eleni's heart beat rapidly as she drove back to the vineyard. All or nothing. All or nothing. She kept repeating those words, talking herself into what the nun had suggested. If Nikko needed assurance of her commitment to him, she would offer it freely. If it took a grand gesture, he would get one. The thought of what she was about to do made her feel like an entire gymnastics team was tumbling in her belly. She pressed her hands against her stomach. If this didn't work out how she hoped, she'd see a humiliation beyond her comprehension. Worse, Eleni would know definitively that she and Nikko were done for good.

When Eleni returned to the house, she quietly snuck in and tiptoed to her room. She found what she wanted at the bottom of her drawer, but as she grasped it, her nerves got the best of her. Shaking, Eleni felt her body break out in a cold sweat.

As quietly as she had entered the house, she exited, following the path to where she had last spoken to Nikko. It was the most beautiful time of day when the sun began to dip below the horizon, creating a canvas of pastel brushstrokes across the sky.

Before Eleni reached the building, Nikko happened to stride in her direction. Her heart nearly jumped out of her chest. This was it—the moment that would determine the rest of her life.

"Eleni," Nikko said, his face contorting in confusion. "I didn't expect to see *you* back here today."

He wasn't happy to see her. That was apparent from the expression on his face. But she wouldn't run again. Eleni had to know one way or another, so she pressed on, moving a few steps closer to him. "I didn't either, but …here I am, and I have something to say. Or rather something to ask. Or both." Eleni waved her hands as if they would erase the words tripping on her tongue in their escape. She inhaled deeply, steeling herself. "Okay. Here goes." She took in a deep breath, building up the courage to continue. "You need reassurance I'm here to stay. That I won't leave you, and that my love for you is stronger than any of my fears or obligations."

"I told you I needed time," Nikko said coolly.

"You did. But time is not what you need," Eleni declared. "You need my unwavering commitment. You need to know I will never change my mind. That my love for you is infinite and unending. So …" Eleni pulled the velvet box containing her parents' rings from the side pocket of her wrap dress and got down on one knee before him. "Nikko Konstantinos Varvos, you are my everything. I came back to this island for you—here, where you were always my closest friend, and where we fell in love and made love. I promise to give you all of me, heart and soul, the way you've given me all of you. You come first, without doubt or hesitation, before everything else. You are and have always been my one and only true love. Will you—"

"Marry you?" Nikko asked, cutting her off. In one fluid motion, he lifted her off her feet, Eleni squealing in surprise. With a bright grin, Nikko drew her close until they were nose to nose, their lips a breath away. "I will marry you," he whispered huskily. "You will marry me. Yes!" he shouted for anyone within earshot to hear. "A thousand times, yes!" He kissed her with all the pent-up passion he'd been holding back for far too long. When he broke the kiss, Nikko took the ring box from Eleni's hand. He removed the emerald-cut diamond engagement ring and slipped it onto her finger.

He kissed her again before resting his forehead against hers. "I've waited so long for this," he breathed. "I gave up all hope that it would ever come true."

Too choked up to form words, she silently mouthed, "I love you." Eleni's relief was palpable. She, too, had thought it was too late for them and that he would never forgive her. But love prevailed through distance, sorrow, and a string of misunderstandings. If Eleni had the power to stop time, she'd pause the clock indefinitely to revel in this beautiful moment. But this was just the beginning of a lifetime of unforgettable moments.

"We're getting married!" Nikko announced to the heavens, his eyes sparkling with joy.

"We're getting married!" Eleni beamed.

Nikko set her down and took her by the hand. "So let's go! I'll call the priest and tell him we're on our way."

Eleni laughed. "What's the rush? I'm not going to change my mind. We don't have to lock this down now," she joked. "Besides, I think we need to tell your family first."

"Sure, let's tell the family what they already knew years ago." Nikko rolled his eyes, though they twinkled with amusement.

Eleni giggled. "Well, not only will we hear a resounding 'We told you so,' but your *mamá* and *yiayiá* will start planning the wedding before we even get the words out."

"And that's fine by me as long as the arrangements don't take longer than a week."

Eleni poked him playfully in the chest. "I was joking before, but you really want to lock this down right away, don't you?"

"I do. Don't you?"

Eleni nodded. "We've wasted enough time."

"Speaking of wasted time," Nikko said, closing in on her with one of his smoldering looks.

"And just what did you have in mind?" Eleni asked, narrowing her eyes. The stiff bulge pressed against her stomach told her all she needed, but a little fun was in order.

"Don't you think we need to seal the deal?" Nikko whispered while trailing kisses down her neck.

"Isn't that what the engagement ring is for?" Eleni teased.

"I suppose we can wait," Nikko relented. "If you don't want this." He took her hand and cupped it over his erection. "Or this," Nikko added, reaching under her skirt to dip his fingers into her panties.

"I want it," Eleni said, barely able to choke the words out.

Nikko took her hand, guiding her briskly back to the building he had come from. Eleni could hardly keep up with his frantic pace.

"Missed you so much," Nikko growled as soon as they were inside, tugging the ties on her wrap dress to expose Eleni's nude lace panty and matching bra.

Eleni felt the heat of his lustful stare, and that response permitted her to wantonly unzip his pants. Nikko stepped out of them while simultaneously tearing the sheer bottom garment from her body. He backed Eleni up against the wall, entering her with a deep, carnal thrust. He wasn't gentle or apologetic. Nikko took what he wanted— what he craved. And Eleni hungered for everything he gave, meeting him stroke for delicious stroke as he drove into her, filling her completely. She had missed the intimate connection between them that only sex could satisfy. Muffling his groans in the crook of Eleni's neck, Nikko rhythmically pulsed deep inside her. His orgasm ignited hers like a tidal wave crashing to shore in the most exquisite bliss.

Wedged between the wall and Nikko, Eleni was sated and boneless. She rested her head against his chest and sighed. If he let her go, she'd fall like a rag doll to the floor. "Was that makeup sex or engagement sex?" Eleni panted.

"Whatever you want it to be. You choose, the other will come next." Nikko grinned.

"Is that so?" Eleni smirked.

"We have years to make up for," Nikko said, helping Eleni adjust her dress. Her panties were now but a shredded scrap of discarded fabric on the floor.

"That sounds like a long overdue dream come true." Eleni ran her fingers through her mussed hair. "Do I look presentable enough to tell your family our news?"

"Sure, once you comb your hair and fix the mascara smudges under your eyes," Nikko chuckled.

"I must look a sight," Eleni complained.

Nikko pulled her in for a kiss. "You're breathtaking. You look like the man who loves you was just buried deep inside you."

"When did you become so irreverent?" Eleni playfully slapped his arm. "But never stop." She reached up and brushed her lips over his. "I'll be eternally happy if you still say those things to me forty years from now."

"I can promise it will be for even longer." Nikko took her by the hand. "Come on, let's head to the house. Knowing them, our news won't be much of a surprise," Nikko said, shaking his head.

"Just for the record, when we tell the family, I want it clarified that, in no uncertain terms, this was completely and solely our idea and had nothing to do with their machinations."

"Absolutely, my gorgeous Brooklyn girl," Nikko agreed.

"I'm not from Brooklyn," Eleni reminded him, shaking her head with mock annoyance.

"I know." Nikko kissed the tip of her nose. "You're one hundred percent Kefalonian now, exactly as it should be."

"I have found the one whom my soul loves." Song of Solomon 3:4

EPILOGUE

Eleni

Six months later

Eleni stood dreamily in front of the cheval mirror while Maria and *Yiayiá* Thalia fastened the dozens of satin buttons running down the length of her wedding dress.

"*Ftou sou, ftou sou,*" Thalia sounded out, pretending to spit—a gesture intended to keep evil away whenever a compliment was offered or hinted at. Children and brides were the usual recipients of the superstition, and today, Eleni was getting *ftou soued* left and right.

"I never saw a more beautiful bride," Maria declared joyfully. "My Nikko is a lucky man."

"It's me who is fortunate to have all of you in my life," Eleni said. She looked over to Angela, who approached with her veil. "It means the world to me that you're here," Eleni told her friend.

"Where else would I be?" Angela took her by the hand. "Now, sit so I can fasten this to your head correctly."

The hip-length veil was attached by a delicate seed pearl head-band with matching adornments scattered over the tulle. It had been Maria's, and Eleni was touched she had offered it to her.

Suddenly, a rush of young women filled the room. Eleni had made some good friends over the last several months, along with the many

263

Varvos cousins who wanted to be included in the wedding party. This brought the number of bridesmaids to nearly a dozen. One over-enthusiastic young woman parted the cloud of women dressed in white satin and tulle and handed Eleni a pair of wedding shoes and a marker.

"What is this for, Athena?" Eleni was puzzled.

"You write the names of every eligible bridesmaid on the bottom of your shoes," she explained eagerly. "Whichever name has not worn off by the end of the reception will be the next to marry."

"Oh! In America, we toss the bouquet to find that out," Eleni said as she began to write on the soles of the proffered shoes.

"One last check of hair and makeup, and I think we can head out," Angela suggested.

"The men are already on their way," Maria said. "It's tradition to make the groom wait for just a little while."

"I'm ready," Eleni said excitedly. "Lead the way, *Yiayiá* Thalia."

Soon, they were strolling down a path to the church. Thalia and Maria began to sing cheerful wedding folk songs, and the brides-maids immediately joined in.

"What are they singing?" Angela whispered to Eleni.

"Traditional songs of love and weddings," she explained.

Angela looked back. "Do you realize there's a trail of women following behind?"

Turning, Eleni laughed. "I guess they weren't joking. *Yiayiá* Thalia and Maria told me this would happen. They are all guests and maybe a few curious onlookers."

When they arrived at the church, she found Nikko and Yanni standing outside the doors with the priest and an army of men surrounding them. Beaming, Nikko stepped away from the crowd and over to Eleni. Smiling broadly, he presented her with a beau-tiful bouquet of fragrant gardenia, peonies, and lilies of the valley, garnished with a spray of olive leaves.

Eleni gazed at Nikko with so much love that she thought her heart would burst. It took everything she had not to lean in and kiss him. Instead, she laced her fingers with his as they walked hand in hand to the priest, who recited a betrothal prayer. With his golden Bible in hand, the priest blessed the union, then Eleni and Nikko went into the church, the masses following behind with delighted anticipation.

For the next forty-five minutes, Eleni stood beside Nikko, occasionally wiping back joyful tears as the *stefana* were exchanged over their heads, the rings placed on their fingers, and most especially when they circled during the Dance of Isaiah. Eleni and Nikko walked together, united by the ribbons binding the *stefana* on their heads; she took in what this meaningful, symbolic ritual meant. This was their first steps as husband and wife—the first of thousands together for a lifetime. Eleni grew misty-eyed, thinking back to how, not so long ago, she had stood in this very church, watching another couple perform this ritual and secretly wishing she and Nikko would be standing in their place someday. It had been up to her to take the leap—to be brave enough to fight her fears and the ghosts that haunted her. Eleni overcame them in the name of love, and she felt her family's presence now, but not in the form of sorrow, which had held her back for so many years. They were here in spirit, their souls wrapping her in a comforting embrace. Eleni was finally at peace. She was happy.

The reception was held at the vineyard. Maria and Thalia had decorated each corner of the patio with potted white hydrangea trees. Blush peonies in low-sitting vases were placed at the center of each table, and floral garlands were strung high above along the perimeter, illuminated by twinkling fairy lights.

The festivities continued late into the night. Over two hundred guests attended, including relatives, family friends, neighboring vineyard proprietors, and the many shop owners who had become friends with Eleni and the Varvos family.

Angela tapped Eleni on her shoulder. "Let me check the bottom of those shoes. You've been on that dancefloor all night. If my name has worn off, I'm blaming you for losing my chance at love." She gave Eleni the stink eye before bursting out into laughter.

"You can joke about it, but why do I have a feeling you're dead serious?" Eleni asked. Her friend would have no problem finding a suitor tonight if that's what she wanted. With her golden-bronze skin, topaz eyes, and an enviable, shapely figure, single men had clamored around Angela all evening.

"Have you met my cousin, Demos," Nikko asked. "He's right over there." He pointed to the bar set up off to the side of the tasting room entrance. "He hasn't stopped staring at you all day. Should I introduce you?"

"That's another cousin? What do they put in the wine here?" Angela asked, shamelessly ogling the man.

Nikko laughed. "Follow me," he said, escorting Eleni and Angela toward the man. "Did I happen to mention he just accepted a position with a major financial institution in New York City?"

"No, you did not!" Angela gave Nikko a playful slap on his arm.

"Four glasses of Robola, please," Nikko asked the bartender as they approached.

"Right away." He nodded, opening a new bottle.

"Demos!" Nikko called over the crowd, beckoning his cousin over. "I want to introduce you to Angela, Eleni's closest friend. She lives in New York City."

Demos took Angela's hand in his. "It's a pleasure. How lucky it is for me to meet you. I happen to be moving there next month."

Eleni pressed her lips together to suppress a smile. Angela was flustered. And that didn't happen to her often. Before her friend could respond, the bartender slid four glasses across the bar.

"A toast to long marriages and new possibilities," Nikko said as he handed each of them a goblet. "*Yamas.*"

"*Yamas,*" they toasted, clinking glasses. Eleni looked back and forth between Angela and Demos. They hadn't taken their eyes off each other. "My *pappou* often said there was magic in each glass of Robola." Eleni nudged Nikko. "And with that thought, we'll leave the two of you to get acquainted."

But before Eleni walked away, she tapped Angela on the shoulder, picking up her foot to reveal the sole of her shoe. Winking, she smiled. Angela's name was the only one still completely visible.

"Is it our turn to play matchmaker?" Eleni asked Nikko with a sly smile as soon as they were out of earshot.

"We only introduced them. The rest is up to them," Nikko conceded. "You are the only one I want to focus on at the moment." He kissed her.

"Only at the moment?" she teased.

"This one and every single one after from here on in."

Eleni didn't want the night to end, but she had forever with Nikko. And she understood better than anyone how each day was a precious gift never to be taken for granted.

The End.

GLOSSARY OF GREEK WORDS
AND EXPRESSIONS

Agori mou - My boy.

Babá – Dad

Dolmathes - Grape leaves stuffed with rice or rice and meat.

Éla – Come

Éla mesa - Come inside.

Éla, pethí mou - Come, my child.

Elenitsa mou - adding an 'itsa' to the end of a name is a term of endearment. Adding the mou strengthens the emotion.

Ellinítha - a Greek woman

Erhomaí - I'm coming

Fíle mou - My friend.

Frappé - A Greek foam-covered iced coffee drink made from Nescafé instant coffee.

Ftou sou, ftou, sou - A superstitious gesture of pretending to spit on the devil to keep him away. This is often done when giving a compliment so as not to jinx it.

Galaktoboureko - A custard-based dessert made with milk, eggs, and semolina set in between layers of phyllo dough and ladled with orange-infused simple syrup.

Gamísou - Fuck off

Glyki mou - My sweet. A term of endearment.

Hárika - Pleased to meet you; pleasure to meet you.

Horta - Wild greens, usually dandelion.

Kafé - coffee

Katse - Sit

Koukla / kouklitsa - Doll; little doll. A term of endearment.

Yamas - a shorter version of stin ygía mas - to our health. Used when toasting.

Yiayiá - Grandmother

Kalamaria - Squid; calamari.

Kalimera - Good morning

Kali mera - Good day

Kalispera - Good evening

Kaló taxithí - Good trip; bon voyage.

Káva - Cellar

Koutali - Spoon, but in the context used in this story it means wooden spoon.

Koumbari - The couple sponsoring the bride and groom during the ceremony. Similar to a best man and maid of honor but with more religious context. They exchange the crowns on the couple's heads in a symbolic ritual and take the Walk of Isaiah with them. Koumbaro is the male. Koumbara is the female.

Mamá - Mom. Mána is also used for mom or mother.

Mandoles - The famous sweet treat of Kefalonia. Red sugar-coated caramelized almonds.

Manoula mou - A general term of endearment though in literal terms it means my mother.

Matí - the evil eye

Mavrodaphne - A sweet red dessert wine made primarily in Kefalonia and on the mainland in Patras.

Melitzanosalata - A traditional eggplant dip.

Mesimera - the literal translation is midday, but it's the time of day when everything shuts down for a few hours and quiet is requested. Also known as a siesta.

Meze / mezethes - Appetizer / appetizers. Small plates of food similar in concept to tapas. Often mezethes are set out on a platter with a variety of offerings.

Mou - My (added after a person's name it becomes a term of endearment).

Ne - Yes

Païdákia - Lamb chops

Paraklasis - Supplication service for the Holy mother, or any other saint, particularly on their feast day.

Pappou - Grandfather

Pethí mou - My child.

Po, po, po - An exclamation Greeks use regularly in many contexts.

Proxenió - Arranged marriage.

Psémata - lies

Robola - White grape variety grown only on the Ionian island of Kefalonia.

Skorthalia - Traditional Greek garlic dip or puree made with potatoes or bread as the base.

Stefana - Greek wedding crowns/wreaths, symbolizing unity and the blessing the couple receive from the Holy Trinity. They are crowned king and queen of their home, which they will govern with love and faith.

Stin ygía mas - To our health. Used as a toast.

Stremmata - A unit of land measurement. One stremmata is 1,000 square meters which equals a quarter of an acre.

Strígla - a witch or a vixen

Taramosalata - Traditional Greek fish roe dip

Tha fas xýlo - "I will hit you." It's one of those saying though where the literal translation makes no sense. It literally means you'll eat wood.

Vre, Ynaíka - Vre is a word of exasperation. Ynaíka means woman.

Zeibekiko - A dance of the soul, of passion, and a way of expressing the joys and heartaches of life. It's a solo improvisational dance that in the past was only performed by men.

Turn the page for an excerpt from Effie Kammenou's novella,

Don't Want to Leave her Now.

DON'T WANT TO LEAVE HER NOW

By Effie Kammenou

PROLOGUE

Christmas Eve 1956

Plato believed humans were originally created with four arms, four legs, and one head with two faces. Zeus, feeling threatened by these beings, split the body in half. Feeling as if a vital part of themselves was missing, the humans searched for their other half. And so, this is how the belief came to be, in all its romanticized fantasy, that one soul could recognize another on a transcendental level. That in the form of an undeniable and inevitable connection, whether for a lifetime or merely a few hours, the lure of the soulmate held great power in the universe.

It was a frigid evening in late December, Christmas Eve to be exact, and New York City sparkled with holiday spirit. From the ornate store windows and the towering lit tree at Rockefeller Center to the gently falling snow and the warm, comforting smell of chestnuts roasting on street corners, Manhattan seemed as if it had been created by movie magic.

Earlier that afternoon, two pregnant women had rushed to the same hospital, both equally advanced in their labor. Questions were fired at them by triage staff, identification tags clasped onto their wrists, and they were both wheeled down to the Labor and Delivery Unit simultaneously. As they waited for the double doors to the unit to swing open, the women made eye contact, one stoically attempting a smile, the other expressing her fear reflected only by the anxious look in her eyes. From this momentary unspoken communication, a bond had instantly been formed between the two women.

Several hours later, two infants were wheeled into the nursery and laid side by side in clear bassinets—a girl, given the name Noelle, and a boy who was yet to be named.

Twelve babies filled the newborn nursery in total, yet the staff couldn't help but take special notice of Noelle and the boy beside her. There was something unexplainably exceptional about them. Although only a few hours old, the nurses could swear they were reaching for each other, turning in the other's direction, or trying to make eye contact. If they'd let their imaginations run wild, they would have believed the two had an unspoken language, a connection, an energy between them.

"Impossible," Nurse Rosa dismissed, waving off the idea as ridiculous. Yet she had witnessed some unlikely behavior between them herself. If she hadn't seen it with her own eyes, she wouldn't have believed the look of recognition when the newborns' eyes connected through the Lucite crib, though it was a given fact their sight wasn't fully developed at this stage.

During her shift, Rosa usually walked around the room, checking each child individually. There was always a child to calm, rock, diaper, or feed. It was on one of these shifts that the strangest thing happened. For a good solid hour, the room had remained unusually quiet. The silence was eerie, and it concerned her. It wasn't likely that not one of the twelve babies was stirring or fussing.

Suddenly, Rosa was jolted from her thoughts when a scream ripping from Noelle broke the hush. The nurse immediately ran to her, lifting her from the crib to soothe her. When the baby had calmed, Rosa set her down, but Noelle kept, almost frantically, attempting to roll toward the edge of her bassinet. Rosa looked at the boy in the next bassinet as though Noelle had compelled her to. As he seemed to prefer, the child had pushed his way to the edge of his mattress to face Noelle. With one last glance in her direction, the infant closed his eyes, peacefully taking his last breath.

Some have theorized that everyone has a soulmate. Destiny determines how, when, and if these two souls unite. But what if your soulmate lives at the opposite end of the earth? Or was born in a different era? Or what if your soulmate never had the opportunity to live at all?

CHAPTER 1

Cape Cod

Summer 1971

Every year since she could remember, Noelle's parents had loaded up the car with their luggage, along with plenty of snacks and travel games to keep her two younger brothers entertained for the seven-hour drive to Provincetown, Cape Cod.

Noelle occupied herself by reading, listening to the music on the car radio, or daydreaming as she stared out the window. At fifteen, her interests were pretty much the same as most girls her age—fashion, makeup, and boys. But some girls made all of that work in their favor, and others, like herself, hadn't quite figured it out yet.

"How long until we get there?" Kevin, Noelle's ten-year-old brother, asked.

"Don't ask me again," their father snapped.

These vacations were supposed to be fun, but the boys would always fight in the car over who touched who, before their mother would turn up the music to drown them out, and their father would shout and threaten to throw everyone out of the car.

Noelle wished they were on their way to Disneyland like a few of her friends. Or Italy, where her best friend, Nina, was headed to visit family. But year after year, they returned to the same place—the same hotel, the same restaurants. True, it was all they could afford, but it was also the place her mother called 'her little corner of heaven.'

Dan and Marcia Henning were a typical middle-class couple. They had three children, two cars, and one paycheck between them. To the outside world, they seemed to have an ideal marriage. The reality hidden behind the suburban illusion was somewhat problematic, though. Dan was conservative, whereas Marcia was a free spirit. Marcia, who was socially conscious, was also nurturing and friendly. Dan was a loner; he laid down the law in his household and preferred to keep his circle of friends to a bare minimum.

The Doors' 'People Are Strange' came on the radio. The DJ had been looping Morrison's songs continually since his untimely death only a few weeks ago. It was a song Noelle related to when she was in a certain mood, during those times when she'd quietly observe strangers as they went about their lives, appearing to be, in her estimation, so confident of where they fit into the world.

"Okay, kids," Dan said. "Chop, chop! Change your clothes, and we'll head out to grab a bite to eat."

They had arrived at the hotel not thirty minutes before and her father was already barking orders like a pissed-off drill sergeant. Noelle changed into a pair of dark rose hip-hugger bell bottoms. The black and pink floral peasant top was cropped short enough to show some belly and incite some reprimands from her father. Her large-brimmed floppy hat and pewter peace sign dangling from a black leather choker completed her ensemble.

Noelle wanted to blend in with the eclectic bohemian crowd of P-town—the hippies, the artisans, and the everyday townspeople who seemed to live life on their own terms.

Less than an hour later, they were at their favorite restaurant, Plain & Fancy, on Commercial Street, pulling lobster meat from its tails and dipping it in melted butter.

"I'm spending tomorrow afternoon with Kara at her studio," Marcia told Dan. "Take the kids to Macaroni Beach. Kevin wants to take surfing lessons. Brian might want to try it too once he sees his brother doing it."

Kara was one of the main reasons her mother insisted on visiting the Cape each year. Kara and Marcia had been friends for as long as Noelle could remember. They had much in common; both were interested in art, studying, and creating. The difference between them was that Kara was fully immersed in the art world, whereas her mother only dreamed of it. Noelle often caught a look of sadness or longing in her mother's eyes that she could only speculate as regret.

"I'll come with you, Mom, if that's okay," Noelle said. "I can walk around town while you're at the studio."

"You can always bring your sketchpad and draw," her mother suggested. "Or Kara can set you up with an easel and some paints."

"Maybe tomorrow. Today, I'd rather browse the shops."

* * *

The beaches of Provincetown didn't hold the appeal for Noelle as they did for her brothers. They could splash in the water all day, play Frisbee, and hunt for sea creatures. Her father enjoyed the museums and taking long, peaceful bike rides. Noelle, however, was drawn to Commercial Street, which, it could be said, was the heart of the town. There was a vibrant energy flowing here that didn't exist anywhere else. At least not anywhere she had been. And certainly not in her own very provincial town back on Long Island.

Commercial Street was lined with old buildings painted in bright colors, some splattered with psychedelic patterns. Noelle passed on the homemade taffy shop, opting for the ice cream parlor instead. She rummaged through her macramé bag and found two quarters to pay the girl behind the counter. Licking the pistachio scoop from the bottom to avoid dripping, she continued down the street, looking in a boutique window.

She wondered how she would look in the outfit on the mannequin staring back at her. The micro-mini skirt would show off a lot of skin, but her gangly body and stick-thin legs wouldn't do the garment any justice. Sighing, she walked away.

"Tie-dye halter tops!" a woman shouted. "Only five dollars."

Noelle stopped to look at the rack of multi-colored garments. As she rifled through each one, deciding on a color, the saleswoman addressed her. "Try this one on," she said. "The violet hues mixed with the sage green would look beautiful on you."

"Thanks," Noelle said, taking the item from her. "I like what you're wearing, too."

The middle-aged woman looked entrancing in a gold and orange tie-dyed maxi dress, belted at the waist by a burgundy sash. Each of her arms was adorned with what had to be at least twenty bangles, and gold feathers hung from her ears. Her wild, wavy hair framing her cosmetic-free face reminded Noelle of Carol King.

The next shop she stopped in was called Spiritual Elements. A neon sign flashed 'Palm Readings,' catching her eye. Inside, one wall was dedicated strictly to angels. Statues, plaques, paintings, and angel tarot cards filled the shelves, while on the other side, crystals, and gems of all colors and sizes, each with a special meaning or power, crowded the stands. In one corner, an odd-looking machine stood. "Put your feet on the markers, and for one dollar, you can have your aura read," a self-proclaimed psychic wearing a loose-fitting floor-length tunic explained.

Noelle did as the woman told her. At once, lights flashed and swirled like strobe lights at a dance club. The woman ripped a paper report that had been printed out from the bottom of the machine.

"Pink interspersed with gray," the psychic read. She took Noelle's hands in hers and closed her eyes. After a moment, she snapped them open, startling Noelle. "You are connected to the spiritual world. You have a healthy sense of balance between the important and the frivolous. But ..." she said, waving a finger in warning, "you have anxiety—worry and melancholy—that must be expelled." Closing her eyes again, she lifted her hands, her palms facing upward as if calling to a deity. "Trust in the universe," she said solemnly. "That's all I can say for now."

Noelle didn't take much stock in what the woman had told her. It was probably an act she used on every customer, but she took the paper from the woman, thanking her politely as she left. But a heaviness settled in her chest, accompanied by a nagging despondency that manifested itself within her. It wasn't an unfamiliar feeling, and it happened at the most random of times. Noelle supposed that, in this case, the psychic's words had triggered the mood. As she watched couples walking by, parents as they wheeled their babies in strollers, and friends sharing a meal at the outdoor cafés, Noelle never felt so alone.

Her attention was drawn across the street to an unremarkable, white building, which stood out merely for its lack of color amongst the surrounding shops. It was plain compared to the other mural-decorated storefronts, but something about the place piqued Noelle's curiosity. She crossed the street and hopped up its four creaky wooden steps. A sign above the entrance was scrawled with the name Heaven's Gate.

Walking inside, she noticed a rack with large-brimmed hats, sunglasses, and beach cover-ups on the left. To the right, a display of leather wallets and belts was set out on a distressed table. Noelle roamed around, stopping to lift a candle to her nose and breathe in the sweet vanilla aroma. Corked test tube perfume samples were suspended in the holes of a chicken wire grid, the whole display resembling a lab experiment. One by one, Noelle pulled the cork off to sample the scents. Patchouli, musk, sandalwood, and lavender invaded her senses. Fanned in a bouquet, aromatic sticks stood in a mason jar next to fragrant cone-shaped incense wrapped in decorative paper.

Hidden in the back of the store was paraphernalia used for smoking marijuana and hash—pipes and roach clips, rolling paper, and bongs. Noelle's father would surely kill her if he spotted her studying the contents of the glass showcase.

The aroma from the burning incense gave the place a comforting vibe. Music played in the background—loud enough to sing along with the words but not so ear-splitting that you couldn't ask the clerk a question without shouting.

Near the cash register was a compartmentalized wooden box showcasing an array of silver rings. Noelle occupied herself by trying on each one. Unconsciously, she hummed to Gordon Lightfoot's 'If You Could Read My Mind.'

Sensing she was being watched, she turned and noticed a man looking at her as though her every movement was of earth-shattering interest to him. He smiled and averted his eyes away from her, continuing to fold the graphic t-shirts he was straightening on a shelf.

Inspired by the trendy woman who had sold her the halter top, Noelle tried on various bangles. She took a second look at the rings by the register when 'Something' by the Beatles filled the room. It was her favorite of all their songs, and she couldn't help but smile. The man who'd stared at her was now behind the counter ringing up a customer's purchase.

"I see you like it, too," the man behind the counter said.

Noelle looked up. *Was he speaking to her?* "The ring?"

He shook his head. "No, the song. I think it's the most beautiful song ever written."

"Are you a Beatles fan?" she asked.

"Isn't everyone? But it's the words of this song that speak to me. I'm a fan of love," he answered. "The peace, beauty and harmony of it." He pointed to a copper plaque overhead. Hammered into the metal were three symbols: a heart-shaped from a pair of angel wings, a dove, and a star dangling from the moon.

"Did you make that?"

"I did. Love in all its forms is precious. But I can't think of anything more meaningful than being loved as deeply as this song conveys."

Noelle had never been spoken to by anyone in this manner. He shared his opinion and engaged her in conversation as if she were a casual friend, not a child or a girl at least ten years his junior.

"Which one do you like best?" he asked.

"Which what? Song?"

"No, which ring. Can't decide?"

"They're all so pretty," Noelle said.

He leaned over the counter. "I'm Raphael, by the way," he said, extending his hand to her.

"Noelle," she breathed, speechless as Raphael clasped her hand in his. An energy emanated from him that couldn't be explained. She found warmth and comfort in his touch and a power that mesmerized her. A large silver and turquoise ring sat on his third finger, similar in design to the buckle on his belt.

"That's a beautiful name."

His sun-kissed face was lit up by a genuine smile that reached his sky-blue eyes. He was more than handsome. She had never met anyone so beautiful. Yes, he was beautiful, she decided; she could almost envision rays of light radiating from him.

Noelle shook herself from her overactive imagination. "Thank you. I was born on Christmas."

"I know," he said. Swiftly raising a hand to clarify when her eyes flew to his in surprise, he explained, "I just assumed since most girls named Noelle were born on that day."

Raphael rummaged through the ring box. Finally, he chose one and held it up to her. "Try this one," he suggested. "It doesn't look like much, but I think it's special."

She took the ring from him and slipped it on her finger. "I like the design. Does it represent something?"

"It's a puzzle ring," he told her, gliding it off her finger. "Let me show you."

Noelle's eyes widened as he pulled apart the five silver wires that held the ring together. Raphael held one thin band between his thumb and forefinger while the rest dangled below.

"That is so cool!" Noelle exclaimed.

"I'll bet you are trying to solve your own puzzles and mysteries," Raphael said. He began winding the pieces back together as he spoke. "Each one of these bands is imperfect, but together, they fit. It's a lot like life, don't you think?"

His voice was deep but melodic. A sense of calm washed over her as she listened to him. A beam of sunshine streamed in through the front window. Hints of golden highlights reflected off Raphael's thick, dark hair. There was an ethereal and mystical quality about him that entranced her. Chills ran down Noelle's spine, realizing this exchange, this tiny blip in time, would stay with her forever.

"I want the ring," she said. "If you could just show me one more time how to put it together, I'd be happy."

Raphael smiled. "I'll even give you a diagram in case you forget." He pulled a small ring box out from under the counter.

"I don't need that," Noelle said. "I'll wear it now."

"Good decision. Better yet, you should always wear it as a reminder that even when we think we have our lives figured out, there are still pieces of the puzzle to work out."

"I will," she said. "Wear it, that is."

After she paid him and he handed her a few cents change and her receipt, Noelle thanked him.

"It was a pleasure to meet you," Raphael said.

As Noelle exited the store, she turned and glanced at Raphael one last time. A peaceful feeling washed over her as he smiled back at her, nodding his encouragement. Raphael made an impression on her, and she was sure he was someone she would never forget.

CHAPTER 2

"Dan, lighten up! We're on vacation," Noelle heard her mother complain.

Marcia and Dan were standing on the small patio area beyond the sliding glass doors of their motel room. The door was cracked open, and from what Noelle could make out, her mother wanted to go out that evening, but her father wanted no part of it.

"It's not my scene," Dan said. "You know what this town is like at night."

"I do. It's fun," her mother said. "Something you've forgotten to have."

"Watching men perform in drag is not my idea of a good time," Dan groused.

"It would be nice if you at least gave it a chance. We could go to a comedy show instead," she suggested.

"The last time we did that, I was disgusted. I'm surprised the place wasn't raided."

"When did you lose your sense of humor?" Marcia asked. "Listen, Noelle is perfectly capable of caring for the boys for a few hours. Let's stay for a drink and see how the night goes."

"Whatever," he said, sighing heavily.

Surprisingly, the boys fell asleep watching TV in bed shortly after her parents had left. Noelle pulled out her sketchpad and began to draw.

Two hours and three sketches later, she examined her artwork.

Raphael had been on her mind for the remainder of the day. With deliberate strokes of gray charcoal, she had captured his essence: the gentleness of his expressive eyes, the lush waves of his hair as it grazed his shoulders, and his large hands flooding warmth into hers as he held them. It was an image of a modern-day god, recreated from her perception of him through the careful strokes of a pencil.

Noelle and her mother headed to Kara's art studio the next day. The boys were going for a bike ride and later would climb the Pilgrim Monument with their father. A sense of foreboding nagged at her. Day by day, she could feel her family splintering. The vacation wasn't bringing them together. If anything, it only accentuated how truly fractured her home life had become.

"What's wrong, Mom?" Noelle asked. Her mother had been quiet for the entire walk.

"Oh, Noelle." Marcia's tone held sadness. "You're grown enough to see and understand what your brothers can't."

"Your fights with Dad?" she asked. "The boys hear them, too."

Marcia spotted a bench by the curb and motioned for Noelle to follow her.

They both sat, and Marcia tweaked Noelle's chin. "But you're old enough to understand that relationships are complicated." She rubbed her forehead before she continued. "Your father is a good man. I'm just not sure he's good for me. One minute I'm convinced he's a saint, and the next, a son of a bitch."

Noelle wasn't sure where her mother was going with this, but she was certain she didn't want to hear more.

"When I married your father, I didn't think I would have to give up my dreams. I wanted to sculpt, work in an art gallery, and one day own one—or at least manage one. Once I had you, he insisted I stay home and give up any thoughts of returning to work. Later, your brothers came along, and my idea of pursuing those dreams was shattered."

"Do you resent Dad? And me?"

"Not you! Never you," Marcia assured her. "You are my greatest work of art. But your father can be overbearing. Sometimes I feel so trapped that I can't breathe."

"The son of a bitch moments," Noelle murmured, more to herself.

"Yes," she validated. Vacationing here year after year is his concession to me—my one week of artistic freedom. And although he and I never speak of it, he knows that my friendship with Kara is a complication."

"He doesn't like her much, does he?"

"No, but he lets me get my time with her 'out of my system,' as he states."

Her mother's cryptic words were laced with resentment, anxiety, and even a bit of guilt. Noelle rubbed a finger over the wires forming the design of her new ring. One more puzzle to unearth, she thought.

Kara greeted Noelle and Marcia as soon as they stepped into the studio. A weekly pottery class she instructed had just been let out, and the students were still gathering their belongings. Kara kissed Noelle on the cheek, but when she embraced her mother, she noticed they lingered a little longer than necessary.

"Kara," Marcia said, "I want you to look at Noelle's drawings."

Kara took Noelle's sketchpad and assessed the pages she'd been working on the night before. "These are exceptional, Noelle." She turned the pages between three drawings and asked, "Who's the model?"

"His name is Raphael," Noelle said. "I met him at Heaven's Gate, around the corner. Do you know him?"

"No," she dragged out. "And I know almost everyone. At least I thought I did."

'All You Need Is Love' serenaded Noelle through the studio speakers. "If you had met him, you'd remember," Noelle said. "He's not someone easily forgotten."

"Someone has a crush." Kara smiled.

"It's not like that. He's special in a way I can't explain," Noelle said.

"Ah, you might have a karmic affinity, a connection from a past life," Kara said.

"I'm not sure I believe in all of that."

"Don't be in a rush to rule out what you don't understand," her mother said. "Kara and I knew each other …before."

They looked at one another in a way Noelle had never noticed before. She felt a flush come over her face. Sweat beads formed on her neck, and she felt lightheaded, as though she would pass out.

"We had a past life regression session to verify it," Kara said.

When had her mother lost her mind? "Okay," was all Noelle could think to say. "I need to go. I promised to meet Dad by the Pilgrim Monument."

Noelle shot out of the studio as though a fire alarm had sounded an evacuation. Briskly, she strode away, her sketchpad tucked under her arm. Noelle didn't stop until she turned the corner by an outdoor picnic table on a café deck. Slamming her drawing pad down, she sat, her mind racing with speculation. Droplets of tears fell from her eyes, landing on her ring finger. As she wiped away the salty liquid from the silver band, she felt a hand resting on her shoulder. Turning, she was met by a pair of compassionate blue eyes that only God, in all his glory, could create.

"Raphael?" Noelle questioned, confused to see him standing before her.

"What's troubling you?" he asked.

"How did you know to find me here?" Noelle stared at him, tall and imposing in his bell-bottomed jeans and a tight-fitting black t-shirt that read 'Let It Be.'

He sat down beside her. "I was taking a walk. It was happenstance. Fate, if you will."

She laughed humorlessly. "What is it today with everyone talking of fate and karma?"

"You don't believe in it?"

"I'm not sure what I believe anymore," Noelle said.

Raphael took her hand, rubbing his finger over the ring she wore. "Remember what I told you about the ring?" he asked.

Noelle nodded, looking up at him through unshed tears.

"You've reached an age where everything changes around you. Your body, your emotions. You're taking the next step into adulthood—probably considering what you want to do with your life. Right?"

She nodded her head in agreement.

"On top of it all, there will be changes you can't control, decisions others will make, and choices that will affect your life. All these components make up the puzzle I spoke of yesterday."

"What are you trying to say?"

"That it's up to you to map out your life with the circumstances you've been given. You can choose to crumble or you can choose to survive." He lifted her chin with his finger, forcing her to meet his gaze. "You need to see your beauty. I don't think you do. Especially what's on the inside. What's in here." He stabbed at his chest. "When you see that, you'll reach your full potential, regardless of any misfortune that comes your way."

"Are you a prophet? I feel like I'm being warned of an impending disaster."

"I thought you didn't believe in such things." He grinned. "No, just think of it as a little advice from someone older and wiser."

He reached for the drawing pad, but Noelle tightened her grip.

"Please don't," she said.

"I can't see your work?" he asked. "Art is to be shared, not hidden."

"It's embarrassing."

"Never be embarrassed by what you've created from your mind and talents." He dislodged the pad from her grip and flipped to the first page. It was a scene of ocean waves crashing to the shore and two boys kicking their feet by the water's edge. Raphael turned page after page, examining each sketch closely. In between his examination, encouraging words of praise fell from his lips. But he was stunned into silence when the image of himself stared back at him.

Noelle covered her face. "I told you."

He peeled her hands from her eyes and looked at her sternly for the first time. "This is nothing to be ashamed of," he said. "I am flattered that this is the way you see me. I'm honored that you would think of drawing me."

Noelle ripped the portrait from the pad and handed it to him. "I want you to have it then. I have two others." She turned the page over. "See? But this is my favorite. You should keep it."

Raphael rose from his seat. "Thank you. I'll treasure it," he said. "I have to get back now." He looked at her as if he was trying to memorize her face. "I hope we meet again one day. But if not, I want you to know that no matter what happens, you are loved. You're being watched over."

A gust of wind nearly snatched the drawing from his hand. "I have to go."

As Noelle waved goodbye, an unfamiliar melancholy settled over her. Wondering what he meant by saying she was watched over, she turned in his direction to call him one last time, but he was nowhere in sight. Raphael had vanished.

To continue reading *Don't Want To Leave Her Now* for free, sign

up for my newsletter through the link or QR code below.

https://www.subscribepage.com/effiekammenoubooks

OTHER BOOKS BY EFFIE KAMMENOU

The Meraki Series:
Love is What You Bake of it
Love by Design
Love is Worth Fighting for

The Gift Saga Trilogy:
Evanthia's Gift
Waiting for Aegina
Chasing Petalouthes

The Magic of Robola

If you enjoyed *The Magic of Robola,* please consider leaving a review on Amazon and Goodreads.

Feel free to connect with Effie Kammenou on social media

Website - www.effiekammenou.com
X - @EffieKammenou
TikTok - www.tiktok.com/@effieeverafter
Facebook - www.facebook.com/EffieKammenou/
Instagram - www.instagram.com/effiekammenou_author/
Goodreads - www.goodreads.com/author/show/14204724.Effie_Kammenou
Bookbub - www.bookbub.com/authors/effie-kammenou

Sign up for Effie's newsletter to learn about promotions and events - https://www.subscribepage.com/effiekammenoubooks

For additional recipes follow Effie's food blog
https://cheffieskitchen.wordpress.com

Printed in Dunstable, United Kingdom

78230669R00178